PRAISE FOR *SINCE YOU'VE BEEN GONE*

Since You've Been Gone is one of those heart-stirring stories that makes us question everything we know to be true in life. At the same time it wakes us up, it also teaches us the power of resiliency and faith. As any good author manages to do, Christa Allan gives us the tools we need to move through the world with eyes wide open.

—Julie Cantrell, *New York Times* and *USA Today*
bestselling author of *The Feathered Bone*

Poignant and steeped in mystery, *Since You've Been Gone* will make you laugh, cry, and know God has a plan for us all.

—Liz Talley, RITA Award finalist and author of
Charmingly Yours

Since You've Been Gone will grab your heart from the first line and won't let go until the very last page. Christa Allan pens a beautifully written story of heartbreak and redemption that will stay with you long after you've closed the book. Incredible prose, characters who become your friends, and a tale that makes you laugh and cry. Allan is a master.

—Jenny B. Jones, award-winning author of *Can't Let You Go* and
A Katie Parker Production series

SINCE YOU'VE BEEN GONE

ALSO BY CHRISTA ALLAN

The Edge of Grace

Test of Faith

Threads of Hope

Walking on Broken Glass

SINCE YOU'VE BEEN GONE

CHRISTA ALLAN

Waterfall
PRESS

Text copyright © 2016 Christa Allan

Published by Waterfall Press, Grand Haven, Michigan

www.brilliancepublishing.com

Amazon, the Amazon logo, and Waterfall Press are trademarks of Amazon.com, Inc., or its affiliates.

ISBN-13: 9781503937673
ISBN-10: 1503937674

Cover design by Jason Blackburn

Printed in the United States of America

To Michael, Erin, Shannon, Sarah, and John, who
make this mother's heart happy

PROLOGUE

My Granny Ruth says we always have choices about falling in love. So maybe you and I should have just fallen in like.

That would have been less painful and less expensive. Because, of course, the wedding and the reception still have to be paid for, even if nobody shows up.

Well, the rest of us showed up. But not you.

That qualifies as grounds for legitimate bridezilla anger.

When the phone shrilled at five o'clock that evening, there was a wisp of hope. Like the scent of perfume after someone's walked through a room and, for as long as the fragrance lingers, you look around to see who's there. But then it's gone, and you know hope's a memory.

An unrecognizable voice from an unrecognizable phone number said you'd been found.

Dead.

Fifty miles away. Headed in the opposite direction of the church.

And on the backseat of your car, a package wrapped in blue.

Baby-blue sailboats.

CHAPTER 1

Some people lead charmed lives. Lives that unfurl like endless bolts of silk.

I'm not one of them.

My hopsack life had snagged upon disaster. And, for the past month, the threads frayed faster than I could stitch them together.

The appointment I'd just finished left no doubt about the tangled mess ahead.

I found a bench outside the side entrance of the West Shore Medical Building, wished it wasn't the middle of heatstroke-humidity June in New Orleans, and called Mia. Mia of the upscale bohemian wardrobe, wildly curly hair the color of wet sand, and funky rectangular violet eyeglasses. My best friend, who moved six hours away to Houston, has abandoned me in yet another crisis.

Please answer. Please answer. Please . . . don't go to voicemail. By the fifth unanswered ring, I'd mashed the cell phone against my ear, jamming my earring post into my neck. My silent pleadings were on the verge of running out of my mouth when I heard her voice.

"Hey, Livvy. I'm with a client. When can I call you back?"

The more her design business increased, the more our ability to have conversations decreased. I couldn't bake outside much longer. I was sweating in places I didn't know existed. My mother would be mortified to know I was even thinking about such unladylike bodily functions.

"Sweetie, ladies don't sweat," she'd tell me, the word *sah-wet* dripping off her tongue like sour grape juice. "We glisten." I learned to expect *Gone with the Wind* flashbacks from the woman whose mother named her Scarlett Ellen.

But *sah-wetting* would soon be the least of our lady issues, considering the news I was about to drop on Mia.

"I'm pregnant." I held my breath, willed my somersaulting heart to steady itself, and waited for a sign of life on the other end of the phone.

"Hold on," said Mia, her voice less chirpy. "Wait, no." Her tone now impatient, her fingers probably drumming her desk. "I'll call you back in a few minutes."

My anxiety on pause, I stood and peeled my damp cotton skirt away from my legs where the bench's wrought iron slats had embedded themselves in my thighs. The nearby glass door groaned open, and a gaggle of scrub-dressed people spilled out, yammering about lunch options. The receptionist in Dr. Schneider's office who'd scheduled my next appointment waved to me. I nodded and produced a suggestion of a smile. The least I could do for a woman I'd never met until an hour ago, who now knew more about me than my best friend and my parents.

Mia's name flashed on my phone. I perched on the edge of the bench, and before she could speak, I said, "I'm pregnant." Only this time the weight of the words settled in my throat like broken glass. "What am I supposed to do? I can't believe this is happening to me. My life's already a mess. Isn't it somebody else's turn?" I sounded like a person in the complaint department of humanity attempting to return a defective life.

If God were as compassionate as my mother believed Him to be, then He'd dole out tragedy on a rotating basis. You'd stand in line, then He'd reach into His bushel of adversity, hand one over, and you'd go to the back of the long stretch of mankind. You'd have time to deal with it, dress it in different clothes, ignore it, shove it someplace in your heart before your number was up again.

But no. God dished the trifecta of trials and tribulations in my life. In the past month, Wyatt died on a highway (without leaving a clue as to where he was going), I traded wedding white for funeral black, and now, instead of being a wife, I was going to be a mother. I stopped wearing mascara twenty-eight days ago because I woke up every morning with a tear-stained pillow, cried during the day any time I thought of Wyatt (which was about every ten minutes), and cried myself to sleep at night. After today's revelation, I didn't expect I'd need eye makeup anytime soon.

"You're still there, right?" I walked back inside the medical building, a closer source of cold air than my car on the far end of the parking lot.

"Olivia . . . I almost don't know what to say."

I knew Mia well enough to know she'd just said volumes.

"I'm not ready for this. I lost Wyatt, and today I found out part of him is still with me. How am I supposed to handle that?" I sat in a chair in the corner of the lobby and hoped I had something in my purse to wipe my already leaky nose.

If only I could be like Holly Hunter in *Broadcast News* and schedule my cathartic crying. My eyes dripped, my underarms dripped, and my emotional reserves dripped. All in a medical building lobby as I waited for Mia to come up with a plan, and I wiped my face with a crumpled Starbucks napkin. I counted on her to save me from myself. Now wasn't the time for her to forgo the life vest when I was drowning in the sea of my own irresponsibility.

"I can only imagine how your parents will react when they hear this. When are you going to tell them?"

The door opened and ushered in the sultry heat and a woman with twins. Her "Sit there and don't you dare move" resonated in the room, and even I shifted in my chair.

"I'm not sure. I need time to process this. What if I lose the baby? Maybe I should wait a few more weeks."

I must've sounded as if I were asking for her permission because, even without seeing her, I knew I'd awakened her hand-waving, finger-pointing, mouth-spitting wrath. "And what if you don't," she snapped. "Postponing the inevitable is always an option. A dumb one. You have to tell them now."

Reality fell over me like the sticky silkiness of a spider's web. "Today? A few days? What's the difference?" I'd lowered my voice so as not to be the main attraction for the audience of three seated near me. "It's not like I'm a pregnant, unwed teenager who . . ."

"You're right. You're a pregnant, unwed twenty-eight-year-old."

The bite in her voice pushed me against the chair. I picked at a loose thread on my skirt, nibbled my lower lip, and reminded myself to breathe.

"I'm sorry," Mia said, her voice barely above a whisper. "That was mean of me. But in all the years I've known you, your first reaction is to procrastinate. And it's your worst one because you make yourself and me crazy with all your what-if scenarios."

"I know. I know." She made me face my fears but somehow managed to soften the blow. I hated and admired her for that.

"I'm sorry to do this, but I have to get back to Mrs. Nicholls. I told her that while I was taking your call she should pull fabrics she sensed would increase the positive energy in her home. At the price per yard she's looking, her husband may feng shui me into another universe," she said, her wit as sharp as her style. "Go talk to your parents. Call me after you do, okay?"

I promised her I would because she'd be relentless if I didn't. I dropped the phone into my purse, looked up, and made eye contact with one of the twins. She sucked her thumb, forefinger hooked over her nose like a hanger, lids half-drawn shades over her eyes.

I envied her quiet contentment.

Every day since Wyatt died, a tsunami of grief assaulted me, sent me crashing into memories, and sucked my dreams away in its undertow. I didn't know when or how I'd ever experience the soft swell of happiness and comfort without him.

CHAPTER 2

Mia, her future husband, Bryce, and I met during our freshman year at Louisiana State University when we waited tables at the Magic Mushroom. By day, it was an unassuming, though always quirky, eatery that New Agers could've hung out in for personal transformation, social consciousness, and gourmet pizzas with names like Aura Artichoke.

As soon as the sun set, the football crowds, karaoke singers, and book-weary students getting turnt up for the weekend guaranteed generous tips. Most of the time, being there didn't seem like work at all. Bryce said some nights he felt like he was earning money just for hanging out with his friends.

After graduation, I moved home for a summer internship with a public relations firm. Bryce and Mia married in August, then moved to Houston where he worked saving the environment, and she opened a design studio to decorate habitats in the environments her husband saved.

And two years later, I met Wyatt, whose first words to me were "Excuse me, would you care for a mushroom stuffed with walnuts and pesto?" Well, he actually spoke to Bryce, Mia, and me, because we were together at the second annual Hope House charity art auction. The center provided support services for abused children.

Bryce, who knew firsthand what those kids experienced, was a generous contributor. Mia and Bryce had donated the catering, which was being provided by his younger brother, Colin, who'd started the business the year before.

My boyfriend at the time, Evan Gendusa, predictably unpredictable, had begged off hours before to study for his bar exam. I was certain he meant as in *law*. Bryce disagreed. "Stools, Livvy. He meant barstools." Either way, I wasn't invested enough anymore to care. A shame, really, considering he turned more heads than I did when we'd walk into a room. We'd known each other since high school, and his parents and mine were friends. We had been together over a year. I couldn't compete for attention with his ego or his law classes.

Being dateless turned out to be perfect. I could devote all my eye time to Wyatt.

On his next pass, Wyatt served mini crab cakes and nodded in Bryce's direction to ask if my husband would want one. Bryce, engaged in an intense discussion of ping drivers and his improved golf game, wouldn't have known what his own wife wanted much less her friend.

My lips slid into a smile—like the ones I'd seen in the Victoria's Secret catalogue because with those bodies, who wouldn't flirt with the camera —and I told him Bryce was my friend's husband. When he walked away, I checked my mirror to make sure remnants of spinach phyllo weren't wedged between my teeth.

Later, as Mia brushed spring roll crumbs from the top of her baby bump, landing zone for whatever missed her mouth, she asked, "That waiter over there," tilting her head toward Wyatt. "Is he worried you're too thin? You seem to stay in his flight path."

"He's sweet. And, come on, he's not hard to look at, either. What's not to like about a man with blue eyes?" And thick, wavy black hair that just brushed his collar, a grin that could melt chocolate, and a body made for biceps. Of course, I'd have to take that starched white tuxedo shirt off, one button at a time, to know for sure . . .

"Hel-lo, Miss What's Not to Like Over There." Mia waved her hands in front of me. "How about . . . he's a waiter?" She said *waiter* like it was synonymous with *drug dealer.* "For all you know, he has someone like me"—she paused to pat her belly—"waiting at home."

Wyatt himself, the possible philandering druggie, saved me from answering by swooping in with a tray of desserts. "Ladies?" He offered an array of coma-inducing indulgences.

Mia reeled in a towering brownie, a slab of red velvet cheesecake, and a mini éclair. "Olivia, do you want something from . . . I'm sorry, what did you say your name was?"

"I didn't." Wyatt's eyes met mine for the length of a heartbeat, then he smiled at Mia. "My name's Wyatt."

"No, thanks." Adorable. I glanced at his left hand. No ring. Not even an untanned suggestion of one. I tipped my wineglass in Mia's direction. "I'll share hers."

Mia glared at me. "Only if the baby's full." She slid a benign fruit tart off the tray and handed it to me. "Just in case."

Sometimes with Mia, resistance is futile. I held the tart on my lap like a bomb that would detonate if I moved. One blueberry toppling onto my dress, and I would explode.

Wyatt lingered for a moment, but no chance was I navigating this tart to my mouth while he stood in front of us. His eyes grazed me. My skin shivered watching him. Then he said, "Enjoy," and turned to the next table.

"Was he referring to the dessert or your staring at him?" Mia examined the éclair as if it might be defective, then sent it down to the baby. "You're actually blushing. Hormonal adolescent jolt?" She looked at me wide-eyed, as if she hoped the answer weren't the one she suspected.

I relocated the tart to the table, stood and smoothed the front of my gown, and scanned the crowd for a broad-shouldered waiter with ink-black hair. "I'm getting a drink. Want anything?" And without wait-ing for her to answer, I said, "It's been months since I've been able to engage in harmless ogling. Really, where could this go?"

Mia shrugged. "Bryce was a waiter when I met him. That's where it could go."

The three of us stayed after the auction officially ended so Bryce could talk to Colin. That's how we learned Wyatt and Colin were friends. They'd met during high school, then later worked together as cooks at a French Quarter hotel. When Colin left to start his catering business, Wyatt offered to help.

The next morning Bryce and Mia had reservations for the Sunday jazz brunch at the Court of Two Sisters. Colin had invited Wyatt, and the night before, I had invited myself when Mia told me their plans.

I met them at their hotel. Bryce opened the door, looked at his shoeless wife, and tapped his watch. "Reservations, remember?"

Mia huffed and puffed, demonstrating an alarming contortionist move to reach her bare foot. "If there wasn't a volleyball in my stom-ach, I might be able to buckle these sandals." She leaned back in the chair, her arms flopped over the side, her face waved the white flag of surrender.

Bryce looked at her, his expression a caress so tender I felt as if I'd just intruded on a private moment. He kneeled in front of her, propped one leg up, and helped Mia with her shoes.

"And this," Mia said to me, "is the kind of man you want to be the father of your child."

As we were leaving their hotel room, she informed me she'd Googled Wyatt and unearthed as much information as she could, "for your own good since you seem so fascinated with him."

By the time the elevator doors opened to the lobby, she'd ticked off all the details on her list: He was twenty-three, she couldn't find any siblings, there was no mention of college, and he worked as the sous-chef at one of the Brennan restaurants. Oh, and there were no known ex-wives or felonies.

"But Livvy," she said, "he may not be Mr. Right. Maybe he's just Mr. Right Now."

"I can live with that," I said as the door opened, and the humidity swooped by to frizz my hair. "I'm not looking for forever."

I learned to be careful what I asked for. Sometimes it arrived in the most unexpected ways.

CHAPTER 3

I always wanted a baby.

But, clearly, I wasn't specific about the *when* part of the want.

And now to break the news to my parents. My churchgoing, Bible-quoting, choir-singing mother answered my call before the first ring ended.

"Sweetie, of course your dad and I will be home if you're coming over. I'll send him to the club to pick up dinner. It'll be so much nicer to eat at home. Just the three of us. Oh. My. I'm sorry. You know I didn't mean to suggest three was better than four. I meant it would be more enjoyable and civilized for us to eat at home instead of having to listen to all the racket in the Grill Room. You know, those young parents let their children have their own heads and run around like little heathens . . . Well, shame on me. That's not the kind of thing I should be saying . . ."

She paused for a breath, so I jumped into the void. "Mom, I'm ten minutes away. We'll talk when I get there, okay?" My mother's conversations were bait and capture. Interrupting her wasn't impolite; it was survival.

But despite all her yammering, my mother's heart never failed to listen. She shielded me from guests' endless questions after the almost wedding, from the decisions of what to do when the caterer had prepared food for three hundred and no one was there to eat, and from making decisions about Wyatt's funeral because we were the almost family—the only family he had.

I turned past the long stretch of white picket fence that marked the entrance into Wildwood Country Club. Pulling into my parents' driveway, I felt as if a slab of granite had landed on my chest. And I didn't expect that I would leave feeling any better.

"Hey, I thought you liked Carlo's Eggplant Parmesan," my dad said as he picked up my plate. "Your mother's going to have to sew weights in your clothes to keep you from floating away."

"I'm full, really. I'll take the rest home. I won't have to cook for days. And I'm sure I have enough ballast to stay grounded." I sighed, remembering Lily as a volleyball in Mia's tummy.

"Your grandmother will be home in a few days, so you might not have to cook ever again." My mother laughed, but I knew she was serious.

She had grown up in a house where food equaled love. And if someone didn't eat much, Granny Ruth took it personally. Happy people ate, and, unless you wanted to be the focus of her rapid-fire questioning to exorcise the demon blocking your stomach, you ate.

"Maybe you should have joined her on that cruise. It might have been nice to have a change of scenery," said my mother.

"Watching everyone on the Oldies but Goodies cruise dancing to 'Macarena'? No. But it was sweet of her to invite me along," I said.

Mom leaned across the table and patted my hand—a whisper of her familiar almond and cherry lotion followed. When I was younger, she would come into my room at bedtime, rest her warm hand on my cheek, and kiss me good night. The scent would linger even after she walked out.

"Are you sleeping well? Your face looks so drawn," she said.

"I'm sleeping. Mostly."

She and my father exchanged looks. The emotional telepathy of thirty-five years of marriage. Their eyes conveying the words they left unspoken. Would Wyatt and I have experienced that connection?

I'd never know if we would have shared that moment when our hearts could speak for us, because when Wyatt died, his secrets died with him. I hated that answer. I hated it because it was true. I hated it because it swallowed my life whole.

"Well, okay, honey. But remember, Dr. Welsh gave you those pills—"

"Of course, Mom. I remember." How could I forget? The pills I didn't take because numbing the pain of losing someone I loved didn't make sense to me. The grief reminded me what it meant to be alive. And now I couldn't take the pills because I was responsible for the life Wyatt had left me.

"If you think you need something else, maybe something stronger, we can call him. Not now, because his office is closed—"

"Scarlett, we can discuss our daughter's drugs later." He turned and winked at me. "If you get the coffee started, Olivia and I will clear the kitchen table."

For a second, she looked like someone coming out of a trance. In her mind, she had already scripted her conversation with Dr. Welsh's nurse tomorrow, made the appointment, and driven me to the pharmacy.

"Sure. In fact, I just bought a new flavor . . ."

Off she went in the direction of the pantry, her glasses pushed up like a headband, her dark brown hair gathered into a stub of a ponytail.

My dad elbowed me as I stood next to him rinsing dishes. "She means well, you know."

I nodded and handed him a bowl. "I know, but thanks for the distraction." He smiled, and I wanted to shout, "Please don't be so nice. I'm about to rock your world, and there's no distraction for what I'm going to tell you." Instead, I returned his smile and added one more brick to my wall of guilt.

My mother brewed her Southern Bread Pudding Coffee, the aroma of cinnamon and raisins trailing behind the steaming mugs she and my dad carried to the porch. Its wall of windows faced the tee box behind their house where they watched the sun set. They relaxed in their matching leather recliners facing the golf course, and I sat cross-legged between them on the oversize ottoman.

"Did you two play golf this afternoon?" Since the sun didn't set until a few hours after they closed the office, my parents often came home and played nine holes.

"I wanted to, but my hip wouldn't cooperate." My mother sounded as if she were scolding a disobedient child.

"Scarlett, you make it sound like it has a mind of its own. You really need to make an appointment with that orthopedic doctor." My dad's tone matched hers, as did the look in his eyes.

I pretended to be invisible, having learned years ago that taking sides in these verbal exchanges between my parents sometimes ended in an emotional tug-of-war. With me as the rope.

Mom reacted as she often did when she didn't want to admit my father spoke the truth. She ignored him and changed the subject.

"I love that sundress on you. It's so flattering. Doesn't that red look great on her, George?" Mom leaned over the chair arm and riffled through the basket of *Good Housekeeping* and *Redbook* magazines on the floor.

Dad glanced at me over the rim of his coffee mug. "Um . . . yes, very nice."

"It's great to see you dressed up. Not in those yoga pants and . . ." She paused, tilted her head and scrunched her mouth in that way she did when she was suspiciously curious. "So, did you do something special today?"

I drank some water to wash away the anxiety that lined my mouth. But there wasn't anything I could drink to dilute the sludge in my gut.

"You're looking puny. Are you feeling sick? George, you don't think anything was wrong with that dinner, do you?" My mother's eyebrows edged toward each other, a sure sign an inquisition was pending. "Is it indigestion? I'll check the medicine cabinet—"

"Mom," I said, my hand on her arm stopping her from getting out of the chair, "I'm not sick." One breath. Two. "I had a doctor's appointment. I'm pregnant."

Her gasp after the word *pregnant* created a mini tidal wave of coffee that lapped out of her mug and splashed onto the hem of my dress. "Oh my goodness. Look what happened," she said. In her attempt to lean forward to blot it, the mug leaned with her, spilling more coffee in my lap.

I jumped up, more from the surprise than the warmth.

"Now what have I done?" Her voice vibrated, and the flush in her cheeks spread to her neck. "Don't move. I'll find a towel."

"Mom, it's fine. Just wet, that's all."

"You might still have some clothes here. I'll go look. We'll get it clean. It's going to be okay," she said, but her hand trembled, and the mug she placed on the end table performed a little tap dance of its own.

"Are we still talking about the dress? Mom, you heard me, right?" My words scratched like fingernails against a chalkboard.

"Scarlett, Olivia, both of you, please sit," said my dad, folding his newspaper in half, then in half again, creasing the edges as he did.

The silence swelled between us.

We both sat.

I blotted my wet dress with a napkin, glad to have a reason to avoid eye contact. I didn't want to know what I'd see in my parents' eyes.

My dad placed his hand under my chin and lifted my face. "You've walked through hell for weeks. The worst part of it for us has been watching you suffer this pain and not being able to save you from it. Wyatt's accident and being robbed of one of the happiest days of your life . . . you had no control over any of that. But you had to live with the consequences."

He looked at my mother whose quiet tears streamed down her face and spotted her blouse. "But this, Olivia. You had control over this. I don't understand," said my mother, her face drawn in disappointment.

"I didn't ask you to understand. Nothing about this makes sense. Wyatt and I loved each other. We were getting married. It's not like we were irresponsible teenagers."

"Exactly, Livvy. You weren't. You were irresponsible adults," my mother said. "There's a reason sex outside of marriage is discussed in the Bible. This is one of them."

Somewhere between the words *irresponsible* and *Bible,* I dropped the reins of my seething anger, and let it rip. "Not the God talk. Not today. Maybe not ever. You know, if Wyatt hadn't died, we'd both be here telling you about this baby. And, whether we were married or not, you'd be thrilled." God had ruined my life. I didn't care anymore about anything He said after He had let Wyatt die, leaving me alone.

"Olivia, you knew your father and I disapproved of your moving in with Wyatt before the wedding. We certainly didn't think you slept in separate bedrooms. But it's obvious to all of us now that our plans often don't work out the way we expect. It would be foolish to think there wouldn't be consequences for your actions." She folded her arms across her chest, her back erect, shielded by her self-righteousness.

My father stood on the sidelines like a referee at a tennis match that was disintegrating into a vendetta. "Scarlett, Livvy, both of you calm down. We can handle this better if—"

"Dad, it's too late for that." I held my hands out in disbelief. "Mom, that's it? That's your compassionate Christian response? If it is, then why are you shocked I'm not buying into this God of yours who's ruined my life?"

"Olivia, please—"

She reached toward me, but I backed away.

"No. I don't have the energy to fight about this. Wyatt's death should be punishment enough for whatever wrong I've done. Or he's done. Or we've done. I don't even know." I placed my hands on my stomach, "But this baby . . . this baby . . . I refuse to let you make this baby a punishment, too."

"We don't have to do this to one another," my dad said. "Scarlett, can we stop with the accusations? All of this fighting isn't going to change the facts."

"Exactly, which is why it's time for me to leave." Before I walked out, I lowered my voice, laced it with sarcasm, and snarled, "By the way, this new life you're ashamed of? It's your grandchild."

My father flinched. The recognition of what this child meant flashed through his face when I said those words.

"Olivia, don't you think there's something very important you've forgotten in all of this?"

It wasn't a question my mother meant for me to answer. When she spoke with such deliberate softness, whatever she had to say would be anything but.

"Wyatt's car wasn't headed in the direction of the church when he had that accident. And we still don't know why. If he hadn't died, you'd be just another bride who'd been jilted at the altar."

CHAPTER 4

Jilted at the altar?

I wanted to run back into my parents' house and scream, "Did *you* forget something? I didn't have a chance to get to the altar."

The only person on the altar that evening was my father. Over an hour after the ceremony was scheduled to start, he announced to the guests that there wouldn't be a wedding, while I curled, fetal-like, on the bed in the bridal suite. A frothy crescent of beaded lace, swathed in layers of embroidered tulle, my expensive and time-consuming makeup application smeared on my illusion sleeves like an Impressionist painting.

My mother's playing the Bible card tonight followed by her "just another bride" comment were two sticks of contention with enough friction to spark a fire in my gut.

I pulled the front door shut behind me, opened my car door, then flung my purse down on the passenger seat. Bunching the front of my damp, coffee-soaked dress, I slid behind the wheel and stabbed the button to start the car.

My dad stepped out of the house carrying a white bag in one hand and waving the other. "Olivia, wait. Wait."

I opened my window and stared out the windshield. "I'm not going back inside."

"I know," my dad said, his voice gentle with understanding. He held up the bag. "You forgot the leftovers."

"Keep them—"

"No. You're going to take them because you need to eat," he said with a hint of sternness.

"Don't lecture me." I rolled my eyes, not much differently than I had as a teenager when he expounded on late curfews and generous allowances.

He set the bag on my lap. "You know, it's not just about you now. That's my grandchild, too."

I couldn't ignore the tears in my eyes any more than I could the ones I saw in his.

"Give her time, Livvy. She loves you." He tousled my hair. "We both do."

As soon as I turned onto the highway, I directed the phone's voice activation to call Mia. I'd learned to enunciate all syllables in her name or risk arguing with the annoying female voice who'd keep repeating, "Call Me. There is no one by that name on your call list."

"Well? How did it go?" Mia's confident curiosity was about to kill someone's cat.

"No more advice unless you're going to be here to witness the fallout for yourself," I said. My stomach already grumbled at the pungent smell of basil, garlic, and eggplant in the bag. *Why isn't my sickness limited to mornings?*

"It couldn't have been that bad," Mia said.

"You're right. It was worse." I started my play-by-play of the night, then I heard Bryce's off-key singing and water splashing in the background. "Please tell me you and Bryce aren't bathing while we're having this conversation."

She laughed. "We might as well be. I should wear a swimsuit when it's Lily's bath time. It's like a water park in here. I'll let Bryce finish so we can talk."

Seconds after a subdued conversation with her husband, Mia found quiet, and I continued my story. I finished with surprisingly few interruptions and waited for her response as I drove past the country club entrance, taking my time navigating the snaky road in the dark.

"Okay, in my defense I said you needed to tell them sooner rather than later. I never said they'd be happy to hear that you're pregnant. But, really, what did you expect?"

I wasn't sure if it was the intensifying smell of Parmesan cheese or Mia's answer that incited a new tiny riot in my stomach. "If you were so sure it was going to be a train wreck of a conversation, why didn't you warn me ahead of time? I might have felt less blindsided."

"What? Are you kidding me? I don't understand why, in the name of everything holy, your parents' reactions shocked you. And I was supposed to *warn* you? Come on, Livvy . . ."

"A little compassion would have been nice—from all of you." I pressed my lips together, hoping the sour taste coating my mouth wouldn't escape.

"Girl, you know I couldn't love you more if you were my own sister. So I'm going to talk to you like one. That 'little compassion' business works both ways. Your parents are the ones who met the police at the scene of Wyatt's accident before they'd even changed out of their wedding clothes. They're the ones who identified him in the morgue to spare you having to do it. They're the ones who finished paying for a wedding, then helped pay for a funeral. And, all the while, watching their daughter experience something I would personally die to save Lily from, and I'm sure they felt the same way."

"But she still had to remind me that Wyatt was driving away from the church . . ." As soon as those words stomped out of my mouth, I regretted having sent them out to battle. I sounded pathetic, petty, and ungrateful.

Mia groaned. Or maybe she snorted. Either way, I suspected she was done. With me and with our conversation.

"Call me tomorrow. I'm going to hang up because Lily's finished her bath, and I don't like you very much right now."

We were finally even. Because I didn't like myself very much right then, either.

Thanks to Wyatt's fascination with technology and Bluetooth, I didn't have to fumble with keys or memorize numbers to open our—my front door. The lock and my cell phone talked to each other with more harmony than Mia and I had earlier, and voilà, I was in.

Since I had moved back after staying with my parents for almost two weeks, NASA might have mistaken my house for an unnamed star at night because I rarely turned off the outside lights and inside lamps. The lights comforted me. Reminded me that I was alive.

I put the leftovers in the refrigerator, where everything else languishing in it couldn't summon the energy to be glad someone new joined them. They joined an unopened bottle of Champagne, a bottle of wine I'd uncorked two weeks ago, and an open-jawed pizza box that revealed four slices with their triangle points turned up like elves' shoes, the veggies on them so glazed they looked plastic. A bowl of green grapes—most were on their way to becoming raisins. Two wheat bagels sat atop a block of cheddar cheese spotted with fuzzy blue-and-white mold.

None of these met the pregnancy nutrition guidelines the nurse had given me earlier that day. Neither did Nutty Caramel Swirl, the only container of Ben & Jerry's in the freezer not spiked with icy stalagmites rising from the surface. But if I didn't rescue it before it suffered freezer burn, it would linger in the ice cream graveyard with all the other flavors. The ones Wyatt and I had bought days before the wedding, laughing about having stocked up on our future late-night dinners in bed.

I grabbed a spoon, the ice cream, and my cell phone, then stopped in the laundry room to ditch my coffee-flavored sundress and pull on my girlie boxer shorts and a faded LSU T-shirt.

On the way to the room where I now slept, I bypassed the bedroom Wyatt and I had shared. I'd toted his pillow into the guest bedroom the first night I slept by myself in the house. Laying my cheek on the pillowcase, smelling the fading scent of him was the closest we'd ever be for the rest of my life.

But then came the day when my parents revealed more about the direction Wyatt was headed.

I hadn't known that hours before the ceremony, Bryce had called Mia to ask if we had talked to Wyatt. The groomsmen were meeting at the Carousel Bar in the hotel before the photographer arrived, and Wyatt wasn't there, and he wasn't answering his cell phone. Colin told Bryce that Wyatt said he had one more thing to do, but he'd see them all at the bar.

My few calls to Wyatt had gone unanswered as well, but we'd spoken when we woke up that morning. I figured he was hanging out with the guys.

Days later, instead of waiting for a canoe to deliver breakfast to our bungalow in Bora Bora, I was serving coffee to my parents and their minister, who was helping us plan Wyatt's funeral. My mother, who thought I might have been serious about dyeing my wedding dress black so I could wear it somewhere other than the hotel room, bought me a sedate black sheath. And, leaving nothing to chance, she took my wedding dress to the cleaners. I haven't seen it since.

At first, my parents told only my grandmother that Wyatt's car wasn't headed toward the church when he'd been found. They waited until days after his funeral to break the news to me because, as they said,

"It didn't change the fact that Wyatt died. We didn't want to heap still more onto an avalanche of so much tragedy."

I didn't believe them at first and wished they'd kept it to themselves, because knowing that changed everything.

After they told me, I came home that night, yanked off the pillow-case, and washed it. Later, fueled by rage and betrayal and too many glasses of wine, I rifled through every pocket of every piece of clothing in his closet. I hurled each one onto the bed when I finished.

Memories lingered in all those familiar things he wore. Soaked through my skin, coursed through my veins, and settled in my heart. The green-plaid flannel shirt he wore to the Christmas tree farm last year. His "No White Flags" shirt in honor of Steve Gleason, the Saints player with ALS, which he put on every time the team played. The blue linen Armani shirt that defined his broad shoulders and narrow waist, and my hands against his chest. Sometimes I had to toss things he'd worn before my hands felt scorched by so much left of him in them.

The clothes covered the bed in a tangled mountain of pants and shirts and jackets as if they'd been tossed out of a dryer. As I stared at the mess, my anger surged, pushed against my lungs until only my screaming provided relief. "What were you doing? Why did you do this to us? To me? Sometimes I hate you." I stopped when I had shredded my throat raw.

I found nothing but aspirin-size fuzz balls, faded receipts from grocery stores, movie-theater ticket stubs, and more than twenty dollars in bills and change. I turned over every pair of shoes and shook them, unrolled socks because I remembered my grandfather hiding money in his, and dumped the contents of his dresser drawers on the floor.

My hands were sieves filtering the life he left behind, desperate to find one chunk of evidence, of suspicion, of mystery. My neck and back ached from hours of being hunched over the detritus of a man I loved who, by dying, had become a stranger.

Because if Wyatt hadn't died on his way *to* me, then where was he going? And why? And who was he?

CHAPTER 5

After forty-five minutes of waiting, my grandmother arranged for one of the limousines to pick me up at the back of the church and deliver us to the hotel. My parents stayed, assuring me he could still arrive.

Ruthie convinced me to take off my dress. "You don't want to look as if you've been rolling down the street when you walk up that aisle."

I wanted to believe her. With the help of a Valium and tenuous hope, I imagined I'd be the bride I'd been planning almost a year to be.

Two hours later, my father sat next to me on the bed in the bridal suite, where I was cocooned under the covers in my monogrammed white jammies.

He still wore his tuxedo, but now anguish was etched in his forehead and eyes. One look at him and I turned my head. I didn't want to hear what I saw on his face.

"Olivia, I need to talk to you," he said. His voice was soothing, but I knew it belied the message he was about to deliver. "I just spoke with my friend Roger who's with the Louisiana State Police. A call came in from Middleton Parish. They might have found Wyatt's truck."

I closed my eyes. Shivered under the layers of sheets, blankets, and down comforter. Pictured Wyatt's crooked smile, the small scar over his left eyebrow, where he'd run into the monkey bars instead of over them when he was ten. The question I didn't want to ask refused to be silenced. It grabbed my heart and strangled it until I couldn't bear the pain and had to let it go.

"They didn't find Wyatt?"

His answer was in the way his broad hand cupped my warm cheek to turn my face toward his and the gravel in his voice.

"We don't know."

I pushed myself up until my back rested against the upholstered headboard. "What does that mean? You don't know if anyone found Wyatt? Is he missing? Or you don't know if whoever they found *is* Wyatt?" I curled my fingers, my nails pressing like dull knives into my palms. I needed to feel something besides the emptiness that consumed me.

He looked above my head, and that's when I realized my mother was standing near the bed. I stared at him staring at her. Turned to face her and saw her hold one hand with the other to stop them from trembling.

"What? What? What are the two of you not telling me?" With every word, my heart accelerated and my voice deepened.

My mother stepped closer to my father. She placed her hand on his shoulder like she needed to steady herself, not so much as a gesture of affection. "We're telling you all we know, honey. A red truck went off the road someplace about an hour from here. An accident. From what they can tell, it involved only that vehicle."

"Well, is Wyatt there or not?"

"Your mother and I are going there . . . to find out. We think it's better if you stay here with Ruthie . . ." My father kissed my forehead. "We'll call as soon as we know something. I promise."

Wyatt was there. My parents identified him. I don't know why the photo of him wasn't enough. The one taken of the two of us at the rehearsal dinner just the night before. We were smiling.

Hours later, I don't remember how many, they called. Ruthie answered since I was barely conscious between the Valium, not eating, and stomach-wrenching surges of grief and rage and bile.

I knew. I just knew he had died. There were only a few reasons Wyatt would not have been at that altar waiting and watching as my father and I walked down the aisle.

Right foot. Pause. Left foot. Pause. Just like the wedding coordinator had insisted.

He had either been kidnapped, fallen into a deep well, or he was dead. But our little town wasn't a haven for terrorists, and we were already below sea level, so even if someone tried to dig a well, they'd hit water at three feet.

We all stayed one more night at the hotel. The thought of walking out the door terrified me. One step over the threshold, the one Wyatt was supposed to carry me over, meant facing a new reality.

At some point during the night, my mother handed me a glass of water and a pill. I didn't remember much after that, so I guess it worked. Except that when I woke up, I wished it would've lasted longer. Weeks maybe. Sadness filled every pore of my body. I could barely breathe for the weight of it.

That morning Mia came to my room. I think it was mostly to give my parents and Ruthie a break while they ate breakfast. "They're probably afraid to leave me alone. Like they'll come back and find me dangling from the light fixture by my wedding dress."

I sat cross-legged on the bed with Mia kneeling behind me pulling out the army of hairpins that Rory, my stylist, had tortured me with the day before.

"That's ridiculous, Livvy. You're too short to even reach that high. The best you could do would be to suffocate yourself in it." She leaned over and hugged me. "What would you do without such compassionate friends?"

I smiled. Grateful that she talked to me as she usually would without resorting to the maudlin crap I knew I would be hearing for days.

She finished brushing my hair, then pointed the brush in my face as she lectured me. "You know, people are going to say incredibly stupid things to you. They mean well. Really, they do. So remember that before you're tempted to unleash your inner gargoyle on them." She pulled my hair into a ponytail and tightened it until I thought my eyebrows would move closer to my temples. "Unless, of course, they say something criminally idiotic."

"And then I can pummel them into a pulp?" I loosened the elastic in my hair, then flopped back onto the bed and yawned. I wanted my heart to stop breaking.

"Hey, princess. You can't stay locked away forever." Mia tossed a pillow at me. "Time to get moving." She handed me two plush towels on my way to the shower that she demanded I take. "And shower, no bath. I'm rusty on my CPR classes, so I can't promise I still know enough to resuscitate you."

I stayed with my parents after the wedding that never was because I refused to even drive down the street where Wyatt and I lived.

Once lived. In the house we'd bought barely two months ago in a neighborhood on its way to reviving itself after the hurricane. A neighborhood where houses still boarded up and marked by rescuers flanked freshly renovated shotgun doubles and camelbacks. Where we lived among artists and movie-set designers and the occasional petty thieves on bicycles. My parents wanted me to buy a gun for protection. Turns out, that wasn't the kind of protection I needed.

Most days I vegetated in one or another of my worn college T-shirts and yoga pants or shorts, sometimes nights, too. If I couldn't remember when I last showered, then I figured it had been too long, and I'd at least wash my face.

No one insisted I eat real meals, probably because I spent all day grazing. My old bedroom was a recycling station for smashed soda cans, bottles of too-warm beer, smudged paper plates, crinkled candy wrappers, empty Cheetos bags, hollowed-out pints of gelato, and anything else I could carry and consume. A few oversize bags of popcorn that advertised itself as "skinny" but totaled over six hundred calories. Two of those a day, and I could reach my recommended calorie count.

On the seventh day of sleeping, snacking, and the occasional one beer away from being overserved, God created the unceasing doorbell tune of church bells growing louder. My bare feet stuttered over the floor to my bedroom window. Granny Ruth's new silver Lexus graced our driveway, so there would be no ignoring that insistent ringing.

After I examined my mouth in the bathroom mirror to make sure popcorn kernels weren't lingering between my teeth, I squirted a dab of toothpaste on my tongue and plodded downstairs.

I opened the door and before the word *hello* could even make its way out of my mouth, Ruthie wagged her forefinger in my face as she elbowed past me.

"When you find my granddaughter, Olivia, the pretty one with the bright eyes who doesn't smell like a locker room and who doesn't dress like"—she pointed to me—"that, please tell her I'm here to take her to lunch."

She always seemed to tower over me when I was younger, and even now, though I stood a solid five inches taller, I still felt like she was hovering above me. Lifted by her four-inch heels and her spunkiness.

"Hey, Ruthie." I leaned over to hug her, but she backed away.

"Honey, no telling what you've been rolling around in." She pointed to my T-shirt, mottled into a leopard print by food stains.

"And you must be saving that bottle of Chanel perfume I gave you for Christmas—"

I mentally rolled my eyes. "I didn't know you were stopping by. I just woke up . . ." My voice trailed off when Ruthie herself rolled her eyes as I spoke.

"Well, that's almost a relief because I'd be mortified to know you've been prancing around town like that." Hands on her hips around her designer jeans, she fixed her laser stare on me. "So, the first step in solving a problem is admitting you have one. I know because I paid my therapist a hundred and fifty an hour for that information. Now that you've admitted you'd still be in bed"—she looked at her watch—"at almost noon, we can do something about it."

Ruthie locked her hand on my arm and steered me to the stairs. "You are going to resurrect my granddaughter. Be back down these steps in thirty minutes, then we are going to lunch. Someplace you don't eat with your hands, so dress appropriately."

Over spring rolls and Sesame Chicken at P.F. Chang's, Ruthie informed me, sounding as if she'd just left a TV station news desk, "By the way, did you know there are over two and a half million weddings a year in the United States?"

I stirred my sweet and sour sauce and waited to hear what happened to the other two million, nine hundred and ninety-nine thousand, nine hundred and ninety-nine brides. "No, I didn't . . ." I answered and bit into my roll rather than bite my own tongue.

"Well, I didn't either. But I found out that one hundred thousand of them end in broken engagements," she said.

"My engagement didn't shatter like some crystal vase on a marble floor. It was pulled off life support. It died."

Ruthie told me the time had come for me to join the human race again. "Your parents think they're helping you by letting you dance alone at your pity party. They're only 'enabling' you, which is another pricey therapy term I picked up that I'm giving to you free."

Maybe it was the throat-searing hot sauce, but more likely it was my grandmother's assessment of my life that made me cough until my eyes were as soggy as my lettuce. I wiped them with the corner of my napkin.

"Seriously? You think I'm being a drama queen when just weeks ago the man I was supposed to marry died? And I find out later he wasn't even on his way to the church?" I impaled my chicken with chopsticks as I spoke. Mostly to avoid the temptation to use them as weapons, and I didn't want Ruthie to see the anger that spiked in my eyes.

"Of course, you're grieving. But you can't bury yourself in it. You're isolating yourself from those of us who are still here. Wyatt died. And we're incredibly sad. But we're watching you die a little bit every day, and that's just painful."

"What do you want from me? To pretend my life is wonderful? It's not going in the direction I planned, and I don't understand why this had to happen. Or why it had to happen to me."

Ruthie leaned against the cushioned booth, pushed her plate toward the center of the table and grabbed me with her eyes. "Why you?" she asked. "None of us are exempt from terrible things happening in our lives. Leading a charmed life is a myth. Sooner or later, something will swallow us whole. And sometimes the only way out is like Jonah in the whale's belly. We just find ourselves thrown up on the shore of something solid that we can build on."

I handed my plate to the waiter who'd glided over to our table and who must have sensed the tension, because he simply nodded and walked away as quietly as he'd arrived.

"No Sunday-school Bible stories, okay? I'm already assaulted by Mom's arsenal of scripture verses."

"Livvy, I'm not expecting you to start singing the 'Happy' song or even forget what you've lost. But at least wake up in the morning, wash your face, brush your teeth, get dressed, and leave your bedroom. Call your boss at Virtual Strategies and tell her you're ready to go back to work. Do something."

And that's when the idea that the "something" I was going to do would be figuring out the clues Wyatt left behind.

Nothing. I found nothing to explain where the hell Wyatt was going the morning of our wedding.

Who or what compelled him to drive almost fifty miles, his tuxedo in the backseat, away from home?

Somehow, some way, I would find the answers. On my own. I hadn't told anyone about my playing detective. If and when I discovered something, I wanted to be the first to know.

Propped up on the pillows against the headboard, my pint of Chunky Monkey on the nightstand, I opened my laptop to continue the hunt for where Wyatt might have been headed. He'd told Colin that he'd meet them at the bar. Taking into account the time the autopsy indicated Wyatt died, I figured his destination couldn't have been much more than a few miles from where his car was found if he intended to be back in time. And I refused to believe that a man who hadn't left his tuxedo behind didn't plan to return.

The accident happened off Highway 98, a stretch that ran from where we lived in Lake Morgan and the city of Oakville. The two-lane road ribboned between thick stands of pine, sweet gum, and beech trees, edged in places by water elms and wax myrtle and underbrush. A few miles just before Oakville, the road took a sharp veer to the right. The police told my parents the locals called the surprising turn Dead Man's Curve for a reason. Driving on an unfamiliar—or one we presumed to be—road slick from an earlier rainstorm probably contributed to Wyatt's car careening off the highway and into a patch of unforgiving forest.

I fell asleep that night surrounded by pages of maps I'd printed and woke up to my laptop half under my pillow and a soupy half-empty carton of ice cream perched on my nightstand. The dust bunnies were already cavorting in the sunlight streaming through my shutters, so I must have hit Snooze on my cell phone more times than I thought. I needed to leave in the next fifteen minutes to stay on schedule, but my stomach wanted to stay in bed. Now that I knew I was pregnant, I wasn't sure if my insides' roiling was a classic case of morning sickness or simply knowing I'd be spending the next few hours retracing what I suspected was Wyatt's route.

I skipped putting on a face to have time to drive through PJ's Coffee for my one allotted latte and a breakfast biscuit. My goal was to leave at about the same time I imagined Wyatt might have hung his tuxedo on the hook over the backseat window. I checked to make sure the neighbor's kid hadn't left his new hoverboard in the path of the car, then I backed out of our driveway and turned right onto Jackson Street, which led to Interstate 15.

When my GPS chick announced that the exit to Highway 98 was two miles ahead, the steering wheel quivered beneath my trembling hands. Panic slid next to me, slipped one sweaty hand over my mouth and nose, and tried to shove me into a river of fear with the other. I pushed through. Refused to go under.

At the exit was a gas station. I pulled off to the side past the pumps to a parking spot near the entrance of the Subway attached to it.

I'd been driving for less than an hour, and in a few miles, I'd be there.

There. The last place Wyatt was alive.

Between here and there, the road lapped up the last moments of his life. And in those moments, what did he regret? Not arriving or not returning?

CHAPTER 6

The pristine day belied the treacherous curve ahead, making it seem all the more sadistic in its capacity for destruction. Negotiating the hairpin turn, I held my breath as if it could somehow make me and my Jeep smaller, more compact as the wheels crunched gravel on the road's edge. I understood now how easy losing control could be, especially on a slippery stretch, to turn right around thick-trunked pines that jutted from scruffy-bottomed brush and not see that the road behind them folded back into itself.

Once safely past the curve, I pulled over to a spot mottled with concrete and thick grass that looked like it could have been a driveway once. My skin felt two sizes too small. The car's air conditioner was set on arctic freeze, but my internal thermometer was somewhere between hell and purgatory.

I found the box I'd dropped into my purse before I left home, convinced myself that opening the car door was the only real way out, and demanded my feet hit the ground.

I walked back to the gap of scarred and broken trees left after Wyatt's truck had been pulled away. The few cars that passed me didn't even slow down, as if a young woman moving through high weeds toward a fresh white cross in the swampy silt wasn't unusual.

I reached the spot where my parents, days after the accident, had left the cross with Wyatt's initials. Brushing aside damp pine needles, a thin blanket of leaves, and assorted crud, I lowered my butt to the forest's idea of carpet and sat cross-legged, twirling the brown box between my hands.

Not that either of us chose to be here, but it's June and the humidity is already pressing on everything, hot and heavy, like every angel in heaven turned on a steam iron at the same time. So I might have to make this quick.

I wanted to come here to talk to you because, well, this was the last place you were alive. The mausoleum's atmosphere just doesn't do it for me. Besides, I couldn't sit there and have a private conversation with you with the whole wall of people you're with listening to me.

I set the box in front of me, looked around the little wooded alcove and saw, for the first time, the broken branches and saplings. Some of the larger trees were gashed, their wrinkled bark ripped away exposing their smooth core. Funny. Wyatt's death damaged them, too. I knew how that felt. To have your skin sliced open by the jagged edge of something unexpected, your insides turned outside.

This is so much harder than I thought, but I have to do the hard things now. Alone. And I'm not happy about that. Because wherever you were going, for whatever reason . . . did it have to be the day of our wedding? Some people are saying you were a runaway groom. But I don't believe that. I won't believe that. I think that's the one thing you would have been honest about, not wanting to marry me. But, I wonder now . . . why didn't you trust me?

I opened the box and took out our matching wedding bands. Both gold with a brushed center band and polished edges. Both inscribed with "I love you forever."

Colin gave my band to my parents after the non-wedding, who then gave it to me before Wyatt's funeral. They thought I might have wanted to place both bands in the coffin. I thought that was entirely ridiculous.

For days, I wore Wyatt's band on my thumb. They thought that was entirely ridiculous.

I told them we'd evened the score for absurd ideas.

At first I considered burying our rings near this cross. That's why I brought them here. But on the way over, I changed my mind. I don't know how things work on your side of the universe . . . like you may get the breaking news before I do . . . but I'm pregnant.

So, I guess you didn't leave me all alone . . . Maybe our son or daughter will want these one day. Maybe not. I'll let you know. Or maybe you'll let me know somehow—

I heard the sliding crunch of gravel and the thump of a car behind me. I hoped the thump meant it had stopped and wasn't headed in my direction.

Well, you sure didn't plan for what to do when you were alone smack dab in the middle of nowhere, and your only weapons were two wedding bands, a box, and your not-so-genius brain for leaving your cell phone in the car.

The first thing I spotted when I turned around was a shiny gold badge, which was enough to convince my stomach to work its way back up from the bottom of my feet where it had dropped.

Actually, two shiny badges, one belonging to a ruddy-faced man with the physique of a professional wrestler, and the other to a tall black woman with close-cropped hair whose brown eyes scanned me before she said, "Excuse me, miss. Are you okay?"

People generally never asked that question unless they already suspected you weren't okay. My okay-ness in that minute, though, had more to do with being terrified I might be trying to figure my way out of someone's trunk than what I looked like sitting on the side of the road as if I'd been talking to a tree.

"Yes, I'm fine." I stood and wiped the ground debris off my damp butt. My eyes bubbling with tears, and my face likely as pale as paper, I doubted what they saw matched what I'd said.

They looked as cautious as I felt, which was understandable considering the circumstances.

"I'm Sergeant Gonzalez," said the male officer. "This is my partner, Sergeant East. We're with the Oakville Police Department."

She nodded, pointed to the highway, then looked back at me. "This really isn't a safe place to be—"

"Oh, I know. I'm Olivia Kavanaugh. My . . . my fiancé . . . well, had an accident here . . . a few weeks ago . . . on our wedding day . . ." I moved away from in front of the cross where they'd found me. "My parents put this here, but this is my first time . . ." The longer I talked, the less coherent and more nose-running, throat-constricting, hands-shaking I became.

Their suspicious gazes shifted to sympathetic ones, their stances relaxed, but something about the telltale way they looked at each other unsettled me. I shoved my hands in my jeans and waited.

"We're both so sorry for your loss. We . . ." Sergeant Gonzalez eyed his partner, removed his black-visored hat, and, as if it were some signal between them, Sergeant East continued.

"We got the call that day."

Realizing who I was must have filed the rough edges of her voice into smoother, softer tones, but what she said stunned me. Of all the patrol officers, these two had not only found Wyatt, they also found me. What were the odds? But it made sense; they worked in a small town. Probably a small force.

The thoughts zapped through my brain, but my body moved in slow motion. "I don't want to know," I said, rubbing my arms to dispel the chill freezing under the surface of my skin, making the hairs on my arm stand at attention. "Please, no details."

Sergeant Gonzalez shook his head. "Of course not. We just wanted you to know we understood what you were telling us," he said in apology.

"We're as surprised to meet you as I'm sure you are to have us find you. Your parents didn't say much about whether you'd want to come here. We told them they could call us, after we gave them what we could, you know, so you would have it—the tuxedo and that gift—"

"Gift? You gave them a gift?" *What a strange thing for a police department to do when someone died.*

The two officers exchanged that look again.

"The gift wasn't from us. We found it in the back of the car," said Sergeant Gonzalez.

Why would Wyatt have a gift? My wedding present from him? Why wouldn't my parents have told me about it, given it to me? My confusion seemed to make them nervous.

"Guess they might have forgotten about it with all they had to do," I said, though it felt like a question more than an answer.

"Oh, I'm sure whoever that baby gift was meant for will understand if it's late," Sergeant East said.

I reached for the nearest tree to steady myself. Shook my head as if the words I'd heard were jumbled, and if I could just rearrange them, my world would make sense again. Impossible. Unless he'd been suddenly endowed with a sixth sense, Wyatt couldn't have known about my pregnancy.

I recognized the churning in my stomach, the curdled coating that filled my mouth, and the sweat pulsing through my body that made me shiver. I bent over, my hands on my knees, but I couldn't calm the acid waves in my gut. My breakfast landed between my feet. A putrid mess.

I didn't want to imagine what I looked like . . . snotty and gagging, wiping my face with my bare hands. My eyes stung, my nose burned, and my dignity deflated.

Sergeant East scooted me away from the mess and lowered me to the blanket her partner brought from their car. "I'm so sorry. I didn't mean to upset you," she said as she handed me a box of wipes.

"No. No. You didn't upset me," I mumbled and pulled out one of the little towels and swiped it over my face. Wyatt upset me. My parents upset me. This revelation upset me. "I must have gotten that virus that's going around." Sure. Pregnancy was always going around. Somewhere.

"You want to come back to the station with us before you drive home? Rest a bit? Or maybe we could get someone to take you home," Sergeant Gonzalez said.

"I'm okay to drive. I actually feel better now," I said, hoping I sounded more convincing than I felt.

A squad car bringing me home might embellish the "jilted bride, deceased groom" stories. Give the neighbors a new twist. Then again, I might need to be taken away by the police after I finished talking to my parents. No need for them to make two trips.

After escorting me to my car and supplying me with several bottles of water and their phone numbers, and my promising to call when I reached home, the officers headed back to their car.

The rancid smell of vomit followed me to my Jeep. I started the car, opened the sunroof, then sat in a catatonic stupor during two songs with totally unrecognizable lyrics on the radio.

In one of those moments when a flash of awareness lights up your brain, I knew what I had to do.

Please still be here. Please still be here. Please still be here.

They were.

Whether waiting for me to pull away or just taking a break, the two officers hadn't left. When they saw me running in their direction,

Sergeant Gonzalez opened his door and looked behind me as if expecting to see a bear or a ghost chasing me.

"Nothing's wrong," I said a bit breathlessly as I reached their car. "I changed my mind about going to the police station. I want to go." I needed to go. "Are you going there from here? Can I follow you?"

"Sure. It's just about five miles up the road," he said.

I wanted to read the case file for myself. To not give my parents any opportunity to tell me I misunderstood.

Less than an hour later, I was headed back home to Lake Morgan. But it didn't feel like home. Home was a place where you were supposed to feel safe, protected, accepted. Not the place where lies lurked and truth was held hostage.

On the passenger seat was the manila envelope with copies of the file. The copies that showed my parents signing off on having received Wyatt's tuxedo and a wrapped gift. Sky-blue glossy paper with sailboats covered the box, which was about the size of a basketball, tied with oversize white and blue grosgrain ribbons that flopped to the sides.

It wasn't at all fair of me to blindside them, but they'd kept me blind for weeks. Just the picture of that gift sliced my heart open.

Who was this meant for? Wyatt, who the hell were you? How much about you didn't I know?

Who could have guessed that the people I loved, who thought themselves so different from one another, ultimately became more alike?

My parents and Wyatt.

All three of them harbored secrets that were destroying my life.

CHAPTER 7

At breakfast the day after the fundraiser, Wyatt and I had found common ground in food, being only children, and each other. We entertained ourselves, mostly forgetting that Mia, Bryce, and Colin were at the table with us. He looked even more appetizing dressed in a starched shirt the shade of butter and jeans that hugged his body parts without being X-rated, topped by a smile that widened when we walked through the doors of the restaurant.

When I dropped my napkin, we both leaned to retrieve it, and when his hand brushed against mine, I felt a shiver of electricity so intense, I could barely make eye contact for fear he would see the heat rising from my neck to my cheeks. And for fear he wouldn't.

After that, I wasn't all that upset with Evan, who'd bowed out of the fundraiser the night before, making it possible for me to notice Wyatt. Evan and I had dated on and off for years, and having known one another for so long, we were comfortable together. His sense of humor was sharp and quick, his ability to schmooze my parents was legend, and he knew what delighted me: snowballs in the summer, hot chocolate in the winter, weekend trips to the beach.

Sometimes I wondered if I loved the idea of Evan more than Evan himself. Because he was around, I never had to obsess over plans for the weekend or who'd be going to a social event with me. Sometimes, though, I wondered if knowing so much about each other robbed us of that seductive mystery new couples experience. Then law school, studying for the bar exam, taking the exam, and waiting for his scores monopolized his attention more than the silver-sequined, strapless contoured minidress I wore for New Year's Eve.

Evan must have recognized the emotional distance between us because when we met for dinner, and I told him our relationship seemed like it was on life support, he didn't flinch. In fact, he said he'd been interviewing with a firm, and he expected an offer soon, which meant we'd be seeing less of each other than ever. Our relationship died with dignity.

Wyatt called a week later and invited me to dinner at his apartment. I was astounded that he managed a five-course meal in a kitchen about the size of my parents' closet. How he managed to kiss me until I wanted our clothes to drop to the floor between us. And how I managed to leave fully dressed. Evan's preoccupation with his new status as an attorney would have never been as electrifying as Wyatt's preoccupation with kissing my collarbone.

When my parents first met Wyatt, they admired his self-assurance, but his career path . . . not so much. My mother became expert at steering our conversations into the lane she'd named Wyatt's Lack of Ambition.

"Olivia, honey, don't you think after all that financial struggling, he'd want more out of life than to be a cook?"

In the beginning, my parents were surprised Wyatt and I continued to date. They had met him when we stopped in at one of the club's Friday night buffets. When my mother or father didn't recognize someone's last name, it led to a slight head tilt followed by the question

"That name doesn't sound familiar to me. What does your father do for a living?"

When Wyatt answered "Nothing," I knew my mother was thinking he was either a trust fund baby or someone going after a trust fund baby. Fortunately, before she almost had to start chewing on her size-seven shoes, Wyatt followed up with, "I just wish he was living. He and my mother died more than eight years ago."

His parents both died in a car accident—who knew it would be a genetic trait—when he was a freshman in college.

It wasn't so much that my parents disapproved of Wyatt. He just wasn't the match they had in mind for their only daughter. When it seemed obvious he wasn't going to disappear into the sunset, my parents became much more attentive to my social life.

My father wanted to invite Wyatt to every possible event, including having him over to watch football. I knew his strategy. He always said he didn't trust a man who didn't like football. While my father's attempt was to come to know Wyatt more, my mother's strategy was for me to see Wyatt less. She thought lining up available sons of the professional community would attract my attention. It didn't.

Having spent so much time at college and with my parents' friends, people driven to succeed at any cost, I found Wyatt's contentedness refreshing. He lived in the moment and didn't lose today by worrying about tomorrow. Sunday was his one full day off. He'd sleep until after nine o'clock, and then we'd meet and walk the three blocks from his apartment to the lakefront so we could jog along the sea wall for two miles. On the walk back, we'd talk and sometimes stop at Lucy's Café for po'boys and drinks. We were content cooking on weekends, spending lazy nights watching old movies and, eventually, nights of being less than lazy snuggled on his sofa.

Even before our relationship shifted into serious, I'd decided to postpone my return to Baton Rouge and an MBA so I could find a job where Wyatt and I would be in the same zip code. My parents were disappointed I wasn't collecting degrees behind my name. Their desire for my pursuit of moving up the educational food chain was ironic, considering they were two successful people who hadn't graduated from college themselves.

My father owned an insurance agency, and my mother made sure the doors stayed open. They drove luxury cars, lived in a country club community, and provided a want-for-nothing life for me. I'd always been proud of them because I knew their achievements didn't come without sacrifice, but they persevered. Without the education they insisted was important for my own success.

I started work at a new public relations firm outside of New Orleans. And since they couldn't sway me with other potential spouse offerings, my parents embarked on another tactic: to encourage Wyatt to expand his career options. The weekend the four of us had tickets for an LSU game, which meant an hour's drive, I'd asked my mother if we could suspend talk about restaurant ownership, franchise opportunities, and any other plans she had for him. Fortunately, the Tigers won the game, so the postgame talk trumped Wyatt-talk.

As I'd hoped he would and my parents prayed he wouldn't, Wyatt proposed one afternoon under the leafy umbrella of the ancient spreading oak tree along the lakefront where we often sipped wine and watched the sunset sizzle on the water.

Shortly after that came the question that trumped all questions. We were sitting on the deck outside. My father was grilling burgers while my mother artfully arranged her sliced tomatoes in overlapping circles on a serving tray. Thinking, I'm certain, that she was being demure, she said, "Wyatt, I don't remember you mentioning what church you attend."

Prepping asparagus for my father to add to the grill, Wyatt continued to slice and answered, "I never mentioned attending a church." I admired his ability to sound perfectly charming even while his response wasn't.

I thought my mother might just let the topic die a natural death. But no. She was resuscitating it. She continued with, "Well, what church do you attend?"

When he said, "I don't belong to a church," my mother turned to me, her lifted brows and unblinking eyes conveying her disapproval.

"You know, Wyatt doesn't have to go to a building to be a good person," I told her later. "Going to a church won't make Wyatt a Christian any more than standing in a garage would make him a car."

"You're right, honey, it won't. But what does *not* standing in the garage make him?"

CHAPTER 8

The shorter the distance to Lake Morgan, the more the manila envelope on the passenger seat throbbed with foreboding.

I debated calling Mia, but then decided the conversation could lead to my driving off the road. Especially since I already felt my stomach making its way up my throat. I rubbed my bump as if the baby could feel me soothing it. When, really, it should have been the one soothing me. "I suppose you're as unhappy about this news as I am. But I'd appreciate it if you could somehow make me feel like I'm not a passenger on the Titanic."

A few miles away from my parents' office, I called to make sure they were there. My father answered and, for a moment, I felt guilty because he sounded so pleased I'd be stopping by to see them. "Your mom should be back in just a few minutes. She walked over to that new dress shop to drop off papers for them to sign. I could ask her to pick up some cupcakes at Sweet Delights Bakery for us."

Tempting. Their banana-nut cupcake frosted with banana cream cheese frosting was the bakery version of Valium. But it seemed evil of me to accept food knowing I was going there to emotionally and verbally berate them.

"Guess once you become an adult, you don't worry about sweets ruining dinner anymore," I said.

His voice conveyed the smile I couldn't see. "True. You realize there're more things to worry about than candy before dinner, right?"

He and my mother were about to find out just how much truth he'd spoken.

The silver bell tied to the inside handle jingled when I opened the door to my parents' office, but no one greeted me as I walked in.

Their reception area was empty, a fact I hadn't considered in my determination to confront my parents. Having an agency in the same community for over twenty years meant drop-ins not just for business, but to "visit." Code for catching up on the latest goings-on around town, the center for more breaking stories there than a newsroom.

My mother wasn't in her customary ergonomic chair behind her antique rolltop desk, the only old piece of furniture there. She'd updated the office a year ago, replacing what she considered "institutional" tiled floors with warm oak planks covered with dove-shaded shaggy rugs, changing the wall colors from milk white to soft gray palettes, and adding plump sofas and wingback chairs to the reception area. Nestled in the corner was a coffee station, a pitcher of lemon water, and a basket of fruit. And a candy bowl near her desk.

My dad said her real motive wasn't creating ambience. It was making the environment comfortable when clients had to write large checks and discuss topics that made them squirm—like being disabled and dying and things worse than the two of those—like being someone's caretaker. Sometimes "till death do us part" was costly.

I'd started down the hall to my dad's office when he met me halfway.

"Olivia, so glad . . ." He moved toward me, then stopped as we drew closer to one another. His expression morphed from joy to puzzled as he took in my dirt-stained jeans and my T-shirt splotched with that morning's spilled latte.

"Where have you been? Decided to pull weeds in the garden or start hiking?" He hugged me in that way strangers do when they're uncomfortable with smashing their body parts against yours. In my father's case, it was his attempt to avoid smudging his starched white shirt.

"No. Haven't weeded any gardens today," I said, resisting the urge to get all metaphorical about the weeds I'd discovered earlier. "Where's Mom?"

As if my question had activated her parent radar, the bell announced her arrival. Even without it, I would have suspected she'd walked in because, as it had just now, the lilac scent of her perfume traveled ahead of her.

"I saw your car parked outside. I didn't know you'd be stopping by," she said as she handed my dad a few manila folders. Her eyes didn't look as welcoming as her voice sounded. That she said nothing about the way I looked—and possibly smelled—conveyed more about her disapproval than if she had.

Standing next to me, she looked like the "after" to my "before." Her jeans, with their sharp crease, looked sophisticated, and like my father, she wore a crisp white button-down, hers with classic French cuffs. She wouldn't have looked any different had she been gardening or hiking as my father suspected of me. Her ability to remain impeccable under almost any circumstance was as maddening as it was admirable. My grandmother once joked that my mother's clothes wouldn't dare disappoint or disgrace her for fear she'd banish them from her upscale closet, and they'd suffer the fate of castoffs, relegated to a brown box in the attic.

"You expecting any clients or have any appointments soon? I really wanted to talk to both of you," I said, my voice soft yet deliberate.

My mother looked at my dad in one of their telepathic eye exchanges, but I could tell by his raised eyebrows and almost imperceptible shrug that he wasn't sure what she expected to see in him. Maybe she was just hedging.

"I don't think so, but I probably should check your dad's appointment schedule for the day." She started walking toward her desk, and over her shoulder she asked me, "What is it you need to talk about? How much time do you need?" She flipped a few pages on the desk calendar. I suspected she was hoping to find a legitimate excuse for a short chat.

"Not too much. I just want to make sure that we're not interrupted," I said.

"Your dad is supposed to drop off a policy to Mr. Sutton this afternoon, but we could reschedule that if we need to. If this is going to take over an hour, I can call him to set up another time."

She was uncharacteristically calm for someone who was more accustomed to being the surpriser and not the surprisee. "Let's talk in your dad's office."

I sat on the sofa and they sat on the high-back chairs facing it.

Actually, the only person who sat after I did was Dad. My mother headed toward the small refrigerator in the corner of his office. "Would you like me to get you something to drink? I think we even have some fruit if you're hungry. Are you sure your blood sugar is okay, because you seem a bit agitated or nervous. I'm not sure why you're so shaky. Maybe you should eat something. I don't think it's good for the baby—"

"Speaking of babies," I said and reached into my purse almost enjoying the grand performance in front of such a captive audience. I pulled my copy of the accident report out of the brown envelope I'd been given at the police station. "What do you know about this one?"

CHAPTER 9

My parents didn't do much more than glance at the sheet of paper I slid across the coffee table.

They didn't have to. They both already knew what was written there.

I watched them. Waited for some expression of shock. Some admission of guilt. Even cries of denial as false as they might be.

But nothing.

But that nothing said everything.

My father's wedding band was making its dizzying thirty-first twist around his finger, and my mother stared above my head as if a silent movie played there.

"Why. Didn't. You. Tell. Me?"

My parents looked at each other. When neither one of them volunteered an answer, they stared at me.

"How could you do this? When were you going to tell me about this? What right did you have to keep this a secret?" Every question fueled an already raging fire burning whatever I had left of hope and trust and sanity. I flung questions in their direction like whips. Wanting them to feel what I experienced when something strikes you so unexpectedly, with so much force that your skin rips from your bones.

"Honey, give your mother and me a chance to explain," my father said as he leaned forward, elbows on his knees, hands clasped. For a moment, I thought he was about to lead us in prayer.

"And that's the thing, isn't it? The fact that you have to justify yourselves."

My mother touched my father's shoulder. Her subtle connection signaling she had an accomplice. "We wanted to protect you—"

"Really? So how many more secrets are in that protective vault of yours?" I spit out *protective*, making it sound as foul as the excuse I knew I was about to hear.

"Olivia, please calm down. You have to think of someone else now, not just yourself. It's not healthy for the baby, for you—"

My father, always the master negotiator between the two agitated women in his life.

"Don't lecture me about taking care of my child. Especially not now. I don't think either one of you should be talking to me about good parenting when I had to find out about this from strangers. Strangers!"

"You don't get it, do you?" My mother's back straightened, her rigid posture reflecting the harsh truth she felt obligated to deliver. "We were, and we are being good parents to you. Your dad and I had planned to tell you sooner, but then you came over and announced you were pregnant."

"Like your mother said before, we wanted to protect you. You had enough to deal with, planning a funeral."

"I wanted you to be honest with me. I didn't ask you to shield me from what I had a right to know." I realized I sounded like my parents thirteen years ago. Strange to hear them spout the rationalizations I used during my teen years about telling half-truths in the guise of protection. They'd hear about the party, but not about the drugs.

"It didn't seem the right time to tell you the man you were so in love with had probably cheated on you." My mother crossed her legs, wrapped her hand around her top knee, and leaned toward me for the kill. "And more than that . . . his driving away from the church where you were waiting to marry him with a baby gift on his backseat."

Her arsenal of accusations lifted me off the sofa in seconds. "You're assuming he cheated on me? How do you know that gift belonged to *Wyatt's* baby? Did you open it? Do you have evidence?" The tightness in my chest exploded, cracking my voice, anger and resentment boiling underneath my skin. "He could have been on his way to visit a friend . . . You don't know. You don't know. We may never know. But I had the right to know that gift existed. And both of you kept it from me. Were you ever going to let me know the truth?"

"Well, I'm not sure, Olivia. Were you ready to hear that? No. You're not even ready to hear it now," she said, shaking her head, leaning back in the chair, draped in self-righteousness. "Your father and I have been praying and asking God to let us know how to tell you about it."

My father opened his mouth, but I didn't give him a chance to speak. He'd been mute long enough for me to realize he was letting my mother steer this ship, and he wasn't about to start a mutiny.

"You've been what? Praying about it? Waiting for God to send you the plan? Isn't He, or shouldn't He have more to occupy His time than approving of the two of you lying?" I plopped on the sofa and casually examined the bits of dirt from this morning that hitchhiked under my fingernails.

"Don't be ridiculous." She pushed the cuffs of her blouse almost to her elbows. "We didn't lie to you. You never asked us if anything else was found. Maybe it's a technicality, but if you were a stronger person, we wouldn't need to insulate you from these things."

"You're suggesting that I'm weak? I can't believe you two. I've followed rules, your rules, done things the right way. All of that's wasted, because now God's punishing me."

"Olivia, sin has consequences. We've talked about this."

"So, I've failed you, and I've failed God? It's never enough, is it? I'll never please either one of you. I don't know how I'll ever trust you or Dad or God." I stood, grabbed the police report and my purse.

My father looked from me to my mother and back again. "Olivia, I know this is difficult—"

The front bell sounded, followed by a man's voice speaking to the void at the front desk. "Hello? George?"

"Be right there," my father called from his office door, then turned to me. "Wait just a minute. Let me—"

"Perfect timing. I was leaving anyway."

"Your mom and I don't want you to leave upset."

"You're kidding, right? How could I leave any other way? I drove over an hour thinking I'd implode before I arrived. You think a few more miles are going to matter?"

"I'd drive you home, but Jim's here for his appointment . . ." It was that familiar emotional game of tug-of-war, but this time, my father was the rope.

My mother stood next to him, reached out, and placed her hand on my shoulder. "Let's talk about this later. We can have dinner at home—"

"No. No more talking." I shrugged, wanting her to move her hand. "The only place I want to go is home. My home. Not yours." I walked to the door of his office when it hit me. I'd almost forgotten the very thing I had come for. "That gift. Wherever you've been hiding it, I want it."

My father nodded. "I have it. Here." He opened one of the cabinets near his desk and handed it to me.

Seeing it was like being on that roller coaster at Disneyland, the one that traveled through inky blackness, where you didn't know when the next descent would be that plunged you into a wormhole, then sucked the breath out of your lungs.

With the exception of a smashed-in corner, it looked exactly like the picture in the file.

I wanted to crush it until my hands were bruised from the pounding. Destroy whatever was inside until it was unrecognizable. But the urge to rip it open, to tear into it was just as strong. My Pandora's box. If I opened it, all the truths would be released. And I'd have to deal with them because, even if I shoved them back into the box, I couldn't pretend they never existed.

Before my trembling hands could drop the gift, I bolted. Kicked the door closed with my foot and threw the gift in the back of my Jeep. Whatever it was would have already broken by now, so there was no point in being careful.

There was enough carelessness to go around for all of us.

CHAPTER 10

I woke up on the sofa in my house wearing the same grungy clothes and smelling like a basket of sweaty socks, so I knew I must have driven home from the office. But the distance between there and my den was a wrinkle in time, and I didn't remember getting from one to the other.

My mouth was crusted with drool, my right hand was numb from sleeping with my arm tucked under my head, and my entire body ached from hauling the weight of grief. The room was dark except for the glow from the television and an infomercial for some workout that required more agility than I'd ever have. The streetlight sliced through the silk drapes. The platinum-gray ones I'd angsted over and finally given myself permission to order from Pottery Barn. The ones—when Wyatt finished hanging them—that caused him to say he'd rather hang himself than do that again. The ones that were now guilt-free. There'd be no death by curtains for Wyatt.

I blinked, adjusting to the murky darkness, as I pushed myself to slouching and pressed the button on my phone to check the time. Impossible. It couldn't be only 8:45. But I hadn't Rip van Winkled myself through a time-zone change, so it had to be right.

I checked my missed calls. The usual suspects. My parents, Mia, my grandmother, and—unexpectedly—Cara Coen, one of the owners of Virtual Strategists, the boutique public relations company I worked for. The last time we spoke, I told her she needed to assign my clients to someone else because I didn't know when I'd be ready to return. It wasn't until I listened to her voicemail that I realized two weeks had passed since that conversation. How was it that days that seemed endless turned into weeks that passed in hours? She wanted to discuss some options and asked if I could call to set up a time we could meet. Since she didn't say *options* like it was synonymous with *termination*, I figured her call wasn't a strategy to get me into the office so she could fire me. Gently.

My stomach growled its discontent. If I couldn't remember the last time I'd eaten, then it had been too long. The only things my refrigerator offered were a rush of cold air and the two wheat bagels I hadn't tossed out with everything else in there on its way to becoming lab samples.

I called an order in to Sammie's Burgers, which they promised to deliver in the next twenty minutes. Which meant thirty. Enough time for me to shower.

My wet hair was still wrapped in a towel when the doorbell rang. I peeked out the kitchen window before I opened the front door. An almost habit that started when Wyatt and I moved into the house. He said opening the door before I knew who was there wasn't safe, especially since I was home alone when he worked late at night. "I'm going to install one of those doorbells with a monitor. You can't ever be too safe."

He never got around to that. *Guess you weren't too safe yourself, huh? You should have followed your own advice. You didn't just wreck your truck. You wrecked our lives.*

The car in my driveway had a Sammie's logo attached to the hood. Dinner had arrived early. I swiped my never-ending supply of tears with the edge of the towel, then opened the door.

"Here's your order . . ." The guy on my porch tilted his head, looked at me, shifting from his customer script to a friendly smile. "Hey, Miss Olivia. I didn't realize this was your address."

That this kid could recognize me wearing a canary-yellow towel turban and faded sweats was both remarkable and humiliating. "Yes, but just for the past few months." He looked familiar, but my brain couldn't access the file.

He handed me the bag, the smell of the burger and fries distracting me from focusing on identifying this face in front of me.

"You probably don't remember me," he said, a shy grin that likely charmed his teachers and any girl looking in his direction. "I'm Ethan—"

"You're Evan's brother," I blurted, delighted my neurons connected. "You're so . . . grown." Had it been that long since Evan and I had stopped dating? I didn't remember this kid having to look down to speak to me the last time I saw him.

"Yes, ma'am. I'm a senior in high school. Just found out I've been accepted at LSU. Started working at Sammie's to earn some money to pay for my car, you know?"

I nodded. One thing I admired about the Gendusa family is that they didn't believe in kid welfare. Even though both parents were affluent, successful attorneys, their children learned to work for the things they wanted. That compensated for everyone in the family having a first name that started with the letter *E*, which made for an extravagant monogram on their Christmas cards.

He handed me the receipt to sign. I left a generous tip and, while we weren't making eye contact, asked him how Evan was doing.

"Still living in Baton Rouge." Ethan handed me my copy of the receipt. "He's, um, getting married in December."

"That's wonderful," I said, trying hard to sound like I meant it.

"I gotta make another delivery, so guess I need to take off. Nice to see you again. And . . . I'm . . . We're all sorry . . ." He didn't need to finish the sentence. We both knew what he meant.

"Great to see you again, Ethan. And thanks."

I leaned against the closed door, bag in one hand, wiping tears away from my eyes with the back of the other.

I bet Evan won't be taking any trips the morning of his wedding. And his bride won't be left standing at the altar wondering what happened. He's getting the happily-ever-after. And I got a baby gift.

And it wasn't even for our own baby.

A pepper-jack cheeseburger topped with fried pickles and fried onions and a side of cheese fries was probably not the best meal of choice two hours before midnight. But anyone who might have tried to pry the globs of melted cheese and drippy burger from my greasy hands could have lost a finger or two.

Maybe I was trying to fill the hole Wyatt and that baby gift had posthumously dug in my soul. The gift I left in the car. Like a vagrant trespassing on my property, it wasn't entering my home. It didn't get to be in the one place I shared with Wyatt and no one else.

But keeping it out of sight didn't keep it out of my mind. Or my heart. It was a splinter, burrowed in me, and even when I couldn't see it, I always knew it was there, ready to inflict pain.

I needed, more than ever, to know the truth. About that, my parents and I could agree. But I wanted the truth to prove Wyatt was honorable and trustworthy. My parents wanted it to prove I had been about to marry a man whose deception was cruel and unforgivable.

CHAPTER 11

By three o'clock the next morning, I truly understood why parents wept and moaned when the late-afternoon nap monster descended upon their children.

The long nap plus the food overload meant no sleep for me. Haunted by my grief and everything that had happened, once again giving way to rage, resentment, and bags of M&Ms, I tore through the house like a Tasmanian devil—screeches and screams included—trying to scavenge a clue. Anything I could use as a wedge to pry open a door in the parts of Wyatt's life that I didn't know existed.

I ripped through clipped stacks of papers in our desks and dressers, scrolled through our credit card and bank statements online. Receipts and bills drifted to the floor as I tossed them, one by one. By the end, I'd created a pile of pink, yellow, and white papers, like useless leaves shed before winter. Not one provided even a whisper of a clue. They spoke of clothes and furniture and meals and the mundane. Artifacts of a life stolen from me.

Maybe he had credit cards and a checking account I didn't know about. But if he did, then that answered questions I didn't want to ask.

I left the mess I'd created and walked into our bedroom. My bedroom. Where I dragged my forefinger along the dust covering my dresser and wrote my initials *O. H.* But I never became Olivia Hammond. I smudged the letter *H* out with my bare hand, leaving the *O* by itself. Just as I was now.

All of Wyatt's clothes were still on the bed where I'd left them a few nights before. Someone could have had a sizable bonfire with that pile of rumpled cotton and linen and silk. Like the bonfires we'd watch on Christmas Eve on the levee. Dozens and dozens of them, over thirty feet high. We came home smelling of smoke and night air and memories.

I tugged a blue pin-striped shirt from the bed and slipped it on. Wyatt's eyes twinkled when I wore his shirts. He found it sweet, seductive. I told him he'd been conditioned by too many movies. But later, my eyes would twinkle, too.

Bruno Mars singing "Just the Way You Are" woke me up.

Not the real Bruno, of course, and gratefully. I knew the song told a woman she looked beautiful as she was, but it would be a difficult buy-in seeing me roll off the sofa in sweats with Wyatt's shirt over a T-shirt I used for painting, and hair that pointed in every compass direction.

I'd finally fallen asleep, exhausted more from clicking through hundreds of television channels and wondering why there wasn't one program or movie worth stopping for.

One decision I made before my eyes closed was that I wanted to sell the house. Living here was a daily wrestling match with pain. Here, where the walls pulsed with the energy of our lives together, where almost anything I touched sparked Wyatt's image, and where I wondered who this man was who had loved and left me.

I called our real estate agent, Amanda Green, after I woke up and ate my breakfast of leftover cheese fries. She returned my phone call within minutes. She wasn't surprised I wanted to list the house, but she still wanted to give me a day to think about it to be sure. "Your house may sell before I even have a chance to put up the For Sale sign. Remember?"

The neighborhood had become the place to live. Trendy hipster types next door to grandparents who were next door to upwardly mobile couples with children no taller than the wrought iron fences that kept them safe in their yards. Homes not renovated became teardowns, and not many properties hit the market. Wyatt and I had found out about the house because it was owned by one of my father's clients. We called Amanda the morning she listed it and made an offer. Sixteen phone calls from people wanting to buy the house came in after that.

"I'll think about it, but unless you hear otherwise, let's plan to meet tomorrow to sign the papers."

She said she'd be over in the morning since I wanted time to go to the office to check in with Cara about whatever it was she wanted me to do.

"Do you want me to start looking for another place for you? A house or maybe a condo?" She asked the questions with such kindness, I suspected she understood how difficult this all was for me.

"Not yet. There's still so much I need to figure out."

The scariest of which was learning how to be a single mother. Maybe it would be less frightening if I could depend on my own mother for emotional support. It wasn't just that her moralizing frustrated me. I didn't need a judge in my life. I needed my mother.

I'd just made voice contact with Mia when my doorbell rang.

My grandmother's car was in my driveway, which could only mean she was at the door.

"Oh, this is just what I need right now. A visit from the voice of reason," I told Mia. "Can't I pretend to not be home?"

"If your car is there, and you don't answer in five minutes, she's calling 911 and telling them to bring the Jaws of Life." Mia laughed, but we both knew how close to serious she was.

I said, "You know you're pathetic when someone sees your car and always expects it means you're home. Like I wouldn't have friends who'd pick me up to go somewhere." I didn't even attempt to make that a joke. "She's ringing again. Hold on. I'm going to play the pity card and hope for a reprieve."

I huffed, and I puffed, and I opened the door, hoping my blah-ness was stage-ready. "Hi, Ruthie—"

"About time you answered," she said, her hands already perched on her hips. "Are you going to invite me in, or should I just stand here like I'm passing out Bible tracts?"

"It's not a good day. Would you mind if we get together another time? I'm just not feeling well . . ." I sighed, bit my lower lip, and did my best to conjure my forlorn, exhausted, and in- need-of-solitude self.

She tightened her lips, narrowed her eyes, and, as usual, elbowed her way past me. "Matter of fact, I'm not feeling so well myself. Last night, the girls and I went to Chinese Garden after shopping. Woke up this morning feeling fat as a tick from all that MSG. It's that Moo Goo Pan."

"It's Gai Pan, Ruthie. Gai Pan." Since my phone had been on speaker, I knew Mia wasn't only hearing the conversation, she was relishing every second of it. I told her I'd call later.

"Good luck," she said and clicked off.

My grandmother surveyed the den, measuring the extent of the clutter, her face unreadable. For the moment.

I cringed seeing the room through her eyes. Newspapers scattered on the floor, towels that needed to be folded on one end of the sofa, my pillow and blanket on the other end. A few empty plastic water bottles on the coffee table alongside a bag of chips and a half-eaten apple. My one futile attempt at healthy snacking. The bag from Sammie's still on the floor from the night before.

She moved the bundle of towels off the sofa and onto the lap of Wyatt's dreadful brown recliner. I'd always hated the nubby fabric that covered it because it reminded me of rows and rows of hunched-over, furry caterpillars. Having cleared a space for herself, she sat and asked me, "Who's Guy?"

"Not who. What. The dish you ate was Moo Goo *Gai* Pan."

"*That's* why my order amused our waiter. I couldn't figure out why he was laughing," she said and crossed her arms, her nonverbal *hmmph*.

"Granny, I doubt he was laughing *at* you."

"Well, he wasn't laughing with me, because I wasn't laughing. Maybe he doesn't understand the exponential damage of one scathing review on Twitter." She pulled her phone out of her striped Burberry crossbody purse. She had a wireless network, and she was armed and dangerous.

"If you plan on returning there to eat, you might want to rethink what you're about to post. You wouldn't want your Twitter profile taped over the food-prep station."

"Good point," she said and tucked the phone back in her purse.

Her agenda was on the verge of shifting. I could tell by the way she scooted forward, crossed her legs, and overlapped her hands on her knee. *Just like my mother.*

"Now, the reason I'm here. My yoga class is in an hour. I want you to come with me. You have to get out of this house."

I smiled. "That's exactly what I'm about to do."

CHAPTER 12

"Really? You want to go to yoga?"

I heard the unspoken "Oh dear" in my grandmother's question.

Ruthie liked yoga about as much as I liked Zumba. She hated feeling like a pretzel, and I hated looking as if my limbs were attached in all the wrong places.

Today she wore her favorite Lululemon gray cuffed trousers and matching pullover, but she'd already confessed months ago that the yoga outfits were darling. The classes, not so much.

"No, and neither do you." I moved the pile of towels off the recliner onto the floor and sat, folding my legs underneath me. Wyatt had told me he knew I really loved him when I approved his dragging that chair into our house. At the time, it wasn't the hill to die on in our efforts to move in. But now? I picked at the loose tufts on the chair arm and realized I didn't need his permission to dump it. If he wanted it, he could come down—assuming he was in the upward direction we want to find ourselves in after death—and get it himself.

". . . your parents are so deceitful," my grandmother was saying.

Whoa. Where'd that come from? "Exactly. That's exactly what they are," I said. Finally, an ally. I almost high-fived her.

She stared at me as if my head had just popped off my neck. "Have you paid attention to anything I've been saying?"

"Obviously not." I yawned, then cringed realizing I hadn't brushed my teeth. *Great, Olivia, you're so ready for this mothering thing.*

"I'm not agreeing with you. What I said was you've not placed any blame on Wyatt for his deception, but you think your parents—"

That I paid attention to. The resentment stirring in my gut pushed me forward in the chair. What was it about my family that the issue was never really the issue? "Why weren't you honest with me, and why didn't you tell me the real reason you're here?"

I continued, counting off on my fingers as I spoke, "I'm hungry. I need a shower. I'm in desperate need of a housekeeper. I'm alone. I'm pregnant. Isn't that enough? I don't need anyone else on the team for the prosecution."

I pushed myself off the recliner and darted around the den, picking up trash, folding the blanket I'd slept with . . . anything to move. All of these conversations lately were cranks winding, winding, winding my sanity, my tolerance, my life. I was dangerously close to understanding what it meant to fly off the handle.

"Has it occurred to anyone? Anyone?" I snapped a garbage bag open and tossed in the trash I'd collected. "That Wyatt must have had a reason for that trip?" A straw poked out from under the sofa, but I shoved it back with my foot fearing what might be attached to it.

"Honey, I sure hope he did." My grandmother watched me scurry around the room like she'd scored a front seat at a performance-art theater.

I tied the bag closed and tossed it into the waste can in the kitchen. I sat in the recliner again and started folding the towels I'd dumped on the floor. I wasn't certain how long I'd ignored them and hoped they hadn't retaliated by getting that musky wet-dog smell.

"You're assuming, like my parents, that gift was for his child. That's why you're here, right?" I didn't wait for an answer. I didn't need to.

"Let's not pretend you didn't know about that. Has anyone bothered to consider it was for someone else's child?" But even as I pushed the words out of my mouth, they tasted sour and unconvincing.

"I'd like to believe that's true, but—"

She reached over and scooped some laundry to fold.

"Are you going to talk about what's true? Like you weren't part of that deception with my parents?"

She finished her towel and added it to my stack. "I didn't agree with their decision to not tell you, and I was honest with them about that. In fact, your father wasn't so convinced that not saying anything was the right thing to do. But your mother was insistent. I had to respect their right to make that decision," she said.

"Then why are you here? You're going to pat me on the head and tell me it's all going to work out? To apologize to my parents? That God has a special plan for my life? Because He doesn't. And if this is His idea of being special, forget it. I'll take average. Mediocre. Anything but special."

My grandmother and I called a temporary truce. Her closing remark was something along the lines of not ignoring my faith or not having faith just because "your mother sleeps with a Bible under her pillow and expects it'll move her to the front of the line at the Second Coming."

We made a deal that if I ran errands for her, thereby getting myself out of the house, we could pretend that today was "just another day." She never asked what I meant earlier by getting out of the house, and I decided it was a topic best left until after the papers were signed.

She handed me a grocery list, tickets for her clothes the cleaner was holding hostage, and her credit card with instructions to come back with a full tank of gas and lunch for both of us, which didn't come between two slices of bread.

Almost two hours later, I opened my front door and was stunned. The bags holding our lunches almost slipped through my hands from the shock of what I'd come home to.

I smelled something foreign.

Lemon and ginger and clean house.

During the time I'd been away, Ruthie cleaned my entire house. Including folding all of Wyatt's clothes, then placing them in orderly rows in the closet.

For the first time in months, my wood floors gleamed, my kitchen sparkled, even the granite countertops winked at me. And the dust mites seemed to have been evicted.

All of the groceries I carted in, she had intended for my pantry and refrigerator, not hers.

Looking at her, I understood where my mother inherited her capacity to look like she'd just stepped out of a model shoot, even though she'd been toiling in the trenches. The only evidence that Ruthie had moved from her place on the sofa where I'd left her were a few damp tendrils framing her face and her sleeves rolled to her elbows.

I didn't cry.

I sobbed.

Because when someone knew that all the chaos in your spirit was reflected in the mess that surrounded you and quietly restored your dignity, how else could you thank them?

Ruthie and I demolished our lunches of ribs and green salads with smoked-tomato-and-onion dressing, but left room for the raspberry frangipane tarts I couldn't resist picking up from Angelo Brocato's Bakery. I reached in the cabinet for dessert plates and, thanks to my pods, brewed two cups of coffee for us.

"I had to go into the bakery," I confessed, setting her mug on the table. "There wasn't a line." I knew she'd laugh along with me.

Opened over a hundred years ago, the bakery was home to generations of loyal customers who didn't mind standing outside on sultry summer days or nights for pastries and specialty gelatos, like St. Joseph Chocolate Almond.

I apologized to Ruthie for dumping my anger at my parents, and Wyatt, for that matter, on her. My grandmother was my soul supporter; she listened to my childish rants, my teenage rages, and now, my adult drama.

"I don't want to know what I'd do if I couldn't talk to you," I said. "You've been a friend with benefits. Except that the benefit is you're my grandmother."

"Glad you clarified that. I almost had the vapors," she said, her hand patting her chest. "Oh, before I forget, I brought you a little happy." She found her purse and picked out a small box wrapped with brown paper and twine. "And don't tell me that I didn't need to do this. I know I didn't need to; I wanted to."

Inside was a sterling silver bangle bracelet engraved with my first name. "It's lovely. Thank you." I started to wiggle it on when she placed her hand over mine and stopped me.

"Before you do that," she said, "read the inside, then let me explain."

That was curious, but then so was Ruthie. I turned the bracelet and read aloud, "'Be still, and know that I am God. Psalm 46:10.'" I didn't verbalize my confusion as to why my grandmother chose a Bible verse, but I guessed she expected that response.

"For almost my entire life, I've held on to those words when I had nothing else to hold on to. They make me remember I'm not God, and I'm also not the boss of Him. They're God's way of telling me, 'Sit down, Ruthie, be quiet.' Mind you, I still have to take some personal initiative. The good news is it doesn't all depend on me. When I run out of me, there's God saying, 'Chill out. I got this one.' I'm not trying to push God on you. I just want to push Him in front of you. I wasted too many years thinking God had an A-list, and they were all partying on an island I'd never heard of and never been invited to. Took me a while to realize the invitation had been there all along. I just needed to open it." She kissed me on my forehead. "I wanted you to have and be a part of something important to me."

"Knowing all that makes this even more special," I said as I slid the bracelet over my hand and onto my wrist. "Are you sure this is the same God my mother talks about? This isn't some new and improved God 2.0?"

"I'm not exactly sure what that point system means," Ruthie said, picking up our plates and mugs from lunch and setting them in the sink, "but I am sure that it's not God who changes."

CHAPTER 13

R uthie left, and I celebrated my picture-perfect, lemon-ginger-scented house by taking a guilt-free nap, then returned Mia's call.

A phone conversation with Mia when Lily was tired reminded me of trying to talk to my father during football games.

Pointless.

By the time the commercials interrupted the action, giving me a few minutes of opportunity, I'd either forgotten what I wanted to talk about or it had lost its urgency.

Only Lily didn't understand the concept of commercial breaks. Her breaks between fussing were arbitrary and allowed us barely sixty seconds of talking. Between the whining, rants, and sighs—and those were mostly all Mia—we patched together a conversation.

"We've been interviewing nannies, and a Mrs. Doubtfire's nowhere to be found. Some of them want more money than Bryce and I both earn. One of them asked if we had a summer home and would we provide an annual bonus. Bryce wants to install nanny cams in almost every room in the house and hire someone to do a background check. I'm beginning to wonder if I can work from home or not work at all."

Mia paused. "Hold on. Lily's opened the refrigerator, and she's dragging her stool in that direction. This can't be good."

From what I could discern on my end, it wasn't. Mia spat out *no* like bullets out of a machine gun, while Lily requested almost every item on the shelves in front of her. I considered hanging up and trying again later when I heard, "Look, Lily, it's Daddy!" Judging by her voice, Mia sounded more delighted than Lily.

Bryce's arrival rescued both of them. He promised we'd be interruption-free if Mia would take over later so he could go for a run.

"No problem. Thank you. Kiss. Kiss," Mia said in what I recognized as her mommy voice. I wasn't sure if that voice was delivered along with the baby, but it had been around since Lily's birth. A door closed, followed by a heavy sigh. "Okay, they're off. Now, what's going on?"

I filled her in on my trip to Wyatt's accident site, the drama of the baby gift, listing the house, and the surprise of Evan's brother delivering dinner. "I'm thinking maybe I need to drive back to the town, you know, where I picked up the accident report—"

"And what? Walk into places, show pictures of Wyatt and ask, 'Do you know this man?' You don't have time for that. Plus, in a few months you're going to be waddling in with your pregnant self . . . I don't think that's a good idea," Mia said.

"I know. I can't even drag myself to get a manicure." I examined my ragged cuticles and fingernails, remembering Amanda's magazine-ready hands. "I just don't even know where to start getting answers. Do you think maybe Colin might know something?" I hated hearing myself ask that question. "I don't mean like he's hiding anything. Just, well, he probably knows people Wyatt knew that I don't . . ."

"If Colin knew anything about that baby gift, he would've told me or Bryce. He wouldn't have wanted you to find out about that from a stranger. I'll ask him again if you want me to, but he wouldn't keep secrets like that from us or from you."

I heard an unfamiliar defensiveness in Mia's voice. Maybe my desperation sounded like mistrust. "You're right. Sometimes I just need to hear myself ask the obvious."

"Look, if you really want answers, why don't you stop trying to do this on your own and hire a private investigator?"

"I doubt Richard Castle's available to take my case. Don't you?" One of those times I hoped humor would mask my fear.

"I'm serious, Livvy. What you're doing isn't working, and you're making yourself crazy. Crazier. What do you have to lose?"

Everything.

As long as I didn't know the truth, I could delude myself into believing any number of scenarios. But once I did, that was it. Kind of like being pregnant. You either are or you aren't. There's no "sort of" pregnant. And there's no "sort of" truth. I was already living with one. I didn't know if I was ready for the other.

"Money?" I squeaked out.

"Hmmm. Guess you'll have to decide how much the truth is worth."

More than I was willing to pay emotionally. That was a truth I was sure of.

Selling our house felt like selling Wyatt's dream.

We used the money we'd saved for him to enroll in culinary school to buy the house. But our intention was that the house would be an investment, one that we could sell to redeem that dream when the time came.

That time almost came.

But now it never would.

Even before we talked marriage, we talked cooking schools so Wyatt could one day open his own restaurant. The highly regarded International Culinary Center in New York cost as much as a mid-level priced BMW. And that was for six hundred hours. When we tripped across the Chef John Folse Culinary Institute at a university in Thibodaux, we laughed. At first. Then we realized that if a woman one year shy of being one hundred can graduate from college, surely Wyatt had a chance to finish what he'd started before his parents passed away.

He was in the middle of his freshman year at the University of New Orleans when his parents died driving home from visiting friends in north Louisiana. Wyatt's GPA plummeted, and he lost the tuition opportunity program that made it possible for him to attend college. His father, a housepainter, and his mother, a bank teller, had struggled financially. The only insurance policy his mother had was a small one from work, barely enough to cover funeral expenses.

That's when Colin swooped in to save him by getting him a job as a waiter at Jean Lafitte's in the French Quarter. But it was in the kitchen watching the chefs that Wyatt found his passion. Or, as he would always tell me, his "first passion," the one that led him to me.

Amanda and I sat side by side at my kitchen table, each of us with a cup of coffee, a peach scone, and determination.

"You're ready?" She handed me a pen.

"Let's do this," I said, took a deep breath, looked at my new bracelet, and signed.

She slid papers out of her folder one by one.

Slide. Sign. Slide. Sign. Slide.

"So . . . how far along are you?" she asked me.

I kept signing. "Not far enough. I have no idea where I want to live, and I haven't even thought about packing."

"Oh, of course . . ."

I looked up, and she blushed.

"That's not what you meant, was it?" I handed her the last sheet.

She made a ceremony out of making sure the papers were aligned. "Olivia, I'm so sorry. That was intrusive of me—"

"How did you know?" I smiled so she'd know she hadn't upset me.

Amanda's shoulders relaxed as she leaned against the back of the chair. "It's always been something I sense. I've been wrong, but usually it's because the woman I ask doesn't even know yet. But as soon as we sat here, I felt positive you were pregnant, and since the feeling didn't go away . . ." She clasped my hands in hers. "For whatever it's worth, I always knew my sister was pregnant before she did. And you look beautiful."

"Thank you," I said.

"For . . . ?"

"For not telling me everything was going to be okay or saying 'omigod, whatareyougoing-todo' or 'God never gives you a cross so big, blahblahblah.'"

She laughed. "I'm going to give you permission to borrow my sister's answer to the 'cross so big.' Brelyn flashes her sweetest smile and says, 'You're so right, and I'm guessing He must have sent you to help me carry it.'" Amanda shook her head. "I always regret I'm not around when she says it."

"That one's worth writing down," I said.

"I'm certain she wouldn't mind sharing it," she said.

She scanned everything I'd signed. Her manicured nails, the color of raspberry sherbet, scurried down each page and stopped at my signature. "Okay, we're all set. The sign's in my car, and I'll put it up on the way out."

We stood, and she hugged me.

"And Olivia," she said, her hands on my shoulders, "I really believe it's true . . . what my sister says about people coming along to help. They're not always who we expect them to be, but they show up."

It had been weeks since I had a reason to look in the mirror to do more than brush my teeth. I finished my makeup and stepped back. "Well, there you are." After feeling invisible for so long, it was almost startling to see the transformation.

I hadn't cut my shoulder-length hair before the wedding so my stylist could perform his updo magic: a side braid with a bun, twisted tresses, and tendrils. I kept my head down so long while he worked, I thought I'd be staring at my navel for life. Now my hair was even longer, and it framed my face like curtains. With my highlights fading, the color reminded me of the brown paper bags my mother had used for my school lunches. I pulled it all into a low ponytail, trying to put my professional on for my appointment with Cara. And, lucky me, to be able to wear leggings with a ruffled tunic. Totally in fashion and totally hiding the baby bump.

I managed to have myself business-ready two hours after Amanda hammered down the For Sale sign in the front yard. Any other day walking outside and watching cars crawl by my house, passengers staring out their windows, I'd be flattered or neurotic, depending on my appearance. This afternoon, I would have been more surprised not to see a few house-hungry buyers cruising the street. One car had parked across the street, and a couple stood on the sidewalk and waved to me as I slipped into my car.

Virtual Strategies' office had been carved out of a renovated old warehouse repurposed into commercial units. With exposed brick walls, concrete floors, industrial lighting, and office furniture the color of Skittles, the space elicited the wow factor that Cara and Alice counted on.

The last time I'd been here was the week before the wedding, my arms and Wyatt's cradling wedding presents from the office shower as we walked to the Jeep. Later, my grandmother had tried to return the gifts, but they weren't having it. Alice told her I could return them all for gift cards, toss the breakables off the roof, whatever I wanted to do with them. Except give them back.

I was supposed to return post-honeymoon. Somewhat tanned, armed with hundreds of boring photos, and officially Mrs. Wyatt Hammond.

Instead, I came back zero out of three.

CHAPTER 14

Cara twirled from side to side in her green ergonomic desk chair. In her tan linen dress, she looked like a tall, thin reed pressed against someone's lawn. With the intensity of a five-year-old, she poked through the chocolate stash she hid in her desk to avoid the tirades from the office anti-sugar groupies and looked as delighted as one when she found a Tootsie Roll. "Want one? They're my new drug of choice."

"No, but thanks. So, my new job title would be Reputation Manager?" I crossed my legs and tapped my foot on the floor, regretting I hadn't stopped in the bathroom. How could something not quite the size of a kumquat be the boss of my bladder? "Is this a title you and Alice invented to legitimize my salary?"

"We're a start-up, remember? Eliminating a salary would make more sense for us right now than inventing a reason for one. Here's the thing we're finding out. Since most of our clients are fledgling businesses like ours, they don't have the time to monitor all the social media that can impact their bottom line. But they can't ignore it, especially if it's a hit to their business they can't recover from. After we do our work establishing their brand, giving them a public face, somebody needs to make sure it's kept clean."

"Like the vacation rental owners who were posting on Facebook about their house being haunted, then asking us why the number of inquiries was decreasing?"

"Yes!" She'd found another Tootsie Roll, so I wasn't sure if she was agreeing with me or cheering for her success. "Exactly. Would that make you want to stay there?"

I shook my head. "No. No. And no."

"Here's the best part. You can work from home for as long as you need. Most of this work involves you and your laptop. At first, you'll probably want to meet with the business owners, maybe even schedule a workshop with their employees about social media. If we absolutely need you here, we'll let you know."

She wanted to discuss the clients we'd start with, which I told her I'd be happy to do after I reacquainted myself with the bathroom.

I returned a few minutes later. Cara watched me, her head slightly tilted, brown eyes focused. Like darts. For a moment, I wondered if someone was tiptoeing behind me. I smoothed my tunic, made sure it wasn't hiked up in the back of my leggings. Checked my shoes. No bath tissue followed me. It wasn't until I sat down that she leaned across the desk and said, "Is everything okay? As in you—are you okay?"

"I'm fine. All things considered," I said. "Why?" Was she concerned about my emotional stability?

She tapped her pen on the palm of her hand and returned to her side-to-side chair-swaying. "Just checking. I don't know. Somehow, you seem different."

Lovely. Another baby whisperer.

"My hair's longer?"

"No, I don't think that's it. But you'd tell me, right? If something was wrong?"

"Of course I would." The pregnancy wasn't wrong, unless she agreed with my mother, which I seriously doubted, knowing her history. I planned to tell Cara about the baby, but sometime later. Not like

I'd be able to hide it in a few months anyway. But if I told her now, it would monopolize our conversation, and I preferred to focus on my new job description, not my baby bump.

"Good. Okay, then. Let me get the papers I want to review with you."

She walked over to her file cabinet, and when I looked down, I realized the subtle shift she'd spotted.

I sat with both hands palms down, propped on the baby bump that only I knew was there.

I left Virtual Strategies with a new title, a list of job descriptions—the most important one being to make certain I pushed anything negative about a business to page three on Google search—and a referral to a private investigator.

Until Cara mentioned issues that could be problematic, especially for family-owned businesses, like infidelity, divorce, kid issues, drinking, addictions, I'd forgotten she'd gone through a messy divorce the year she and Alice opened the agency. Her now ex-husband, a druggie who'd moved so far into recreational use he could have won a gold medal if it were an Olympic sport, was also a prominent attorney who managed to insulate himself from scrutiny about his personal life. He'd filed for custody of their daughters, and Cara was determined to leverage whatever she could to make certain that didn't happen.

I told her my father's insurance business might need access to a private investigator. Not that he had asked me, but I didn't think he'd mind my using him to get the information. Legitimate rationalization, right? I slipped the card for J. M. Tarkington into my wallet.

When I had time, I'd call.

Maybe.

A few days later, armed with my laptop and surrounded by pillows on my bed, I started reviewing one of the three files Cara had sent home with me. I'd already spotted a problem on a client's Facebook page. Children First was a local day-care center that approached us after they opened their third location. One of their employees had posted a picture of a waste can full of dirty diapers with the comment "A lot of sh*t went down today." It was on her personal page, but she'd tagged the center.

Not counting that *poopy* would have been a better choice of words, the picture showed the floor around the waste can littered with used facial tissues, scrunched-up fast-food bags, and a pacifier.

I emailed the owner, alerting her to the post, and advised her to immediately ask the employee to delete it. I told her we'd set a date for a meeting soon.

Still scrolling through websites, I heard something I rarely heard in my house. The telephone, the landline we kept because of hurricanes that generally knocked out cell towers and made charging our cell phones a problem after losing electricity. Usually the only calls were telemarketers and wrong numbers. Whoever was calling now was persistent, because after I didn't answer the first time, the ringing started again within seconds.

This, Wyatt, was the reason I asked you not to plug the phone into the jack until we needed it. He probably wouldn't have answered the call if he'd been standing in front of the phone, so odds were he wasn't going to spirit himself down here now.

I pushed myself off the bed, begrudgingly leaving my comfy pillow fort, and plodded to the den where we kept the phone.

An unfamiliar woman's voice asked to speak to Mr. Wyatt Hammond.

"Excuse me. Who?" I asked, my voice as disembodied as I felt. I picked at a cuticle, ripped it away, and watched the raw skin underneath bubble with blood. The burning sting distracted me from the jagged edge of anxiety thrumming in my chest.

"Wyatt Hammond. I'm sorry, do I have the wrong number?" The female voice polite, businesslike.

"No, not the wrong number," I said. "He's . . . he's . . ." My elbows on the table, palms pressed against my forehead, I closed my eyes and mumbled, "Not here. He's not here."

"Oh, well, could you give him a message? We tried to leave him several voicemails, but the service was out."

I started to answer, but she powered on.

"This is Kelly from Babycakes. I wanted to apologize for it taking so long for his alphabet name print to come in. We had to return the first one because the company misspelled the name. Can you imagine? Why would they think there was a *k* in Jacob? But the new one arrived, so he can pick it up anytime."

CHAPTER 15

While Kelly talked, I walked to my bedroom and opened my laptop, searched, and there it was. Babycakes was located in Oakville.

"Just let me know if he wants it gift wrapped, so I'll be sure and have it ready when it's picked up."

I paced, my hand against my chest as if the pressure might prevent my heart from exploding.

"Could you do me a favor? I couldn't find it on our credit card statement, and I just wanted to make sure he paid for it already. Would you have that information?" I squeezed my eyes shut, braced myself as if her answer would come hurtling through the phone and bash me on the head.

"Sure. Hold a minute . . . Let's see, he ordered it April 30, and the ticket shows he paid cash. So it's already been taken care of."

"Great. I'll . . . I'll let you know about picking it up," I said. My teeth chattered as if the room temperature had suddenly plummeted to zero, and I set the phone back in its cradle after we hung up.

I wrapped my hand around the bracelet from Ruthie, repeating, "Be still, be still, be still" to my quivering body. I sank to the floor, my hand sliding down the wall, supporting me because my legs were melting beneath me.

This doesn't mean anything, Olivia. It could still be a gift for someone else. It doesn't mean this child is his son.

He'd ordered the gift two weeks before the wedding, but it wouldn't have been ready until after we returned from our honeymoon based on Kelly's information. He had to have planned to tell me. He had to. That other gift must have also been intended for him, too.

Still, I couldn't tell anyone about this call. Not yet. It would be all the evidence my mother needed to prove she was right about Wyatt.

I needed to know for sure about Jacob.

Jacob.

I remembered hearing about Jacob in Sunday School. He was a twin, and he was born holding his brother's heel. My friends and I were about eight then, and we all decided none of us wanted twins if that could happen.

In the story we read in Genesis, Jacob and his mother deceived his father into granting him his older brother's birthright. I looked up the meaning of the name Jacob: "Holder of the heel; supplanter. A supplanter is one who wrongfully seizes and holds the place of another."

For the first time in my adult life, I was told it wouldn't hurt for me to gain weight. If this was any indication of the rest of my prenatal visits, then I couldn't wait for the next one.

Dr. Schneider, a petite woman whose round eyeglasses made her look like a pretty dragonfly, scanned my chart while her nurse took my blood pressure. "Most women gain about one or two pounds by their second visit. You've lost two pounds."

I was on my back on the exam table staring at a ceiling covered with blown-up pictures of bright-eyed babies with chipmunk cheeks. "You mean I don't have to stop buying cartons of ice cream and Snickers?" My hands were over my little pouch, my fingers tapping as I turned to look at Dr. Schneider, who hadn't responded to my question.

"Only if that's all you're eating." She pushed her glasses up so they held back her springy blonde curls. "No problems with morning sickness?"

"A few times, but nothing recently. Guess I don't have a routine yet. Sometimes I forget to eat."

"Hmmm . . ." She measured my stomach and then helped me sit up.

I stretched my blouse back over my bump. "I hate when doctors say 'hmmm.' I don't know if that means 'Hmmm, you're an idiot' or 'Hmmm, you have a life-threatening disease' or 'Hmmm, I have no answer for that.'"

"Sorry, I forget how annoying that is. It's a habit that follows me home, and I promise you, my husband and kids aren't crazy about it, either," she said. "But, in my defense, I was thinking how to help you feed yourself and this baby. Have you ever tried those online services that deliver boxes of food every week? A number of my single moms have subscribed. Saves grocery trips, and they're eating healthy."

Single mom. I hated hearing that more than "hmmm."

Mia called on my way home from the doctor's visit. I told her the good news: I wasn't a cystic fibrosis carrier, I was Rh-positive, and the baby was due the first week in February, not earlier like we first thought.

"We didn't have any luck hearing the baby's heartbeat, but Dr. Schneider said that's not unusual, and she's sure we'll hear it at my next visit. They're going to do an ultrasound then, too."

"Hmmm . . ."

"Oh, not you, too. What's up with that?" I pulled into the parking lot of the new Trader Joe's.

"I guess every doctor's different. Mine did an ultrasound and blood test at every visit," she said.

I heard the uncertainty. I chose to ignore it. Mia was often overly cautious and fussy. Bryce would have said "phobic and princessy."

"She said I needed to gain weight, so I'm on my way into the grocery to follow doctor's orders. I'll call later and tell you about my new job."

"Wait? You have a new job? What happened to the old one? You never even mentioned you were looking—"

"Whoa. I can't vet everything in my life with you first," I said and followed with a laugh so she wouldn't shift into her defensive stance. "I should have been more specific. Old job. New title. Now go decorate something and we'll talk later."

Shopping for food when the calories didn't matter was almost as decadent as shopping for clothes without looking at the price tag. At least I could accomplish one of the two. I skipped the fruits and veggies because those I could find anywhere. But pretzel bagels, lemon heart cookies, lobster ravioli, frozen mac and cheese, figs with herbed goat cheese, tiramisu torte, and cookie butter rocked my world at Joe's.

I zapped frozen sweet potato gnocchi for supper that night, then treated myself to two chocolate croissants while I scrolled through the food-delivery options Dr. Schneider had suggested. I subscribed to one that would start delivery in a week. By next month, I figured I'd have made up for the lost pounds and then some.

I was on my way to solving at least one challenge in my life.

In the days following the phone call from the children's store in Oakville, I debated whether I should drive there and actually pick up the gift Wyatt had ordered.

That first night after I'd found out about it, I couldn't sleep. Every time I closed my eyes, I saw Wyatt smiling as he held a baby. A baby swaddled in a blue blanket. A baby whose face I couldn't see.

My heart might as well have been made of glass it felt so shattered, shards of it trapped in my lungs, their edges slicing every breath.

But sometimes a wild-animal rage consumed me, and I hated that Wyatt had left me to suffer this alone. I wanted to yank him into the fire fueled by his deception, his irresponsibility, his abandonment.

But I still held on to the hope that Jacob wasn't Wyatt's son.

But what if he was? Somewhere in Oakville or nearby, there was a woman who might not know her child was fatherless.

Like mine.

If I couldn't bring myself to open the baby gift I'd kept ever since my father gave it to me, then I wasn't ready to drive to Oakville to pick up another one.

I called Babycakes, gave them my address, and asked them to mail it.

CHAPTER 16

I hadn't seen my parents since I'd been to their office after confronting them with the police report. My father called more often than my mother, who sent brief text messages. In our usual Kavanaugh family dynamics model, we didn't discuss that afternoon again.

When I listed the house, I put them and my grandmother on notice because, once again, our family code dictated that no one in the family should first hear anything about the family from anyone outside the family. That unwritten rule had gone into effect when I started high school.

My mother had sat me down before I left the house for the football jamboree and said, "Olivia, we might be close to New Orleans, but this is a small town. Your father and I may not know about things you do right away, but believe me, we'll find out sooner or later. And if we haven't heard it from you first, you're going to pray it's later and not sooner."

My father had walked into the den midway during her monologue, sat in his recliner, and picked up his remote. And when she finished, he said, "Don't lie to us. That's the CliffsNotes version."

And I never did lie to them. Except for the times I did. By my senior year, my parents trusted me enough to attend parties I'd gone to anyway. If they'd found me out in all the years before that, it was never an issue. Probably coming home sober and at curfew helped.

When they learned that I was selling the house, they asked where I planned to go when I moved. I told them the truth: "I have no idea." And I didn't. All I knew was I couldn't stay in that house.

With the number of showings Amanda had booked, I hoped the house sold soon because I felt like a human boomerang. Plus, there was that thing of having to keep it ready for a walk-through at any time. I discovered that prospective buyers didn't bother looking in the washer and dryer, so they became my safe places to store clutter and even dirty dishes.

One couple had come back three times. The last time with an architect. Amanda called me after they left. She said they'd told her they would call with an offer by the next morning. "I explained to them that in three weeks I've shown this house to at least a dozen couples and some of them twice. If they're serious, they needed to act."

And they did. They called her that night, offered me more than my asking price in case another offer might be pending, and were paying cash. While I was doing the happy dance in my kitchen, Amanda added that they wanted the act of sale in three weeks.

"Three weeks from when? Today?" My dance music disappeared.

"Yes. They want to make some changes to the house before they move in, and their schedule's tight due to his job transfer. They're paying cash, so we don't have to wait for loan approval."

I couldn't pass up the offer. I signed the contract, rented a storage unit, then sat on my bedroom floor and cried.

I summoned the courage I didn't use when I avoided driving to Oakville and invited my parents to my soon-to-not-be-my house for coffee and dessert.

I told them about the contract I'd signed and the conditions. "I wanted to ask you—"

My mother held up her hand. "We know. You want to move in with us. Right? Why else would you invite us over after we've not seen or hardly talked to you in two weeks? When we drove up and saw the Sold sign, it didn't take us long to figure out." Her expression waiting for my reaction was as blank as my date calendar.

My father traced the parquet pattern on my kitchen table, looking up only when she finished talking, his eyes moving from me to my mother to the table.

"I'm not asking for forever. This happened sooner than I expected—"

"Like some other things in your life," my mother said before taking a sip of her coffee.

"Scarlett Ellen." My father used those names together like a reprimand. His lips formed a tight seam across his face. He shook his head, the slow version he reserved for when he didn't want to call someone out in front of others. It accompanied the dismal look of deep disappointment. Even at my age, I'd rather bear the force of shouting that could blow leaves off trees than endure the shame and guilt of knowing I was responsible for such emotional devastation.

"As I was trying to explain, it's temporary until I decide where I want to move." I sliced a slab of my dad's favorite lemon Doberge cake, seven layers of lemon pudding and eight layers of cake covered with buttercream and ganache.

"Whoa, Livvy," he held the plate up until it was at eye level. "I'm not sure I can eat all this."

I was about to tell him I'd seen him in action with that cake, when he winked and set the plate back on the table and said, "But I'm sure gonna give it my best."

"And how long is 'temporary'?" my mother asked.

"I didn't know you'd want me to define it." I served her a sliver of a piece, but she scrunched her nose and waved it off.

"I'm still full from dinner. There's also a luncheon at the club next week, and I don't want my skirt to be tight. Watching what I eat for a few more days."

Any other time, I might've joked that I noticed those extra eight ounces on her, but her sense of humor left on the first flight out with a one-way ticket the night I told them I was pregnant. Instead, I added her sliver to my Goldilocks "just right" slice and casually mentioned I was under doctor's orders to gain weight.

"I'm thinking a month, six weeks would be enough time," I said, taking a bite of cake and letting my mouth be happy.

"What if it takes longer for you to move?"

"What if it does?" I was already calculating the number of cakes Dad and I could consume in that period of time. I should've paid less attention to the cake and more to her face or I wouldn't have been as shocked by what she said next.

"Your living with us makes it seem as if we're condoning your pregnancy. And I've been clear about where I stand on that."

An army of ants crawled up my backbone. For a moment, I was incoherent while my brain processed this latest offensive comment. "As if you're what? I'm not believing this. What you're telling me is you're more concerned about what your church friends are going to say about you at Women's Fellowship?"

"Don't turn this around. You're the one who sinned," she said, the accusation in her voice unmistakable.

On the verge of a total meltdown, I pointed at my father. "And where are you on all of this? Is she doing the fighting for you?"

"Your mother needs to—"

"Shut up. That's what my mother needs to do." I stared at my father, but my mother's audible gasp drew our attention.

Impassive no more, my mother sat on the edge of the chair, her coffee cup pushed to the side. "Olivia, that was disrespectful. And I deserve an apology."

"What you deserve is to listen to me. Not just hear me. Listen. What century are you living in? Wyatt and I were getting married. You call yourself a Christian, yet you're denying me and your grandchild a few weeks in your home?"

"Let's take this down a notch. Calm down." My father turned to my mother. "Scarlett, let's not act rashly. We don't have to make a decision tonight. You can think about this."

"'Think about this'? She shouldn't have to think about this. She's my mother." And I needed her now more than I wanted to admit. How could she not know that?

"We can barely spend an hour together without butting heads over something. What do you think would happen after a month or longer? As for what century I'm living in, the last I checked, the Bible isn't undergoing revisionist history." She slid her chair back and stood facing my dad. "This isn't going to work."

"Where am I supposed to go in three weeks? I can't believe you're doing this," I said and stared at her, the mother whose love shielded me after Wyatt died. Her face was familiar, but her heart was unrecognizable. I remembered when I was a child and wandered away from my parents when we were Christmas shopping. I spotted a woman wearing black pants, worked my way through swarms of shoppers until I reached her. But when I tugged, instead of my mother's face, a stranger's looked down at me. That same panic, disbelief, and confusion exploded in me now.

"You'll find your way," she said with the warmth of a rock.

Now it was my turn to stand and stare. "I was never enough, was I? You wanted more children, but I was it. And as much as you tried, I couldn't or wouldn't be you. I can't do anything right in your eyes or God's."

⚜

I didn't wait to see my parents leave. I walked out of the kitchen before they did, made my way to my bedroom and closed the door.

When I stopped the ugly hiccupping and the heaving crying, I did the only thing I knew to do next.

I called Mia.

CHAPTER 17

I stretched out on my unmade bed, turned on my side, and faced the space occupied by my memories of Wyatt.

I told her everything.

I started with the call from Babycakes, then the offer, then my parents. Their lack of an offer.

"I have a plan. You can move here with us. And don't tell me no before you've heard me out. We're still frantically looking for a nanny. You could help us with Lily. Really. And you wouldn't be in our way. There's an apartment over the garage. It's even detached from the house. You'd have your privacy, and we would, too."

"Mia, I know you want to help, and I love you for that. But I can't take advantage of you and Bryce."

"Are you kidding me? I need you. Don't make me fly over there and drag you to Houston myself. You're our friend. You're having a baby, and you need help. This isn't forever. You and that kid aren't going to grow old in my garage apartment. You'll have the money from the sale of the house, and we can look for a place for you to live in Houston. And you can talk to Cara and ask if you can work from here."

"Is Bryce okay with this?"

"Would I be talking to you about moving here if he wouldn't be?"

I loved the way Mia framed that answer. Because "wouldn't be" meant she hadn't discussed this with Bryce first. But, as in most things Mia, she'd overcome any objections he might have, and Bryce would end up wondering why she had asked for his approval in the first place.

"Give me some time to think about all of this," I said, looking around my house and imagining the exhaustion of packing boxes, moving the furniture, the clothes, the artwork . . . I hadn't even started and I was already tired. "Cara didn't expect me to stay away from the office months at a time, so I'm not sure what she'll say about my working long-distance. Plus, Wyatt is buried here, which is dumb to even say because he's not going to miss me. But I'm still no closer to finding out where he was going when he died, and I don't know how I'll do that hundreds of miles away . . ." I was rambling.

"I didn't expect to pick you up at the airport tomorrow. Though it would make my life less complicated. See how unselfish I can be?" I heard the smile in her voice. "I hate to say this, but—"

"Mia, anytime you start a sentence with those six words, what you really mean is 'You're going to hate to hear this.'"

"I know you want to solve this mystery with Wyatt, but you can't do it alone. You may not be able to do it at all. There aren't any bread crumbs left for you to follow on the road from there to Oakville."

She paused, but I didn't fill the empty space with words.

"Thing is, Livvy, maybe it's time to stop trying to figure it out. Just let it be. Maybe you're not meant to know. Or, when the time is right, you'll find out the truth."

"I'm not giving up. Not yet. I know there's an answer; maybe I'm not asking the right questions."

The frustration kept me awake at night. Some piece of this puzzle was hiding in plain sight, like my car keys. I'd zip through the house, a cartoon character on fast-forward, lifting clothes and magazines, checking pockets, looking under beds and the sofa, checking every flat surface in the house.

I stopped asking Wyatt for help when, every time I couldn't find something, his response was to ask me where I had it last. I'd slap my arms against the sides of my body and screech, "If I could answer that, they wouldn't be lost, would they?" If Wyatt could have tied a string around me and pulled it, I would have been a human top spinning until exhaustion.

It was only when I surrendered in defeat that my head or the veil over my eyes would clear. I'd remember that I'd forgotten client files and left them on my desk, or they'd be hanging out with the coffee mugs when I stopped for a refill on the way out.

And every part of me thought the answer to the Wyatt mystery was waiting to be found. I just wasn't sure yet what I was looking for.

That night, propping myself up against the headboard, MacBook on my lap, my intention to review a client's site was waylaid by my searching for hospital birth announcements in Oakville's *Daily News*. Another dead end. The hospital there stopped providing the information to newspapers because of an increased risk for infant abductions and the exposure of the hospital to potential lawsuits.

You still haven't opened that baby gift. Maybe that's the answer. Maybe you'll find the truth there.

But what if I hate the truth? What if the truth destroys me?

A text from Amanda woke me up the next morning. She'd sent me the date, time, and place of the act of sale. Three weeks. In twenty-one days my life would change again. I felt like someone who'd studied French for years waiting for that luxurious trip to Paris. Then I step off the plane, and everyone's speaking Greek. I asked for Paris. For a wedding, and a life with Wyatt, and painting the nursery blue, then pink, then blue again.

Instead, I'm sitting in the Athens airport, tossing my Paris guidebooks into the trash. Wondering if I should spend time learning the new language, or would I expend all that energy only to find myself in another place?

Regardless of where I was headed, I had to leave this place. The home I thought would be my beginning would belong to some other family and their new beginning.

I made a list of moving companies, then started my phone calls to gather quotes. My grandmother beeped in at least six times. When I didn't answer, she left a voicemail. When she didn't get a response to the call or the voicemail, she left a text: I called, and I left a voicemail. Did you get those? Call me!

I suspected she would volunteer to be the intermediary between my parents and me. She wouldn't be offering me a place to stay because she lived in a one-bedroom apartment in a retirement center that transitioned to assisted living as needed.

After so many attempts to contact me, she dispensed with nice-nice when she answered my call.

"It's about time," she growled. "What if I'd fallen down the stairs and cracked my head open? Or had a heart attack? Or was in an ambulance on my way to the hospital?"

"I don't know, Ruthie. I would've apologized profusely and hoped to get to the hospital before they pulled the plug." I waited for her laugh, but nothing.

"You know, I'm an old woman. One of those things could really happen. You wouldn't want to live the rest of your life feeling guilty about ignoring my calls, now would you?"

I sighed. It seemed the only trip destined for me was a guilt trip. And the cost of those was always more than the price I was willing to pay. "Of course not. I have too many other items on my Things to Feel Guilty About list. So, what is it you needed to talk about?"

"Your mother called me. Told me you sold your house, and she said you couldn't live with them. Said she had her reasons. What happened?"

"I guess she's more concerned about her church thinking she's opened a halfway house for unwed mothers than she is her own daughter," I said as I walked around the house collecting tchotchkes and putting them on the kitchen table. A ceramic frog dish, paperweights that weren't doing their job, a mug shaped like a football helmet . . .

"Glory be. I birthed her, but sometimes I don't understand what Bible she's operating from." She followed with her little hums of disapproval. "Look, give her some time. She'll come around. I'll talk to her. Maybe redefine what it means to call yourself a Christian and hope she doesn't kick me out on my keister. Too bad she's too old to put in time-out."

"I don't have time to give her time. I called Mia, and she's offered her garage apartment in Houston. I'm driving there after I sign the papers."

"Your mother didn't tell me about this," she said, her voice rising. "When are you coming home?"

"She didn't tell you about Houston because I spoke to Mia after she and Dad left, and I haven't told them yet." I found an empty box, marked it *Donations* and started loading it with some items that might be someone else's treasures. "As for home . . . in three weeks, my home can be anywhere I want it to be."

"But your family's here."

"No. My family . . . all I have of Wyatt, will be going with me."

CHAPTER 18

Moving was the binge-and-purge syndrome of consumerism for houses.

In the guest bedroom closet, I discovered another box of tchotchkes from my former apartment meant to litter the furniture and shelves with dustables. Collections of angels and owls hunkered down with ceramic pigs. Clearly things not necessary for living a full life.

Other surprises included finding the steak knives I'd searched for after Wyatt and I moved in together (which meant I now owned eleven more knives than I needed), a pair of boots I'd ordered shoved into a box of Christmas ornaments, and a plastic bag full of paper clips.

Buried under the boots, I found a high school yearbook. Wyatt's high school yearbook. I sat cross-legged on the floor in the closet staring at the pebbled cover, holding it as if it would break. I flipped through the glossy pages, black-and-white images of students at lunch, at football games and dances. All the seniors were pictured in their caps and gowns. When I saw Wyatt, the front of his cap mashing his bangs so that they almost covered his eyebrows, I outlined his picture with my fingertip as if he could somehow sense that I was there. Colin's picture was there, too, his cap as crooked as his smile.

A few pages later, I spotted a picture of Wyatt on a page featuring a collage of prom pictures. Maybe I had seen it when he first showed me his yearbook the night we strolled down memory lane to visit ourselves in the past. But this color photograph didn't look familiar. Wyatt wore a tuxedo. The girl's chestnut hair was gathered at the nape of her neck, the ringlets falling between her shoulder blades. They were dancing, her hands clasped around his neck, his hands framed her waist, both of them oblivious to the camera lens. The girl's smile reflected his, their eyes caressing each other.

I shuddered. I felt like an intruder staring at the picture of this intimate moment between them. I wouldn't have been surprised if one of them reached beyond the page to slam the door of the space and time between us.

Who was this girl? Without a caption, I had no way to identify her. And, as obsessed with getting to the truth as I was, it didn't encompass searching through almost a thousand students to find a match. She might not even have attended that school.

Could there have been an intimacy between them beyond these pages? Could they have met again years later? Could she be Jacob's mother?

I knew only one person who might be able to answer at least one of those questions.

Colin.

I was separating my clothes into stacks of What Were You Thinking? and Possible Post-Baby and I'll Eat Four Lettuce Leaves a Day Until I Can Wear That Again when Colin returned my call.

He asked what I was doing, and when I told him, he laughed. "Let me guess, the What Were You Thinking pile is winning. My girl-friend's been on an organizing binge, and last weekend she emptied her entire closet on the bedroom floor. I couldn't walk in the room without wading through puddles of clothes. She had a mountain of outfits she said she must have purchased because she felt sorry for the salesperson."

"Does she hire out?" I was only partly joking.

"Even if she did, she wouldn't have time. She's helping me with catering. But I'm sure you didn't call me to talk about clothes. Bryce told me you may be settling in Houston for a while. Did you need some help moving?"

I thanked him for offering, then went on to tell him the reason I called. I described the picture and asked Colin if he had any idea who Wyatt's date was that night. "A part of me feels foolish asking you to remember something from so long ago. But the part of me that wants answers isn't ready to give up."

"I understand," he said softly. "Her name was Chelsea Sullivan. She didn't go to our school. She went to St. Mary's Academy. Wyatt and Chelsea didn't see each other after graduation. If you're thinking she's the person Wyatt was going to see, it's not possible."

"I'm learning things I thought impossible do happen. How can you be so sure?"

"Because two years after graduation, Chelsea walked into her house, and one of the three men who'd broken in shot and killed her," he said.

"Oh, dear God." I lowered myself to the floor and leaned against the wall between the hills of clothes. I remembered her smile in that picture when she and Wyatt were dancing and didn't want to imagine what it must feel like as a parent to lose a child. "That's so awful."

"Yes, it was devastating. They were eventually arrested and convicted. I think that brought her parents some peace." He paused. "But even though they know that, they still don't know why it happened. Maybe that's a question you, or any of us who knew Wyatt, may never find the answer to."

What people didn't understand was that I went to sleep with *never* and woke up with it every morning.

I left early for my meeting with Cara to discuss my working from Houston and for an appointment with one of my clients who owned an emergency-care clinic.

Whatever doubts I had about my shift to Reputation Manager dissolved when I started checking my clients' social media and reviews on sites like Yelp. After five minutes cruising through Dr. Wayne Yellowstone's clinic, I called not only to schedule a time to meet him, but to ask him to suspend his posting to Facebook, Twitter, Instagram, and other sites.

If he exchanged his white lab coat that may have, at one time, actually buttoned across his expansive stomach, for a red velvety suit and sat in a sleigh led by Rudolph, Dr. Yellowstone could convince anyone he was the real-deal Santa. When he smiled, his eyes almost disappeared into the crinkles that formed at their edge, and his silvery mustache offset his white teeth.

I dispensed with my title and explained I wanted to review his social media guidelines and offer a few suggestions for posts and reviews.

He drummed his stout fingers on his desk pad and looked at me from under his eyebrows as if I'd informed him I was there to perform a lobotomy. On him.

"Olivia . . . Is it okay if I call you Olivia?"

I nodded.

He continued. "We opened this clinic six months ago; of course, you probably already know that. What I know about all that social stuff could fit on a prescription pad, and I'd still have room to doodle. I'm too busy seeing patients to learn, so my granddaughter handles all that for me."

"Not a problem," I said. "Most business owners delegate that responsibility." I opened my planner. "When do you think she and I could meet?"

"Hmmm. Probably when she's out of school. Anytime after three." When I asked what college she attended, he pushed back his desk chair as if to give himself space for a belly laugh. "Oh, honey, she's a junior at the magnet school around the corner."

I bit my lower lip so the question "Does the math teacher do your taxes?" wouldn't pop out of my mouth. Instead, I told him I'd be back that afternoon to meet her.

At lunch later, I told Cara having that appointment beforehand was serendipity. "It explained the Facebook photo of bloody gauze pads and splatters of blood on the floor with the caption: 'What an exam room looks like after stitching up an arm sliced by a box cutter.' And, honestly, it convinced me clients need someone who isn't six hours away to look out for them. I can check their sites anywhere, but scheduling time with them, face-to-face, that's important."

"Your moving to Houston, is that a temporary thing?" She handed her credit card to the server, then waited for my answer.

I waited for it, too, because I had no idea when or if I'd be returning. A bus girl passed our table shouldering a tray of steaks sizzling on cast iron platters, the cloying aroma of melted butter trailing behind her. By then, I didn't know if it was the sickening smell or indecision roiling in my stomach. I drank some water and told her, my voice wrapped in confusion and sadness, "Maybe? It depends"—I closed and opened my eyes like someone in darkness adjusting to the harshness of a sudden light—"on what I want to do."

Not my parents. Not Mia. Not the baby.

Me.

Owning that thrilled me. And terrified me.

CHAPTER 19

Cara hugged me and wished me luck before she left. Together we had decided what at least one of us had already figured out. My position at Virtual Strategies couldn't relocate to Houston and provide local clients the services promised them.

"If you decide to come back, let me know. I can't guarantee an opening, but we'd want you on our team. In the meantime, I'll reach out to some agencies in Houston and contact you if I find out they're looking," she said.

I'd have the money from selling the house, so I didn't panic about being jobless. At least for a few months. Which would coincide with the arrival of the baby in the bump. Then I'd spin out of orbit.

No time to be in a tizzy now.

I changed into my slouchy clothes as soon as I got home, determined to finish the closet purge. The temptation to dive into the tidal wave of clothes on the floor for a brief nap was washed away only by the disturbing thought of having to face it again tomorrow.

One stack later, someone started doubling down on my doorbell. A shrill and insistent noise that rivaled nails zipping down a chalkboard for first place in the "sounds from hell" category. In the seconds it took me to get from the bedroom to the front door, I conjured the evils awaiting the person standing on my porch.

My eyes narrowed, laserlike, ready to drill through whomever had the misfortune to be on the other side of it, I jerked the door open.

No one.

I stepped out on the porch and looked for suspects. Derek, the kid next door, and his friends had never resorted to torturing the neighbors. So why would . . . And then I saw it. Behind one of the large plant urns flanking the sideway leading to the porch. A long brown box. The return address . . . Babycakes.

Despite the concrete scalding my bare feet and the hot, thick air, I suddenly felt like I'd been immersed in an ice bath as I carried the package in my house. I sat on the sofa, the box balanced on my knees, my hands on top like I was preventing it from levitating.

Why did I think having it sent here was a good idea? Do I open it? And then what?

The room was weirdly still. I suspected every piece of furniture was holding its breath, anticipating my response.

Do you want to close your eyes at night envisioning this artwork with Jacob's name?

I carried the box to the Jeep and placed it next to the other unopened gift. I opened the front door, now feeling grateful for the chill of the air-conditioning. I returned to my bedroom, ordering the walls to stop whispering "We told you so" when I passed.

That night I fell asleep dreaming of Wyatt rocking a baby while I stood watching through the window of a house I didn't recognize.

❧

The next two weeks were devoured by packing box after box after box. Taking breaks to stomp on the bubble wrap just because I could. Deciding what followed me to Houston. What stayed was scheduled to be hauled by movers to a self-storage unit.

The morning of the act of sale, I wandered through the house, room by room. The aching loss I expected to experience didn't happen once everything that had belonged to us had been taken away. Selling it gave me freedom. Not to start over, but to start again.

My father, who'd been calling me every other day since the "great divide," wanted to meet for dinner the night before I left for Houston. He desperately wanted to repair the damage between my mother and me. And, even though the rift was cavernous, he persisted.

I met him, my mother, and grandmother for dinner at their country club. In one of my passive-aggressive acts, promising I'd shame myself later, I wore a knit blouse to accentuate my bump. Which, for anyone who didn't know I was pregnant, looked more like bloat.

I picked up Ruthie, since I planned to spend the night at her house. She walked out wearing a soft jersey jumpsuit that tied around her waist, silver wedges, and her elegant sapphire and diamond necklace. And by her strut, I knew that she knew she looked amazing. But Ruthie could pull off strutting and amazing without seeming the least bit smug.

"Tell me why a man has not yet made an honest woman out of you?" My question was equal parts serious and jest. She never remarried after my grandfather died the summer before I started college.

"Maybe I'm not ready to be an honest woman," she said, her tone as serious and jesting as she pulled down the visor to apply her lip gloss. "And, my dear"—she reached over and patted my leg—"I don't need a man to define me."

"Then that's the problem," I said. "You're self-assured, independent, and beautiful. Is that the kiss of death for men of your generation?" I stopped to enter the code to open the gates to the road that led to the club.

"Not for all of them. And I'm not so sure that's limited to my generation. After James died, I realized I'd spent over half my life married. I decided to spend some time with me. Get to know Ruthie again. Thing is, you have to be happy with yourself before you can be happy with someone else. If you're not, then you're going to be blaming the wrong person when you're miserable." She paused. "When that man comes along, I'll let you know."

"What if he doesn't?" I think I was asking that more for myself than for her. She'd already been alone for over ten years. Was that what I was facing?

"I have too little left of my life to lead a 'settle for' kind of life. Really, no one should. If he doesn't come along, then I'll keep doing what I've been doing. Being the best me I can be."

We were at the top step ready to open the door to the clubhouse when Ruthie stopped me.

"It might be a while before we all see you again." She smoothed my hair back, then wrapped her arms around me. "Let's make the best out of tonight. Okay?"

The maître d' led us to our table. My mother hugged me; her elbows close to her sides. The kind of hug dispensed with brief and minimal contact, as if my body might scorch her hands if they lingered. I expected the anger from that conflict at my house to resurrect itself when we saw each other again. But instead, disappointment and sadness rose from the grave of that night.

She'd been my refuge after Wyatt died, made all the funeral arrangements, and never left my side that day. All the while knowing what she did, about where his truck had been found, about the baby gift. When nightmares jolted me awake, she'd come to my room and hold me until I fell asleep again.

I wanted that mother back. If I'd asked her, she might have told me she wanted that daughter back. But those two women were buried under the rubble of unforgiveness.

My father played emcee from appetizer to dessert, making sure everything flowed as smoothly as the wine they sipped. Ruthie positioned herself between my mother and me, sometimes elbowing or eyeing me when she thought I should contribute to the conversation.

When we walked outside after dinner, we were like actors told to play a scene without having been given a script. I kissed my parents, told them I'd call when I reached Houston.

My father shook the change in his pants pockets and stared at my mother. She repeated her earlier imitation hug, then told me to drive carefully.

"You get your tires checked and gas in your car?" My father asked, starting a throwback series of "on the road instructions" dating from my college years.

I nodded.

"Need any money? You have cash, not just your credit cards?"

"I have enough money. And cash."

"If you have to stop, make sure you're in a safe area."

"Dad, I'm driving during the day. I'll be fine."

"You know we love you, right?" He cleared his throat, which I suspected was a prelude to him trying not to shed tears. Then he enveloped me in one of his bear hugs, crushed me against him until I almost couldn't breathe.

It was as if he were trying to hug me enough for both of them.

CHAPTER 20

Random facts I learned about Houston:

- I could eat three meals a day, each one at a different restaurant, for seven years and three months.
- Rush-hour traffic was a misnomer. It was not-rush-for-hours-any-time-of-day traffic.
- Speedometers were pointless. The object of the game was to adjust my speed to the cars around me.
- Not understanding compass directions on the interstate signage will most likely result in getting lost. Often.

I pulled into Mia and Bryce's driveway about an hour later than expected. I hadn't considered extra bathroom stops and thirty minutes of delays due to road construction.

Lily was already asleep, so they helped me unload and showed me my new home. The garage apartment was designed and decorated by Mia, so it was picture-perfect. Completely furnished, the kitchen had everything I needed, and they had even stocked the pantry and refrigerator for me.

They had built it for the nanny or au pair they had hoped to hire, but it had been vacant since being finished. Neither of them had thought trying to find someone to take care of Lily would take months.

"We could have another baby in the time it's taking us to sort through and interview all these prospects," Mia said when she and Bryce were helping me settle in the apartment after I'd arrived.

Bryce paled, the flat-screen television he carried was moving dangerously close to the floor. "You're not trying to tell me something, are you?"

"When I stop drinking coffee in the mornings because it starts tasting like used pencil erasers, I won't even need a pregnancy test," Mia answered. "You're safe. But don't get so excited you drop that television you're juggling. Stop trying to hang it on the wall. Just put it on the stand until I'm sure that's where it stays."

Bryce looked like a kid who'd earned early release from his time-out. No pregnant wife. No fear of dropping the television on his feet. No more having to work from home and take care of Lily when Mia couldn't.

The rest of the evening disappeared between the rush of seeing them again, the emotional and physical exhaustion of driving, and settling in.

Usually sleeping was a challenge for me the first night in a strange bed. But I was up against a triple play. Strange bed. Strange house. Strange city.

Was that the central air kicking on, or did someone kick the front door? Was it raining outside, or did I forget to turn off a faucet? Are those sirens on their way to here or from here?

The mattress was probably as tired as I was from suffering through my pillow squishing, my body twisting and turning. I didn't remember when, but I knew I'd fallen asleep because I woke up to my phone ringing.

"Good morning," chirped Mia. "Lily wanted me to call an hour ago, but I told her we had to wait until nine. I hope we didn't wake you."

"Not really. I should've already been awake." I yawned, but not as quietly as I'd thought because she started apologizing.

Then Lily chimed in. "Aunt Wivvy, Aunt Wivvy, come see. Mommy cooked. And I wearing my pink babing suit."

I pictured her jumping as she talked to me. Every sentence filled with urgency and enthusiasm.

"Bryce already left for work. Just throw a robe on and come on down. I'll have a cup of decaf waiting for you." As Mia spoke, Lily accompanied her with singsong chants of "I wuv Aunt Wivvy."

When I told her I didn't own a robe, she reacted as if I didn't own a toothbrush. "We'll be sure and take care of that today, but come eat breakfast and I'll go over the schedule with you."

I unearthed my go-to yoga pants and a loose tee from my suitcase, my clothes in various stages of finding their place. Moving around the apartment, I felt like I was on vacation, not a staycation for an indefinite period. The buttercream walls and the striped window coverings in shades of coffee, which puddled on the oak floors, reflected Mia's penchant for warm earth tones. A contrast to the home I'd left behind where the kitchen walls were the shade of ripe eggplants, and a cranberry accent wall provided a sharp contrast for the white sofa.

Between the apartment and Mia's back door, the weather was a preview of hell, even this early in the morning. Not much difference in the humidity or the heat when moving from Louisiana to Texas.

Lily rushed out the door, and that tired cliché of "Oh my goodness, I can't believe how much you've grown" woke up in me. Mia had already warned me that Lily wanted to pick out her own clothes for the day, so I wasn't mystified by her outfit. She wore a hot pink tulle skirt with a red tank top over her swimsuit, an orange bow in her hair, and a pair of UGG boots.

I picked her up, and she wrapped her legs around my waist and squeezed her arms around my neck until I could hardly breathe. She smelled like lavender and baby powder and joy. The stinging inside my nose usually preceded my eyes bubbling with tears, and I tried to blink them away before Lily could see them. She, like most kids her age, thought an adult only cried for the same reasons she did. Happy tears weren't on her emotional radar yet, and mine were definitely that.

I shifted her to my hip, and she pressed her little cheek against mine and whispered in my ear, "You are my best fwend."

Mia cooking breakfast must have qualified as a special event, because Lily wanted to call her father and tell him.

"Aunt Livvy's going to think I never give you breakfast," Mia said, a layer of chagrin embedded in her mother-ese voice.

Lily opened her breakfast taco and picked out the bacon. "Well, sometimes Starbucks give me bwekfest." She shrugged. "But, it's okay when we do dat."

I laughed. "Starbucks gives me breakfast, too."

"Not this morning, sister," said Mia as she handed me a plate with scrambled eggs, bacon, and cheese rolled into a warm wheat tortilla. She served herself, then sat next to me and slid her planner between us.

"Sweetie, don't wipe your hands on your skirt. Use your napkin like Mommy taught you. Manners, remember?"

Lily nodded, wiped her hands, and made faces on her plate with the bacon bits she'd picked out.

"And don't play with your food."

"Bwekfast here is not fun," said Lily, finally taking a bite of her taco.

When Mia opened her planner, I silently agreed with Lily. The president's press secretary would have been awed by her detailed agenda. Mia organized like I ate . . . with consistency, determination, and pleasure.

Over the next two days, Mia planned to give me a road tour of her business, Bryce's office, the nearest emergency clinic, the hospital, the pediatrician's office, supermarket, pharmacy, library, park, and zoo. We hadn't left yet, and I already felt carsick.

"I know you won't remember the directions to all of these, but I thought giving you visuals of what you were looking for would help," she said. "Printed these for you to put in your binder."

She handed me maps she'd printed for each location. I sipped my coffee to dilute the lump in my throat. "Binder?" The word sounded more like *handcuffs* than I meant it to.

Mia patted my hand and smiled. "I'll show you that later. Let's plan to leave in an hour. That'll give you time to freshen up. We'll stop for lunch, so you may want to change into something . . . something else?"

We both understood that meant I should wear clothes appropriate to being introduced to the public.

Back in my apartment, I found a cotton sundress and sandals, managed to find enough makeup to not have a naked face, and collapsed on the bed.

Maybe this wasn't the brilliant solution I had thought it was. Mia as friend was one creature. Mia as mom, wife, business owner was intense. My phone timer chimed. I had three minutes to meet Mia for our excursion.

Wyatt, this is all your fault. How selfish of you to die.

CHAPTER 21

By the end of Mia in Motion: Day Two, I seriously questioned my sanity, my ability to mother, and my choice of friends.

The busyness didn't allow much time—in conversations or in thought—to dissect everything happening and not happening in my post-Wyatt life. In telling me about the designated tour stops, Mia didn't mention the Houston traffic, schizophrenic freeways, or road-repair dodges. She'd been away too long to remember that complaining about six stop signs and three signal lights was a way of life in our hometown. In one of my emails to my father after I'd arrived, I told him to open a second office in Houston because, judging by the number of drivers and their speeds, the life insurance industry here should be booming.

The binder.

If she'd planned a test on that monstrous binder, I planned to spirit myself out under the cover of darkness and, if necessary, push my car to the end of the street before starting it to avoid detection. My little nugget of a baby would probably cheer me on to victory.

With each page in its own clear protector and weighing more than a small dog, this was the nanny/caretaker/au pair bible. No translation needed. Accept the words printed on the page and—when in doubt—err on the side of caution. If I could create something like it for our clients to monitor their social media, I'd be the darling of Virtual Strategies.

Mia detailed phone numbers of any person/physician/pharmacist/playgroup/neighbors Lily might or might not need, now or in the future. Lists of medicines, allergies, morning and afternoon snacks, approved meals for breakfast, lunch, and dinner, foods not approved, scheduled wake-up and nap and bedtimes, and even values to be encouraged.

Lily was either a high-maintenance three-year-old or Mia was reading too many parenting books.

While Lily napped, we had Binder 101 class. Mia reviewed each page, after handing me a pen and pad for notes. Stopping to ask if I had questions, she must have noticed my saucer-eyed, raised-eyebrow expression—like she'd poured spaghetti sauce on my head.

"It's overwhelming, right?" She flipped over some of the pages. "I mean, it's difficult to plan for every little incident that could happen when Bryce and I aren't here. Being a mom is a 24/7 watch, but you're never sure what you're looking out for. Then you read all those awful stories about children drowning in pools, in car accidents, being abducted . . ." She pressed her forefingers in the corner of each eye to blot the tears. "Think about how protective you already feel about that sweet baby hanging out with you now."

"You're going through this book about everything that would or could happen to Lily, and I'm wondering how I'm going to do this alone." I grabbed a water bottle from the refrigerator and paced, wishing I had a pacifier I could use to soothe myself. "I can't afford to stay home. I don't even have a home. Yet. But how will I pay for child care, let alone a certified nanny or au pair?" My voice quivered.

Mia closed the binder, and her eyes followed me as I paced. Past the white granite island and the custom cherry cabinets and the chef-inspired elitist oven that glared at me every time I walked by.

"It's going to be okay. You'll get it all together. I can help, and your family . . ."

I stopped and stared at Mia. If I didn't think I'd break every bone in my hands, I would have slammed them down on the countertop. "Please, you're my best friend; don't be so condescending. It's *not* going to be okay. Because I don't even know anymore what the 'it' is. Wyatt doing something so idiotic by driving to God knows where the morning of our wedding? Then he dies? The epitome of idiotic. I find out I'm pregnant? My mother thinks I'm the picture in the dictionary under *sin*? Oh, and let's not forget the baby gifts. The ones that aren't for my baby. Again, only God knows what baby they're for, and He's not providing any information to help. So, nothing is *okay* in my life right now."

I could actually take a breath that passed my throat, but at the expense of verbally throwing up all over Mia. I couldn't win. I had to make someone else feel bad so I could feel better.

"I'm sorry your life is screwed up. I didn't mean to sound patronizing," Mia said, with more calm and dignity than I would have managed under the same circumstances. She pushed the binder to the edge of the table. "Sit down. I'll get some tissues for you."

She opened a cabinet and handed me the whole box of them as I slumped into the chair across from hers. Everything on my face was running. My eyes, my nose, even my forehead participated.

Mia stood behind her chair. Her hands wrapped around its carved wood spindles. "I hope being here will help. I'm in this with you as much as possible. But Livvy, maybe you're investing your energy in the wrong direction. Where and why Wyatt left that morning might be questions you'll never find the answers to, and you can't move on if you're stuck there. Whatever that 'it' happens to be, I know one thing for sure. It's not about just you anymore. You have to think about your baby."

"You're right. Like Wyatt was thinking about the baby that might be his."

"Have room for me in that place of yours?"

I didn't need this to be a FaceTime phone conversation to see my grandmother's expression to know she was serious, which made me both happy and nervous. "Are you planning to visit soon?"

"Hmmph. I might have to look for a place to live with you. Been working over your mother about her stubbornness. She may kick me out of the city," Granny said. "I might have gone too far when I told her Jesus hung out with prostitutes and criminals, not with the righteous who followed the law just because it was the law."

"Sorry I missed that." I laughed, imagining the startled reaction of my mother to her own mother dressing her down. I doubted she pegged Ruthie for someone who'd use the Bible to confront her with her hypocrisy. "She texted me yesterday with the same questions she sends every other day: 'How are you?' and 'Are you looking for someplace to live?' Mia's not as anxious for me to move out as my mother is."

"She won't admit it, but I'm sure she realizes now that you might stay in Houston. Make that your home."

"It doesn't feel like home yet, but it could. I'm too busy with Lily right now to start looking at neighborhoods and the classifieds . . ." The slap-slap-slap of little feet on the hardwood floors meant nap time was over. "It's time for Lily to do something. I can't remember right now—"

"Snack foist," Lily informed me, combing her fingers through her hair and almost touching my nose with her own.

"Go feed that child," Granny said. "And Olivia, maybe try voice contact with your mom. I know you've called your dad, and she does, too. If she's a bit grouchy, don't think it's personal. Unless she's never not grouchy when you call. Her hip's bothering her. I think she's more upset about not being able to keep up with your dad on the golf course than she is the arthritis."

⚜

After a few weeks, the binder didn't haunt me. Sometimes Lily and I stretched the limits. Snowballs weren't mentioned in the good- or bad-food list, so we visited the snowball stand almost every other day. That way, Lily could pick out a new color and examine it on her tongue in the mirror when she finished. Of course, that meant no hiding the evidence. But to Mia, Bryce, and me, snowballs were a summer ritual, and I wasn't going to deprive Lily of that experience. I made sure to write it in on both the list of acceptable foods and the one of acceptable places Lily could be taken.

When Mia had nanny interviews, she'd schedule them at home so they could meet Lily. But mostly for Lily to meet them. During those free times, I'd scout neighborhoods where a house the size of a dorm room didn't cost mid-six figures. Some days I drove in circles because I was lost, and other days I spent in my apartment, investigating jobs, practicing my own naps, and trying not to think about Wyatt. Somehow his image had been layered into the insides of my eyelids, because it was his face I saw any time I closed my eyes to sleep. But the thought of those two baby gifts would shove its way into my night or daydreams, and Wyatt would disappear as my eyes popped open.

Mia hadn't brought up the gifts or Wyatt since my binder-induced outburst in the kitchen. And I didn't discuss her wanting me to let go of finding the truth. When the three of us were together at night after Lily had been bathed, read to, and tucked in bed, I'd ask Bryce's and Mia's opinions, meshing stories of their day with mine. But puzzle pieces were still missing. I'd even brought a copy of the map that showed Oakville. Maybe it would jog their memories of someone or something there.

As time went on, their enthusiasm about the subject of Wyatt waned. His name coming up in the conversation became a signal to switch topics. The glances between Bryce and Mia, the way their eyes shifted to one another and not back to me, quenched any fire I had to ask more questions.

One hot Houston Tuesday, Lily wanted a snowball after her afternoon nap, so while she slept, I checked my wallet to make sure I had cash. The business card from Cara with the private investigator's name was still there. Patiently waiting for me to not ignore it. I sat on the love seat in the den, staring at the card in my open wallet. That dreadful feeling I experienced the day I knew I had to call Mia to tell her I was pregnant resurfaced. But so did that whispering voice inside, the one that quietly tests if you're listening to your heart. The one that assured me reaching out was the right decision.

I pressed the numbers into my cell phone, taking my time between each one, hoping Lily would wake and I'd have an excuse to stop. She didn't. I kept going. All that was left to do was press the green button.

Another voice. Not the soft-spoken one. The screamer who pummeled my resolve. *Stop. What are you doing? Once you press Dial, that's it; you're committed. Are you ready for this?*

I canceled the call.

CHAPTER 22

Lily and I were coloring at the table in her playroom when Mia walked in and said she had a surprise.

"Is the surprise that you're home early?" I smiled and replaced my tangerine gel pen with the silver one to shade the stars on my page. "I have an extra book if you want to join us." I colored mandalas as art therapy. I'd read it was supposed to soothe the soul. Trying to draw one of the circles with those elaborate center designs wasn't bringing me inner peace, so I bought a book with the patterns. Regardless, I appreciated having a semi-legit excuse to buy gel pens in more colors than I knew existed.

She looked over Lily's page. "She has a great eye for color, doesn't she?"

"She does. That's why I'm copying her," I said.

Lily nodded as she continued to fill in the flowers on her page with different hues of orange. "She not color good. But I teaching her."

Lily's nose grew closer to the page as she worked. I made a mental note to suggest that Mia have her eyes checked. Her attitude was beyond checking already.

Mia sat on the chair between us. "Lily, can you give me your eyes so I know you're listening?"

Lily put her hands over her mouth and giggled. "You so silly. I can't take my eyes out."

"I know, sweetie. Remember, I explained that means I want you to stop what you're doing and give me your attention?"

Saying "Look at me" would have been a faster route to the same end, but I stayed quiet because that might have been something I missed in the binder.

Lily and I both stopped and gave Mia our eyes. At dinner last night, she and Bryce informed me they'd hired a nanny who would be starting in the next four weeks. Even knowing that this was inevitable, I already missed Lily and felt a wave of sadness.

Mia reminded Lily about my being here with her, how I couldn't stay always because I would be finding my own house. Her hands clasped on the table, Lily listened intently like a bitty congresswoman hearing testimony, her face void of expression.

"Where's the surprise?" She looked toward the door and around where Mia sat.

Have to adore a kid who cut right to the point.

Mia leaned closer to Lily. "Do you remember meeting Miss Jill at our house? She had short black hair, and she wore those flowered rain boots because it rained that day."

"Yeeesssss," Lily said, a note of caution in her answer.

"Miss Jill called us, and she asked if she could be your nanny because she liked meeting you and knows the two of you could have a wonderful time together. She would be with you when Mommy works, like Aunt Livvy has been. You could do all the same things, go all the same places—"

"Will Aunt Wivvy still live in the backyard?"

Mia looked at me. I took that as a cue. "For a while, but then Jill will live there because I'll have my own house." Jill wouldn't move into the apartment until one month after starting; they wanted to make sure the arrangement was working. That meant I had two months to find something.

"Will you still come to my house?"

"Of course, Lily. You're my coloring-book and snowball buddy. And zoo. And park," I said, but realizing at that moment that between working and having my own baby, my time for visits would be rare.

She turned to her mother, nodded, and said, "Okay," then went back to coloring her flowers.

Mia looked at me and shrugged her shoulders, her face a study in amazement. I bit my lip to stifle a laugh. The night before, the three of us had exhausted ourselves stocking an artillery of answers for the barrage of questions we expected.

We didn't plan on acceptance.

A lesson from Lily.

Lily had an important choice to make, and she had only fourteen seconds left to make it.

I knew the seconds exactly because I learned to set timers to expedite some of these life-altering decisions. "Lily Loo, your time's almost over. You'll be able to count down from ten in two seconds."

"Noooooooo. I not weady." She buried her face in her hands. "I not wooking."

"Whether you wook or not, the time doesn't stop. So, let's have it."

Sitting on her hand-painted flowered Lily bench, she plopped herself over from the waist, head in her lap, her arms dangling like two legs of an octopus, and sighed. "Poorpul."

The buzzer went off, and she bolted upright. "No, no. I mean green. Green. Wivvy. I want green. Honest."

"You, my darling, are destined for the stage. How about today you get both?"

On Friday afternoons, we played the mani-pedi game. At home. Because in the nail salon, she spent fifteen minutes collecting bottles of polish and carrying them to the nail station, finally finding one she wanted, only to change her mind two nails in.

I'd scheduled my third prenatal appointment and hoped, in a week, I'd see boy parts on that ultrasound screen. Even if he would one day want a mani-pedi, I felt sure he'd take less time picking out a shade.

I'd only painted one hand, alternating purple and green, which delighted her, when my cell phone rang. It was tempting to let it go to voicemail because I knew it was my dad, and I could answer the questions before he asked them. "I'm still doing fine; Houston is still great; I'm still looking for a place to live." Everything still *still*.

But this time, he said my name like a warning. I asked him to wait while I settled Lily with a second snack and specific instructions about the nail polish. "Don't touch. Don't touch. Don't touch." I set the bottles on a shelf of her bookcase. "Got it?"

"No-o-o-o-o, I don't got it." She looked at me as if I'd grown fangs. "It's there." She pointed to the bookcase.

"I meant . . . never mind. I'll get you a juice and be right back."

I grabbed an organic, gluten-free, no-GMOs, rabbi-approved as kosher, Apple-y Ever After. I handed it to Lily, then sat in the rocking chair in the playroom.

"Okay, I'm here. What's wrong, Dad?"

"It's your mom."

My stomach twisted like a wet towel being wrung out to dry.

"You know that little wooden stool we have? Your mom had it in our bedroom. Hardhead. Didn't wait for me to get home to hang one of the new paintings she'd bought. She used the stool and forgot to move it, so when she woke up in the middle of the night to go to the bathroom, she didn't remember it was there. Slammed herself right into the wall. And it was her bad hip that she hit."

The roller-coaster ride ended. She'd fallen . . . not died, not had a stroke or been in an accident or any of the other soul-sucking possibilities. "That must have been painful. She okay?"

I watched Lily take a bite of her zucchini bread, then spit it out in her napkin. "Ick. Dat's ick."

Poor kid. She needed a brownie or a doughnut.

"She will be," my dad said. "We went to the doctor today, and he said she's going to need hip-replacement surgery."

"Putting you on speaker," I warned Dad as I trucked to the kitchen again. I found my box of Wheat Thins stashed in the back of the pantry. Put some in a cup and gave it to Lily. You would have thought I'd just served her a slab of chocolate cake. She actually giggled.

I returned to the rocking chair. "Wait . . . surgery because she fell? That seems a bit extreme, don't you think? Maybe you should get a second opinion."

"Honey, we don't need another doctor to tell us what we could see on the X-ray and MRI tests. And between your mother's osteoporosis and the way she hit herself on the side of her hip, it's definite.

"The surgery's scheduled for next Wednesday. Olivia, I am expecting you to be here. For all the differences between you and your mother, it's important to rise above that and come home."

"I'll be there. Of course, I'll be there." It surprised and irritated me that he even thought I wouldn't be. "I'll talk to Mia. She should be home from work in about an hour. We'll make plans for someone to take care of Lily for a few days."

She pointed to herself when she heard her name. I nodded and held up two fingers to let her know I'd be off soon. Sometimes two minutes stretched into ten, but I figured until she learned to read a clock, time could pass slower than Houston rush-hour traffic.

As soon as my father cleared his throat, I knew he was about to say something uncomfortable. Growing up, when I heard that sound, I braced myself because whatever followed, it wasn't going to be news I welcomed. Consequences for low grades or staying out past curfew or telling my mother his business was down at the office or giving me the news about Wyatt.

"What's going on? Something else you need to talk to me about?" I walked over to Lily's play table and motioned for her to throw her juice box in the trash. Figured I might as well stay vertical because I'd be pacing soon enough.

"This is going to be as difficult for me to ask as it will be for you to hear it. Your mother won't be able to go to the office for months maybe, and I can't handle it by myself. I need you to help me. To move back."

CHAPTER 23

L ily and I were both impatient waiting for this phone call to end. She bit the ends of her hair, and I bit my tongue. "Move back?"

"Not permanently, unless that's what you want. Look, I know you and your mother have a lot to work out, so I'm hiring someone to help her at home while we're at the office."

"While 'we're at the office'? Dad, there's no 'we' yet. Maybe not at all. I'm looking for a place to live, possibly even buy. And I haven't had a chance to interview for jobs yet because Mia just hired a nanny."

"I understand, but you already know the business. I don't have time to train anyone or know anyone I can trust to handle things, especially when I'm out on calls. It would help us out. Really. I can't do this alone, Olivia."

I squirmed inside. I wasn't accustomed to his voice sounding so flat, so needy. If not for his having seen the X-rays and been with her when the surgery was scheduled, I would have found the timing of her "accident," no accident.

My mother had pulled a few dramatic stunts for attention or diversion, like when she complained of chest pains the night before my father wanted to leave for a golf weekend or the time she backed into the mailbox, but rattled off stories about people she knew—or said she knew—who were injured in car accidents. By the time she mentioned the mailbox, my father was either so grateful she hadn't died or that the stories had ended that he hugged her and said, "Scarlett, that's so minor compared to everyone else's problems. Run the car by the body shop before work and get an estimate."

In my pacing, I must have missed Lily dragging her chair to the bookcase to reach the nail polish. Fingertips on the edge of the shelf, she was about to hoist herself up when I spotted her. My brain played out the possibility of the entire bookcase crashing upon her in record speed.

"Lily, let go and get down—Dad, I have to go. I'll get back to you. But I can't promise anything."

The bookcase started wobbling, and I dashed over and scooped her up. In all the time we'd spent together, I'd never used that tone with her. Her bottom lip trembled, and she wrapped her arms around her body. I'd probably looked away for less than a minute. Sixty seconds could have meant the difference between life and death for Lily. A lifetime of grief and guilt for me.

Was that it, Wyatt? One minute of distraction meant the difference between staying on the road or hitting the trees?

Lily was burbling now. Tears dripping down her face, she sat on the floor, knees up, holding her feet and rocking.

I sat on the floor next to Lily, my arms around her, and tugged her closer. She resisted, her little body stiff, her face buried in her hands. A pouty mumble reached my ears. "You are mean to me."

"Oh, Lily Loo. Sometimes a scared voice and a mean voice sound the same. I was afraid the whole bookcase might topple over and crush your sweet self. And we would all be very, very sad." I moved her hands away from her face. "Look at me. I love you, Lily Loo, and I don't want anything bad to ever, ever happen to you."

She scooted close and wiggled her way onto my lap; her head rested on my shoulder. Her breaths warmed my neck. She sniffled, then wiped the last of her tears. "I wuv you."

I kissed the top of her head, where the scent of baby shampoo lingered.

Lily looked up at me. "Can we finish our nails now?"

August in Houston wasn't much different than August at home. During the evenings, when the sun finally began to drop itself out of sight, the humidity still dampened everything, the air heavy, blistering, and thick as gumbo.

To relieve their kitchens from becoming ovens, people cooked outdoors during these wicked hot days. You could stroll down the sidewalk of almost any neighborhood, and from the backyards, curly tendrils of smoke from barbecue pits wove their way through the dense air. Bryce grilled steaks and vegetables, joining their neighbors in keeping the heat where it belonged. Outside.

That evening, after I spoke to my father and finished Lily's nails, we fed Lily, and I volunteered to take the nighttime bath, book, and bed routine. We read *The Going-to-Bed Book*, then she fell asleep easily, and I sat a few minutes more on the edge of her bed to simply look at her face.

I joined Mia in the pool, and I related the story to her and Bryce of my phone call from my father. "I don't understand why he can't function at the office without me. Once people know the situation, someone will volunteer to help.

"And as for hiring someone, I'm sure my grandmother could spend time at their house once Mom's home from the hospital. My doctor's appointment is next week, which I'll have to reschedule. I've just started to look at places to live. And he wants me to move back there indefinitely? I'm going to call him tomorrow and tell him I'll be there for the surgery, and I'll help him look for someone to work in the office, but when she comes home, I'm on my way back here."

"Maybe you should give it more thought. I don't want to tell you to pray about it because I know that's not on your to-do list," said Mia.

Bryce waved his tongs in our direction. "Everything's almost ready. We're eating outside or in?"

"Definitely in," said Mia as she stepped out of the pool. "I'll get everything ready inside."

I offered to help, but she told me soaking in the pool was probably as relaxing for the baby as it was for me. A few minutes later, I got out of the water, wrapped a towel around my shoulders, and sat on one of the patio chairs near Bryce.

"Smells great. What is it about grilling meat that lures your senses?"

"I think it has something to do with the fat burning," Bryce said.

"Burning fat? You've now made this seductive aroma totally unappealing. I meant it more as a rhetorical question."

I was getting ready to ask him about Colin when he turned off the grill, then pulled up another chair and said, "We've known each other a long time. We can be honest with one another, right?"

"Of course." I nodded, wiped my wet face, and waited.

"I wanted to talk to you while Mia wasn't here." He turned around to check the door as if she might have tiptoed back. "She'd never admit the stress she's under, juggling work and Lily and the house, hiring a nanny . . . I'll admit, she takes it on herself because she's the problem-solver, and she won't rest until she finds a way."

"We've always known that about her," I said. Bryce wasn't dishing out any new information. "Where are you going with this?"

"I think your going home for a while to help out your parents is a good idea, but Mia may tell you she doesn't think it is."

"Well, honestly, right now I agree with her." I wrapped my towel around my shoulders. "I take it you don't? Agree with her, I mean."

Bryce checked the door again, but still no sign of Mia. "She loves you like a sister, and she'd do whatever she could for you to be happy again. Mia would never admit that she has taken on too much, physically or emotionally. Sometime she doesn't even realize it herself. And I don't think she'd be selfish intentionally, but I know your leaving would be hard for her, even with the nanny coming. She's missed you, and her job doesn't leave much time for making friends. I don't want you to stay because you'd feel like you're abandoning Mia. Really, I think your going home would be best. For both of you."

"Why do I feel like you're kicking me out?"

Bryce leaned back, plowed his hands through his hair, and shook his head. "I'm sorry. That's not at all what I meant to suggest." He leaned forward and said, "Your father is really being honest about his inability to juggle things at home and his office. It's difficult for men like your dad to ask for help, so he must really need it. I don't want you to leave him stranded because of Mia."

The back door yawned open, and Mia stepped outside. Her hand full of silverware, she looked from Bryce to me and back again. "Is everything okay?"

Her eyes bore through Bryce as if she'd already figured out he was responsible for whatever might have happened.

"Olivia and I have been talking, and I said—"

"That he thought going home to help my father was the right thing to do, and he wanted to reassure me that you guys would be okay. Bryce was just worried I'd feel guilty leaving before the nanny actually started." I picked up the platter of vegetables. "But we can talk more later. Bryce is ready to take the steaks off the grill, and I'm ready to eat."

During dinner, I distracted myself by entertaining them with stories of our visit to the Butterfly Museum. How Lily would stand like a scarecrow in a field of wheat asking the butterflies to land on her. "I told Lily that when I was a little girl, I used to call them 'flutterbys.' She looked at me with that classic smirk she gets, you know the one where her nose wrinkles and her mouth tilts up on one side. Then she said, 'That's why dey didn't go by you. Dey didn't yike you got their name wrong.'"

"I hope that means she inherited her mother's genes for remembering people's names. I practically need a cheat sheet when we go places," Bryce said.

"Not practically," Mia said, pointing her fork at him as she talked. "I do give him a cheat sheet, and I put it in his suit pocket before we leave. I even offer to drive, so he can study it on the way."

"I want to be sure and write about that day in her baby book. I need to send you the pictures, too. My favorite part of the day was when we were leaving. She tugged my purse strap and asked if we could sit down so I could answer a question. We sat on a bench outside the museum, and she opened one of the brochures and pointed to the picture of a cocoon. She fixed those eyes on me, the ones that say, 'If you lie to me, I will serve you your conscience every time you look at me.'"

They both nodded.

"Then she asked me, 'Do they cry? Does it hurt to come out?'"

Mia sat back in her chair. Her expression so reminiscent of her daughter's as she watched the butterflies. "Wow, she may have an engineer's brain, but I think she'll have an artist's heart."

"She's only three. We have a few years before we have to put labels on her brain and heart," said Bryce. Taking advantage of Mia's reaction to his answer, her staring at him openmouthed and with piercing eyes, he speared part of her steak and put it on his plate.

"You think you could let yourself melt a bit listening to your daughter's questions? Sometimes I wonder if you dive below the surface of things . . ." she snipped. "By the way, if you want more, next time, ask."

I sliced my asparagus in even sections to avoid eye contact with Bryce. He may be lousy at snatching food, but Mia didn't give him enough credit for seeing the unseen. I'd learned this evening he was more astute than she realized.

"Anyway," Bryce started, "before we demonstrate marital discord during supper, what did you tell her?"

"I told her I had no idea. But I explained the only way it could become a butterfly was to leave the cocoon, even if it hurt. I told her that when she was a baby trying to learn to walk, she fell down all the time. But she stood up and tried again and again and again. Sometimes we have to hurt to get someplace or something we really want."

I'm teaching Lily a lesson I'm still learning myself.

CHAPTER 24

I stared at the ceiling where my mind's eye rewound and replayed scenes from tonight.

I thought of the story I told about the butterflies and of my strained relationship with my mother and of the life I'd been cheated out of.

I closed my eyes, turned off the projector in my brain, and resolved to do something before an ultrasound showed my baby biting her fingernails because she was worried about her mother.

I called my father the next day and told him I'd help in the office but asked if he could give me some idea of how long he needed me to work.

"I appreciate this, honey. I'm sure this is tough for you not being settled with everything going on. But I promise, after the surgery we'll all have a better idea of what her recovery will entail. And if it's longer than you're willing to stay, then I'll do whatever I need to do."

He sounded relieved.

At least one of us was.

The mixer was whirring the icing for the coffee pound cake I was making for dessert when I heard thumping by the back door. Thinking Lily had escaped from her nap, I dashed through the mudroom and found Mia instead. Her arms stuffed with fabric swatches and wallpaper samples, she was kicking the door with the toe of her Ferragamo pumps that might have cost more than the door they were bashing.

"This is what my father used to call 'a lazy load,'" she told me as I relieved her of enough weight so she wouldn't topple over. "Not like I couldn't have made two trips to the car. But if I want to be in a sauna, I'll go to the health club, not outside my house."

We carried everything to her office, then she followed me back to the kitchen. "You're home early today," I said. "Did you give yourself the rest of the day off?"

"I'm still working on that design job for the couple building a house in River Oaks." She settled into a kitchen chair, leaned over, slid off her shoes, and placed them side by side against the wall. She propped her head on her hands to watch me. "You'd think people building a house in one of the toniest areas in Houston would be a bit less stringent about their decorating budget. They were in the shop this morning arguing over a two-dollars-per-yard difference on the fabric choices for a chair covering." Mia grabbed clumps of her hair and pretended to pull. "That kinda day."

"This might help." I turned the mixer off, folded in the sliced almonds, then handed her the paddle, coated with cream cheese and brown sugar icing.

She became as googly-eyed and shiny-faced as Lily when I gave her a treat not listed as acceptable in her binder. Maybe Mia had a binder somewhere, too, and this was not on her list, either.

"Goodness, girl, that's a lot of excitement over icing. Not like I just gave you a handful of diamonds."

"No, but it's just as decadent," she said, running her finger along the paddle, making sure she scooped up as much as she could. "Well . . . maybe not, because it's over much too quickly." She handed me the paddle she'd swiped clean without one drip on her silk dress. Which, now that I looked more closely, was about the same shade as what I was mixing.

"Stop ogling the icing. You're making it feel uncomfortable," I teased and continued turning the cake as I spread the frosting. "If you're good, I'll let you lick the bowl."

She smiled. "That's what my grandmother used to tell me when I visited her. She loved to bake, and I loved to eat the icing." Mia looked away for a moment. "I miss her," she said with a longing that comes from remembering those slices of time with someone we loved.

"I never knew my dad's mother. She died before I was born. And I'm certain my fondest memories with Ruthie will revolve around a restaurant, shopping, or both." I handed her the bowl.

"It won't be long before you'll have a reason to make memories of your own," Mia said accompanied by the background scraping of her spoon against the metal bowl as she scooped up the icing.

I carried the cake to safety, placing it in the corner of the countertop. "Oh, absolutely. My child's going to have fond memories of Mom zapping food in the microwave, having meals delivered . . ." I closed my eyes for dramatic effect, my hands crossed over my chest. "So touching."

She waved her hand dismissively. "You are so silly."

We started clearing the table and loading the dishwasher.

"I called my father this morning," I said as I carried the mixer to the pantry. "I told him I'd be there for my mother's surgery, and I'd help him in his office."

"Are you sure you want to do that? You've just started to get acclimated here, and we were looking for a place for you to live and . . ." She stopped rinsing off the bowls I'd used and nailed me with her eyes. "You're planning to come back, aren't you? Please say you will. I'm going to miss you so much if you don't. And just because Lily has a nanny, you know how much she loves you . . . That's not it, is it? Our finally finding a nanny? I mean, we were honest about that from the beginning. Or is it you really don't feel comfortable here in Houston—"

"Mia, breathe." I couldn't help but smile. We always knew when Mia was wound up because her thoughts flew out of her mouth faster than scarves from a magician's sleeve. And hearing her did help me understand the backyard discussion Bryce and I had yesterday.

"I need to stay for my father. If for no other reason than he's been playing mediator/referee between my mother and me for decades. You and Bryce opened your home and your hearts. You've been generous and kind, and I wouldn't have made it this far without you. But I need to figure some things out on my own, and the time back home might help me put matters in perspective." It was all true.

That weekend, I packed only what I thought I'd need while I was home. Everything else was boxed and stored in the garage. If I returned, the boxes would be waiting for me. If I didn't, I'd ask Mia to ship them.

It all took longer than I expected because once I packed a box, Lily would take everything out of it. On every trip from my apartment to the garage, she followed me, stomping her feet, her voice fussy and loud. "No. No. No. You stay here." She tried to push the boxes out again, gave up, and decided to protest by sitting on the ones still upstairs, figuring I couldn't move them.

She was right.

I planned to leave in the morning, and I wanted Lily to understand something I could hardly understand myself. When there was only one box left to move, I sat on the floor next to her.

"What's up, Lily Loo? I need to move this box to the garage with all the other ones."

She scooted around, her back to me, arms across her chest, looking at her feet. Her polished toenails looked like tiny painted shells peeking out of her sandals.

I moved around to face her, and after a few times of playing the game, she started to smile. And when she did, she put her hands on the side of her mouth and pulled her lips down. "Sssstttooooopppp, Aunt Wivvy."

"If your mommy was sick, wouldn't you want to be with her?"

"My mommy's sick?" Her face collapsed in worry.

"No, sweetie." I picked her up off the box and snuggled her on the sofa next to me. "But my mommy is. And she lives far away. I need to drive there tomorrow and stay awhile to help her and my dad."

Lily twirled her hair around her finger, her head tilted as she stared, not at me, but through me.

She climbed on my lap, placed her hands on my cheeks so that we were facing each other, and leaned over and touched my forehead with hers. "I wuv my mommy, too."

I closed my eyes to soothe the sting of tears. She echoed what only my heart could have said.

I hugged Mia for the tenth time and slid behind the wheel of my car. I leaned out my window to tell her something I'd meant to say earlier. "Why don't you see if the nanny can start sooner than you planned? I think it would help Lily to not have to wait so long to meet her. I know you delayed to give me more time, and I appreciate that."

She wiped her eyes again, cursed her mascara that didn't live up to its promise of being waterproof, and squeezed my hand. "You drive safely. Call or text us as soon as you're at your parents' house. And don't worry about the OB appointment. I'll call tomorrow and cancel it. For now."

Bryce walked over and hoisted Lily up so she could kiss me goodbye. I breathed her in, kissed her all over her face while she giggled. "Come back, okay? I can polish you."

"You already have, sweet girl. You've polished me here." I placed my hand on my heart.

Bryce handed Lily to Mia, kissed my forehead, and said, "Thank you."

CHAPTER 25

My father called to tell me the hospital had admitted my mother a few hours earlier, gave me her room number, and asked what time I'd be in town.

"If I can get through Lafayette and Baton Rouge without any traffic, I should be there around one o'clock. I'll go to the house first to freshen up, then I'll meet you there."

"Take your time. Drive safely. We're *all* anxious to see you." Since he emphasized the word *all*, he was either in my mother's room or wanted to make sure I understood she was included, or both.

"I'd rather not stop for lunch. Is there anything at the house, or should I pick up something to go on my way there?"

"Your grandmother and your mother cooked enough food to feed the entire town and send people home with leftovers. Yesterday they sent me to buy more plastic containers because they cleaned out the cabinet of all the ones we already had. Then our pastor's wife came over with food and told us we can expect more in the next few days."

Bottom line: there was food to be eaten. He asked me to call before I left to meet him in case my mother needed anything. I was bringing myself. Shouldn't that have been enough?

I crossed the Sabine River bridge from Texas into Louisiana, where the speed limit was lower, the roads rougher, and home already felt like the garage apartment I'd left behind in Houston.

It felt odd walking into my parents' house. Especially alone. Like not seeing a relative for ten years and then having to feel comfortable with each other again. As usual, opening the refrigerator did that for me. Even after I went away to college, the first thing I'd do after kissing my parents hello would be to walk to the refrigerator, bury my head in the coolness, and ask, "What's good in here?"

Maybe that's one of the last frontiers of intimacy outside of sex. You know you're truly close to someone when, without asking, you can pull open the fridge and stalk what's in it.

This time, their refrigerator didn't look like I remembered it. I opened the door and was mesmerized by the myriad of containers, labeled and dated and stacked in size order. Veggies and fruits were lounging in plastic zipper bags, and bottles of water stood at attention on the top shelf. I checked the outside of the door to make sure I hadn't missed a chart that listed contents. The only list, attached by a round God Will Always Make a Way magnet, was phone numbers.

I zapped a small container of lasagna and ate it in between texting Mia and my father to announce I'd arrived safely. I didn't bother unloading the car, except for my makeup case. I wanted to avoid any comments about looking pale, tired, or grouchy. A speedy dusting of foundation, blush, a swath of lipstick, and I was on my way.

I called my father as he'd asked, and I picked up the magazines my mother wanted, gum for him, a latte for my grandmother, and treated myself to a cinnamon chai tea latte and a blueberry scone. It wasn't until I parked the car in the hospital garage that my stomach churned, anticipating the curtain opening on the drama ahead.

I texted Dad, and he met me in the hospital lobby. His smile stretched across his face, and when he hugged me, it was as if he scooped up the broken parts of me and put them all back together in the safety of his arms. As much as I used to tease him about wearing his cologne, I missed the warm caramel scent of his Old Spice.

"So happy you're here, Livvy." He stood back, his hands on my shoulders, and measured me with his glance. "See you're . . . um . . ."

"Growing?" I smiled and placed my hands on my pouch. "Yes. Your grandchild is taking over my body now."

"My grandchild," he whispered. He looked like someone who'd held a lottery ticket for weeks and finally checked the numbers to discover he'd won.

I didn't expect the same reaction from my mother, which was fortunate because it didn't happen. Instead, she thanked me for the magazines, kissed me on the forehead, and commented that I seemed to have put on a few pounds.

"She is pregnant, Scarlett. My goodness. I know you didn't forget,'" said my grandmother, who'd already rubbed my belly like I was some sort of good-luck Buddha. "I know she just arrived, but I'm going to steal Olivia to walk with me to the cafeteria and find some sugar for this." Ruthie held up her Starbucks cup.

She nodded toward the door, and I gratefully followed.

"In thirty seconds, I've managed to feel resentful and then ashamed because I feel resentful. How am I going to make it through weeks with her?" I stabbed the elevator button. "Are you sure she's your daughter? Does compassion skip a generation in this family?"

"If it does, then you're safe," Ruthie said. "We need to make sure before the next generation arrives."

Instead of getting off on the first floor, my grandmother nudged me out on the third. "Let's do this instead." She pointed to her right. "The atrium's on this floor, and it's much more pleasant sitting outside. I'll pick up a sugar packet at the nurses' station on the way."

We walked through glass doors into an open space filled with tables, some circling trees, white and lilac azaleas spilling over tall ceramic planters, and the hum of classical music.

Ruthie steered me to a table. "Now, tell me all about Lily and your Houston adventures."

"If I'd known you were plotting a getaway, I would've brought my tea and scone with me."

"Oh, I'm sorry." She started to stand. "We can go back—"

"Sit down, Ruthie," I said. "I'm sure you didn't want to talk to me alone just to hear about what I've been doing."

"Of course not. Your mother isn't the only one who can specialize in ulterior motives." She found a sugar packet on the table and emptied it in her coffee, peering over my shoulder as she did. "Now that's a Dr. McDreamy sitting at that table all alone behind you."

I turned for a quick look. "Granted. But he looks like he could be my father."

"I didn't mean for you, honey," Ruthie said and sipped her coffee. "I'm old, not dead. And dating younger men seems to be quite the rage these days."

"Lucky for you, you look ten years younger than you actually are. Guess that's lucky for me, too, assuming I inherit those genes."

"I better tell you why I wanted to talk to you because if we're gone too much longer your mother's going to suspect I'm up to something. Which I am. But I got distracted window-shopping."

The gist of it was that my grandmother knew my coming back to a place where I didn't feel wanted was difficult. She asked if I could extend my mother some grace while I was here, because her surgery and her recovery affected all of us.

"Look, I'm not going to give you that 'your mother is like an onion, you gotta peel back the layers' foolishness. Your mother's more like . . ." She closed her eyes, then opened them and looked up as if an answer would be floating within her sights. "Maybe this is a stretch but, you know, your mother's like a pineapple. There's a lot of good waiting inside for people who aren't afraid to get past that thorny exterior."

"I'll do it for you. As for that pineapple analogy, I'll just tell myself she's not ripe yet."

"Your mother does miss you. I can see it in her eyes when your dad tells her that he's talked to you. I don't think she really expected you to come back. Right now, your mother sees you and her faith as two trains about to have a head-on collision. She can't figure out a way to save you both. But she will. I know she will."

I didn't want to spoil my grandmother's fascination with analogies, but I don't think my family realized that this train had already jumped the tracks.

CHAPTER 26

My experiences entertaining Lily paid off in my distracting Dad during the almost three hours my mother spent in surgery.

We had breakfast in the cafeteria, we walked around the hospital grounds, we watched the news, we talked sports, we watched sports, he checked and rechecked his email and voice messages, we went to the cafeteria again for snacks. At the brink of desperation, I even offered a mani-pedi.

My grandmother was absorbed in *An Absent Mind*, an appropriate title for how inattentive she was in helping me occupy my father's time. But knowing she was reading a novel about Alzheimer's made me wonder if she was doing personal research.

During one of my father's many hall walkings, I was sitting next to Ruthie checking my messages when she leaned sideways in her chair and told me, "All we can do is pray that pain medication works; otherwise, we might all need to ask for some."

When the intercom in the surgical waiting room called for the Kavanaugh family to meet the doctor in conference room one, the blood in my father's face must have rushed to his toes.

"Why the conference room? Something's wrong. I'll bet something's wrong," he said, knocking over his stack of magazines, frantic to leave.

"Relax," my grandmother said as she patted his back. "That's what they do here. Not like the old days when bringing family to a room meant bad news."

Dr. Epstein, a petite woman whose firm handshake was as disarming as her youth, told us the surgery went well, that my mother was in the recovery room, and we could expect to see her in an hour or so. "She's on some heavy duty pain meds—"

"That's a relief," said my grandmother, as if Dr. Epstein had announced that a Category 5 hurricane had skirted around us.

When we all turned and looked at her, Ruthie said, "Oh my. Did I say that out loud?"

"Yes, you did. But yes, having the drip for pain is a relief," Dr. Epstein said and smiled as if she'd been in on the joke all along. She told us physical therapy would start sometime the next day, and Mom would be home in four to six days.

My father thanked her so many times, none of us would have been surprised if he'd picked her up and twirled her around the room.

Hours later, my mother was settled back in her hospital room, though we were sure she had no idea where she was or who we were. Between IV drips, the compression stockings around her legs that inflated and deflated, the large dressing that wrapped around her, the foam pillow between her legs, and her sallow postsurgery complexion, she deserved to be on pain meds. It hurt just to look at her.

Dad said he planned to spend the night with her, so I dropped my grandmother off at home before going back to my parents' house.

We hadn't left the parking garage when Granny said, "Okay, it's just the two of us again. Tell me what's really going on with you."

I stared straight ahead, not even wanting to glance in her direction, because my eyes would tell the truth my words didn't. "I'm okay. Not great. One day at a time and all that."

"Olivia. Cut the crap. It's me who's asking. Not your parents. And the fact that you're doling out that malarkey tells me more than you think."

"I know. I know. I guess as long as all these thoughts and feelings are still inside of me, I can pretend they're not real. Talking about them, it's like slicing myself open. And then what? I'll never go back together the same way."

At the signal light I turned left and realized I was heading home. Not to my grandmother's or my parents' home, but to the one Wyatt and I had shared. Even after all this time away, my heart wanted to take me to what was familiar. Comfortable. Safe. I didn't think I could bear driving past my old house. I made the next U-turn, but my grandmother didn't question my correction.

"I don't want you to start getting upset while you're driving. Not a good idea for either one of us. Tell you what. About a block ahead is a supermarket. I'll dash inside and get us some pints of Ben & Jerry's. We'll kick back in our pj's at your parents' house with our ice cream, and I'll spend the night with you."

When we were settled later, I told her about the call from Babycakes, then getting the package and stowing it in my car with the other one. About Mia and Bryce telling me to stop searching for what I might never find. About hating Wyatt for being selfish and careless. About wanting and not wanting to know the truth, because I didn't know which one I could survive.

"There's one step I haven't taken. And, really, it's all I have left."

Until I looked up from scraping the bottom of my ice cream carton and saw Ruthie's face a study in anxiety, her spoon suspended over her Triple Caramel Chuck, I didn't realize the meaning she'd attached to what I said.

"Relax, Ruthie." I threw my empty Ben & Jerry's carton away. A shame. The only two men I could count on in my life, and they were doomed to be trashed. "I meant someone I work with recommended a private investigator, one she used." I found the card in my wallet, its paper edges frayed from my indecision, and handed it to her.

She glanced at it. "Is this what you want to do? You. Not your family or friends."

"I do. But what if he tells me something I don't want to hear? Maybe never being sure of something will be easier to live with . . ."

"Do you call what you're doing right now living? Holding on to this card, the gifts, what you want to believe about Wyatt? Has that worked for you?" She poked her spoon in my direction with every point she made. "You're more like your mother than you realize." She shook her head from side to side and then went back to eating her ice cream.

Those words flew at me like a nest of wasps I had just disturbed. "No. I'm nothing like my mother." I retrieved the card from the coffee table where she had set it down.

"Try this on. You're both afraid to let go. You think you're in control, protecting yourself. I can hold on to you with fierceness, even in love, but if my hands are around your neck, eventually I'll kill the very person I want to save." She reached her hand to grasp mine and tugged me to the sofa until I sat next to her.

"Mia and Bryce had good intentions. They love you, and they don't want you to be in pain. But they're wrong thinking that letting go means giving up or that you should accept living in a fog. Letting go means you stop trying to control the universe of outcomes. That you're willing to accept whatever it gives you. It doesn't mean you're a weak, sniveling lump. There's so much more strength and courage in surrender."

CHAPTER 27

S he is not going to be happy when she sees this. Or that." I pointed
to the new additions to my parents' house.

"This" being the straight-back chair that replaced my mother's
reclining one next to my father's. And "that" being the elevated toilet
seat my father had just purchased and was now carrying into the bathroom to install. An item we asked the doctor to tell her she had to use
was her walker because, as Granny said, "I'm too old to dodge that thing
if she throws it across a room."

My grandmother was at the hospital with Mom, so my father and
I could prepare the house for when she was discharged tomorrow. The
house was likely more prepared than we were.

Laura, hired to help my mother at home, was supposed to meet
us there in a few minutes. My grandmother and I convinced my father
that Laura did not need a baptism by fire by starting the day Mom
came home.

The past four days had aged my father by ten years. He wouldn't
stay away from the hospital for more than a few hours. He'd go straight
to his office, then back to the hospital again. The padded bench he slept
on in her room would have been comfortable had he been the size of a

ten-year-old child. Even my mother's nurses fussed at him, threatening to send *him* home under doctor's orders. The few times my father let me relieve him were early mornings or after supper, times my mother was barely awake. I wondered if that was part of his plan.

Had I intended to return to Houston after her surgery, seeing my father consumed with stress would have been enough to convince me to stay. I hadn't expected him to react with such intense worry and concern, and I shared that with him while we finished setting up the house so my mother could negotiate the way with her walker.

"Your mother is a strong woman. None of us doubt that. It wasn't the physical part of this surgery that scared me. I trusted her doctor, and we'd been told enough about the procedure that we knew what would happen. As soon as the doctor told her she'd need the hip replacement, she plummeted into a funk I haven't seen for nearly thirty years. She wouldn't get out of bed the day after the appointment. Telling me how her entire life was about to change because she'd be so dependent on other people." He finished rolling up the hall runner and set it next to the area rug he'd already moved in the den.

I handed him a water bottle and wondered what long-ago funk he was talking about. *Better to ask him later. Or ask my grandmother.* "Don't you think it was the shock of hearing she'd need surgery? It's not like she was diagnosed with a brain tumor or cancer."

"Kind of harsh, honey." He had the expression of someone who couldn't place where he'd seen me before. "Anytime you have to go under anesthesia, it's a risk." He set his water on the fireplace mantel and slid the coffee table against the far wall of the room.

I moved the crystal vase of fresh hydrangeas I'd bought, their star-shaped blooms exploding with shades of blue, to the end table next to my mother's new chair. They were her favorite flower, and I wanted her to see them waiting for her.

The doorbell rang, and my father welcomed Laura into our home. Stepping out from the kitchen where I'd readied glasses for iced tea, I almost stumbled over myself when she walked over to shake my hand. I'd imagined someone entirely different, some stereotype I'd invented of a woman willing to care for my mother. Laura was not that.

Never had I ever described anyone as *willowy*; it seemed a word only appropriate for modeling agencies, fashion runways, and trees. Her dark blonde hair was gathered into a messy knot at the nape of her neck, and when she smiled, her white teeth were perfectly even. She stood taller than my father but lacked that self-conscious hunch that some tall people adopted, as if it could make them less conspicuous. Laura was comfortable in her body, and I ashamedly hoped she had a tiny itsy-bitsy flaw that would make me feel better about myself. But she ruined it all by being kind, charming, and unpretentious.

"Olivia, so glad to meet you. Your father told me how relieved he was you'd be here to help him," she said, looking directly at me, her handshake firm without that monster grasp women tended to use to suggest confidence or authority. "He also mentioned you'd be making him a grandfather soon. Congratulations."

"Thanks," I said and glanced at Dad, who grinned at me like I held the answer to a question he'd waited all his life to ask.

"Before you show me around your home, I have a few questions, and I'm sure you have some for me." Laura took a small notebook out of her purse. "Can we talk in the kitchen? I'm much more comfortable around a kitchen table," she said. "Guess it's all those great meals I had at them."

I wanted to ask whether she'd actually eaten any of them, because if she had, her metabolism was faster than the speed of light. Instead, I offered her tea and coffee and set out a tray of homemade oatmeal raisin cookies and lemon squares, which had to have been dropped off by someone, because the only time baking happened in this house was when we sat in the sun.

Laura set her notebook and pen on the table by her mug of coffee, no cream or sugar, because she preferred to "eat her calories, not drink them." Then she asked if we had any questions or concerns.

"My father may have mentioned this already, but in the conversations we had before and since I came home, I don't remember how you came to be hired," I said.

"Honestly, I probably never even mentioned it. A lot going on—"

My dad walked over and grabbed a cookie before joining us at the table.

"Not a problem, Mr. Kavanaugh. I'll fill in the blanks for Olivia," she said, then turned to me. "One of my friends is a long-time client of your dad's agency. Your dad mentioned needing someone to help in the office and at home, but he wasn't quite sure of your plans at the time."

"Right. Jonas had an appointment the day after we were told your mom needed surgery. He said he might know of someone, but he would be back in touch with me after he talked to her."

Laura picked up the story. "When Jonas told me about the situation, I'd just finished a contract job and was looking for something until school started in the fall." She paused to dunk her cookie in her coffee before taking a bite, which endeared her to me even more because it was something only someone who felt comfortable with you might do. "I enrolled in school for a degree in hospitality management . . . Better late than never, I figured. Before deciding to go back to college, I worked off and on as a nanny and a caregiver for children and adults, some with developmental disabilities."

"I'm a little bit confused," I said. "What's the connection between hotel management and being a caregiver?"

"So is Gary, my boyfriend." She laughed. "Confused, I mean. I enjoy being a caregiver when kids or adults are personally referred to me. But I've come to realize that aside from getting entrenched with the families, it's emotionally demanding. And after a lot of soul-searching, I knew it wasn't something I could do indefinitely. My boyfriend and I met when we were bartending together in a downtown hotel. I loved the energy there and being able to meet people from all over the world. With my degree, I'd have opportunities for traveling. And Gary wants to open a restaurant one day, and I told him I'd gladly manage it for him."

Laura didn't see my dad and me look at one another when she mentioned the restaurant, because she'd walked away to pour herself another cup of coffee.

"I guess that was more information than you bargained for?" She brushed a few cookie crumbs from her white lace tank top and sat between us again.

I shook my head. "Not at all." In fact, I wondered if her boyfriend wanted to open a restaurant because he was already in the food-service industry. In which case, he might have known Wyatt.

Instead, I asked if she knew CPR, which she said she did and offered to provide a copy of her certification.

"Not necessary," my dad said. "Let's talk about your schedule and anything else you want to talk about before you look around the house."

Laura would be with Mom from Monday through Friday, from nine in the morning until four in the afternoon, when my father and I would take turns coming home early. She suggested my dad and I accompany my mother to her first few physical therapy appointments to meet the therapists and to find out what they expected when she was home. After that, Laura said she'd drive her there.

My father showed her the house and told her she was welcome to use the guest room at any time. "I may take you up on that offer when Gary has overnight trips. Hate sleeping alone, even at my age."

I knew exactly how she felt.

CHAPTER 28

If I had any doubts about Laura being a competent caretaker for my mother, they disappeared faster than good intentions at a Ben & Jerry's factory after what we'd later call the "walker negotiations."

That day she came to our house, she'd already impressed me with her conscientious concern about caring for my mother. Then she met my dad and me at the hospital the morning Mom was released so she could hear the discharge instructions firsthand and be able to ask questions.

When my mother saw the aluminum walker, she stared at my father as if he'd told her she had to use the stairs to leave. "No one told me I'd have to use one of those things," she said, pointing to the walker. "And I'm not."

My father reached out his arm. "Now, Scarlett—" But the arm never made it to the destination, which we supposed was her shoulder, before she pushed him away. His arm, face, and ego drooped simultaneously.

"Don't patronize me. Especially in front of all these people." Her lips were set in that thin line that signaled "I dare you." She tugged her blouse, smoothed it over her stomach, and glared at the ceiling. She might have been praying for deliverance from us or processing her next attack.

It was the latter.

"I signed all those release papers. Can we leave now? Where is my nurse? She should be here." Arms folded, she was in her take-no-prisoners mode.

Laura, who'd been sitting in a visitor's chair in the hospital room casually flipping through a *People* magazine, placed it on the bed and looked at my father. "Mr. Kavanaugh, would you mind going to the nurses' station and asking when someone will be available to take your wife downstairs?"

"Happy to do that," he said with the relief of a student who'd just been given permission to leave detention early.

When he walked away, Laura scrunched down in front of my mother in her wheelchair so they were at eye level with one another. "You're a person of your word, right?"

"Of course," my mother replied, sounding more wary than defensive.

"In the discharge papers you signed, you said you'd follow doctor's orders. That walker and everything your family and I do for you is to help you get your life back. You're going to have to trust us, just like we're going to trust you to cooperate." Laura extended her hand. "Deal?"

I didn't realize I was holding my breath until my mother nodded and shook Laura's hand.

My parents and the nurse walked ahead to the car. Laura and I followed, pushing carts jammed with floral arrangements, plants, magazines, clothes, and plastic water bottles imprinted with the hospital's logo because my mother had said, "For what the hospital probably charged for them, I could've bought Waterford crystal. I want them."

As we were loading my Jeep, Laura said she'd forgotten to mention to my mother that she'd set up a girlie day, and she wanted me to invite my grandmother. "A friend of mine owns a salon, and he's coming over this weekend with two nail technicians. I thought your mother could use some primping time, and we could do the mani-pedi thing."

I wanted to hug her, but I wasn't sure if we'd reached the stage where we hugged without awkwardness. "Just so you'll know how thrilled I am that you arranged this, the inside me is twirling and hand-clapping."

"I hoped you would be. Figured we'll all need pampering next week." She closed the back door. "Hey, pop open the back, and I'll load the rest of this in there."

The door yawned open, and I walked around to help her.

The two baby gifts were still there.

I opened my mouth and hoped a lame excuse would find its way out, but Laura didn't mention them. She put the magazines and suitcase in the trunk, pressed the button to close it, and said, "Done."

We survived my mother's first day home without verbal warfare or threats of violence. My grandmother ran interference with the uninvited visitors, some of whom came bearing casseroles as their guest cards. My father and I took turns answering cell phones, and by the end of the day, we realized we should have had a voicemail message that told callers, "Yes, she's home. She's still on medication, so none of us, including her, know how much pain she's in. No, she's not ready for visitors. Yes, we'd love for you to drop off a meal. In two weeks. And thank you for praying."

Laura hovered over my mother, and we stayed out of her way unless she needed one of us. She didn't leave until Mom had eaten dinner, taken her medicines, and was tucked in bed. I told my father he needed to make sure that the friend who had recommended her was rewarded generously and thanked often.

"I doubt I have the financial resources to express how grateful I am. He'd tell me to 'pay it forward,' and that would be the best thanks," my father said. "Same way I feel about you staying here. You know how thankful I am." He leaned over and kissed the top of my head. "I would have hugged you, but I don't think you would have appreciated that." As evidence, he held up his soapy dishwater hands as I dried and put away another plate.

Ruthie spent the night so my dad and I could leave early before Laura arrived at the house.

The next morning, still bleary-eyed, I followed him into the office as he unlocked the door. He whistled as he flipped on the lights, started a pot of coffee, and listened to the voice messages on the business phone. I watched him as he puttered around, looking more relaxed than I'd seen him in over a week. Maybe longer considering the drama before I'd left for Houston.

I stored my purse in the bottom drawer of the front desk, and he looked up from the notebook he'd been scribbling messages on. "I almost forgot you were here," he said, a smile breaking across his face. "Let's get some coffee, and I'll show you the ropes."

An hour or so later, I worried that I might hang myself from all those ropes. I'd helped him and Mom in the business on and off throughout high school and even a few college breaks. But the insurance industry had changed, his client list had grown, and my tolerance for making spreadsheets had waned. I sat behind the desk and did what I felt comfortable doing: arranging the paper clips and pens, and crossing out dates on the desk calendar.

Dad patted me on my back. "Just answer the phone, take messages, and we'll worry about the rest later," he said. "I'm going to clear the piles waiting on my desk. Let me know if you need anything."

I felt like I was five again, and he was leaving me at the door of my kindergarten classroom. "No problem." He'd taken about four steps down the hall when I asked him to come back. "Two things. I have a doctor's appointment next week. And I'll be taking a lot of bathroom breaks because, well, the baby insists. Wanted to give you a heads-up if the phone keeps ringing."

"Got it," he said and poured himself another coffee. "Oh, and if your mother or Laura calls and I'm on another line, let me know."

He made his way back to his office, and I putzed around familiarizing myself with the computer and his files, and doing what I did best: educating myself by being nosey.

I managed to stay busy enough, occupying myself between calls by looking at baby furniture and equipment online. One call was Ruthie telling me she was bringing lunch. She stopped by with chicken panini sandwiches and Greek salads.

"As tempting as that looks, I best get myself home to have lunch with Scarlett. Maybe give Laura a break, too," said my dad.

We agreed. Granny waved to him as he walked out, then opened the bags and said, "Poor man, I didn't have the heart to tell him I hadn't planned on him being here." She handed me a still-warm sandwich, and if that nugget of a baby could cheer, I thought it did at that moment. "Guess we could have shared with him."

"That would have been nice of you." I handed her the Coke Zero in the bag. "He might have had to wrestle me for a bite. How can I be so hungry when I've been vegetating at a desk for hours?"

We munched in silence for a bit, and while my grandmother picked the black olives out of her salad and dropped them on mine, she asked, "When's your appointment with that private investigator?"

I leaned back, took a long swallow of water. "I haven't called him yet."

She neatly folded the paper that had covered her sandwich. "What's the holdup?"

Why wasn't the phone ringing now, when I could use an interruption? "I needed to make an appointment with my OB first." I couldn't look at her because we both knew I trotted out a pitiful excuse.

"Did you make the OB appointment?"

As soon as I nodded, she picked up the office phone and handed it to me. "Good. Then you can call him."

I punched in the number. Hoped I could leave a message, but three rings later, I heard a voice say, "Hello, this is Jim Tarkington, private investigator."

CHAPTER 29

Long ago and far away when I used to run—on purpose—the most difficult part was getting dressed and lacing my shoes. Once I accomplished that, my whining inner child would shut up because she knew the decision had been made.

Making the phone call to the private investigator was like that. Instead of hating to lace shoes, I hated to punch in the phone number. Plus, my grandmother sitting on the other side of the desk meant backing out wasn't an option. That day after she left, I called her. "Did you have lunch with me today because you suspected I hadn't contacted the PI?"

"I don't remember you being such a cynical young woman, but I suppose you're entitled. Bless your heart. Would I spend over thirty dollars for lunch and more than an hour of my day simply to ask you a question? I could do that for free, in thirty seconds with a text or an email without your even having to hear my voice. Can't a grandmother just want to spend time with her only granddaughter? I'm not getting any younger. For that matter, neither are you."

"A simple yes or no would have worked," I said. "But it's okay either way. It's time for me to do something, even if I don't get the answers I want."

By the end of the first day, I learned a few unexpected lessons. Sitting on my butt, which I'd dreamed about some days when I was running after Lily, was not the paradise I envisioned it to be. Plus, it revved up my snacking motor, and I'd almost emptied the customers' candy dish and two boxes of Girl Scout cookies I found stashed in the freezer. As if the box of Thin Mints being frozen would deter me.

My mother, I discovered, still had full use of her cell phone abilities and called every two hours to either check on me and my father or to remind one of us of something we needed to do or should have done.

At one point, Laura called to apologize and said she threatened to place my mother on cell phone probation because she wasn't resting. "And realize that sometimes she's calling after one of her pain pills, so she might not always be lucid."

"That explains the call about keeping track of my hours for the payroll department. The one we don't have," I said.

The next few days at the office, I mostly tried to stay out of my father's way. He was still catching up from being out, and I didn't want to interrupt him, so I did whatever I could on my own. Important tasks like making coffee, dusting, buying candy to refill the dish I kept emptying, filing, checking email . . . the company's and my own. If I stayed another month, which based on my conversations with Laura was highly possible, I thought I should try to acquaint myself with the basics of what the business offered clients. One page into the information about homeowner's insurance, I realized I'd discovered a nonaddictive solution to insomnia. It wasn't exactly fascinating literature, but my father would be delighted if I learned the difference between *casualty* and *hazard*.

When I wasn't swamped with office tasks, which was often, I checked in with Mia. We'd sporadically communicated via text and email, and I'd promised her I'd call after my prenatal visit. She and Bryce had sent my mother an organic spa basket filled with candles, herbal tea, and toffees, bath and body gels and lotions and scrubs, all in a woven hamper the size of a small cradle.

She forwarded pictures of Lily, including one where she held up a sign that said *I miss you. Come back.* I told Mia no more tiny terrorist tactics. Truth was, once the new nanny started, the signs might end and I'd miss them.

Something I already missed about Houston was the emotional distance from my life before and after Wyatt. The distance, being surrounded by the unfamiliar, knowing I wouldn't be blindsided by an aching memory when I turned a corner, made pulling myself away from that *before* life less painful. But being home smeared that boundary I'd started to create with constant reminders of the life that had been stolen from me.

I had someone to talk to in Houston. Someone who knew my life not just in the *before* and *after*, but in the *during*. Someone I trusted. Mia was my closest friend. I never had a wide circle of friends. Never felt the need for that. And when Wyatt and I started dating, we were either with Mia and Bryce or by ourselves. Colin, his friend, and Mia were to be our only attendants at the wedding that never happened.

But now that I was home and not even in my own home, I missed having a friend. A face I could talk to, a body I could do things with, and a spirit that "got" me.

⚜

We had our girls' pampering day Sunday. Laura's stylist brought two nail technicians, someone to do our makeup, and more equipment and products than I'd ever seen in one place other than Sephora.

My father helped them haul everything inside, and five minutes later was dressed for the golf course. "Sorry I'm going to miss the fun. Enjoy yourselves, and I'll be back"—he looked at his watch—"in about six hours. I'm sure it won't take that long to make you all beautiful."

My dad smiled and waved as he walked out the door, and I wouldn't have been surprised if he ran to his car.

"Scarlett, I told you that man kissed the Blarney Stone from the day you met him," said my grandmother, with only a trace of sarcasm in her voice. "Too bad you couldn't have taken a trip to Ireland before your surgery so you could have kissed it yourself."

I braced myself for the return fire from my mother, but she retaliated by laughing. Still managing to look regal even in a wheelchair, she said, "I might have been the first person to make it disintegrate into pebbles."

"Did you give her an extra muscle relaxer this morning?" I whispered to Laura as she covered the kitchen table with tubes and trays and brushes from what looked like oversize tackle boxes.

"Thought about it," she said and smiled. "But no. Maybe her doctor injected her new hip with time-release mellow meds. The past few days she's been amazingly cooperative."

"Are you two talking about me?" My mother wheeled in our direction.

"In fact, we are," said Laura, flashing a beatific smile. "I was telling your daughter what a model patient you've been."

"That's your story?" My mother applied a smile and tilted her head.

"She was. Really," I said. Without adding how shocked I was to hear her say it.

We were saved by Laura's stylist who wanted to talk to my mother about her hair.

While he introduced my mother to the wonders of dry shampoo, Laura and I started our manicures and pedicures. Ruthie served maple bacon biscuits, peach scones, and blackberry muffins she'd picked up at the bakery, along with virgin mimosas for the alcohol-restricted among us, and coffee and tea. When she finished serving, my grandmother was first up to have her makeup done. At one point, the cosmetician asked if she could relax her face, which Laura and I knew meant stop talking long enough for the makeup artist to finish her eyes.

By the time lunch rolled around, I'd forgotten I'd met Laura only a week earlier. Her calm yet assertive personality was exactly what my mother needed, and if I hadn't liked Laura so much I would have envied their easy banter. The wall between my mother and me rose and fell at unexpected times, bruising my ego and my willingness to attempt another breakthrough. Today, though, she acted more relaxed than she had in months. The two of us even joked about Dad's confusion when he did anything outside of Reply and Send in his email.

"The first time I asked him to attach pictures to a document and then forward it, his eyes glazed over," she said. Then, mimicking my father's perplexed expression, eyebrows driving toward one another, her lips pressed together, she continued, "Then he said, 'Scarlett, I can't keep up with all this technology and run a business, too.'"

We laughed, then Laura said as she scrutinized the nail polish options, "I have friends whose kids aren't walking, but they can make sense out of an iPhone. In a few years, maybe his grandchild can teach him, right, Mrs. K?"

My mother sat behind me, so I couldn't see her expression. I shook the Bikini So Teeny nail color, examining the bottom as if, like the Magic Eight Ball I played with as a child that revealed answers, the polish would reveal my mother's reaction to Laura's question.

The quiet swelled in the room until my grandmother punctured it with "Just like my grandchild taught me."

We all stopped to eat lunch while we waited for our toenails to dry and to give the crew helping us a chance to rest. I let them have their way with my hair, shaping it into a feathered bob with tapered bangs, adding highlights and lowlights. The stylist assured me that the minimal dye for the contrasts would be safe to use while I was pregnant.

"Do you know the sex of the baby yet? Are you finding out?" Laura asked as she tore off sheets of foil and handed them to me to cover the leftover salads and sandwiches.

"I have an appointment next week. The doctor said when I'm about twenty weeks, they'll do the gender check. I'm not sure yet if I want to know."

Laura carried the wrapped containers to the refrigerator. "What about you, Mrs. K?"

"I hope she's not planning to have one of those dreadful 'reveal' parties that seem to be the latest rage," my mother said, her voice stretching *dreadful* into a three-syllable word.

I wanted to remind her that "she" was in the same room with her, but the "she" that was my mother had more to say. Of course.

"All things considered, I think Olivia should find out if she's having a boy or a girl. She doesn't have a clue if Wyatt might—"

No more syllables escaped from my mother's lips because my grandmother swooped in and snatched the opportunity. "If Wyatt might have wanted to be surprised or not."

We were shined and polished and dyed and styled and beautified from head to toe. And that's where the changes ended.

CHAPTER 30

"How is it something the size of an avocado can make me gain five pounds in five weeks?" I stepped off the scale, slipped my flats on, and followed Nora, the nurse practitioner, to the exam room.

I sat on the exam table, which was really more like an industrial-size recliner, adjusting myself on the white scrunchy paper that covered it while she flipped through my chart.

"Considering you'd lost weight the last time we saw you, I'd say you're right on track," she said as she wrapped the blood pressure cuff around my arm. "Okay, blood pressure good. Let's see if we can hear that baby's heartbeat. Usually we can detect it on ultrasound as early as six or seven weeks. So we shouldn't have any problems now that you're about eighteen weeks."

In the minute or so it took her to spread the warm gel on my abdomen and ready the Doppler, my own heart tightened, clutched by the "what if?" monster. The one that specialized in worst-case scenarios. *What if she can't hear the heartbeat? What if something's wrong and it doesn't sound like it's supposed to?*

I must have looked as scared as I felt because Nora gently squeezed my arm and said with gentleness, "Hey, Mom, relax." She positioned the probe on my bump. "Ready?"

I nodded.

She swirled the probe around. "Okay, that's your heartbeat."

"I'll take your word for it. Sounds like an electrical storm's going on in there."

A few more swirls, she stopped, and in a blanket-soft voice said, "Listen. There's your baby."

At first, all I heard was the swishing of wind-blown sand. Then a beat, like galloping horses. Fast and rhythmic. "That's it . . . my baby? That's my baby?" I whispered the questions as if in the presence of something holy and sacred. These heartbeats echoed my heart and Wyatt's heart.

At that moment I understood what it meant to be blessed. To be granted something beyond measure, beyond deserving, beyond myself.

And yet, at that moment, even with this incredible gift growing inside me, I had never felt so alone. Fortunately, no one in the room except for me knew that some of the tears I shed weren't all happy tears. Mingled with them were tears of sadness for all that Wyatt was missing and tears of anger for his being so irresponsible.

I couldn't wait until the weekend to talk to Mia. I called before I even left the parking lot to share my excitement.

"I heard the baby today. The heartbeats. I had no idea . . ." But the euphoria couldn't dull the searing stabs of sadness. My throat tightened, and I made ugly, wet alien noises. I couldn't stop the sobs from erupting, and soon I sounded like someone trying to talk underwater. "It'snotfair . . . it'snot . . . it'snot . . ." I clenched my teeth and wanted to pound the steering wheel with my fists until they were bruised. "I hate him. I hate him for not being here to hear his own child's heartbeat. I hate him for leaving me with all these questions. I shouldn't have to do this alone. I shouldn't . . ."

"Oh, sweetie, I know, I understand—"

"No," I shrieked through my sobbing. "You don't understand. You can't. Bryce never left you. Lily has a father who didn't miss her first heartbeats. A father you never had to doubt might have had a child somewhere else. Please, don't think for one minute that you know what this feels like. You don't. And I hope you never do." I dug in my purse and found a crumpled tissue and wiped my nose. Made myself breathe through the hiccupping.

"You're right, Livvy. I don't know what it feels like to be you at this moment. And you're right, I hope I never have to." Her voice was gentle and soothing and wrapped itself around me as if Mia herself was with me. "I'm sad that you're alone right now. You shouldn't be. And it's not fair. You are doing the best you can do. And you know Bryce and I will help you."

"You and Bryce have already helped me. You've been so generous, and you came through for me when I had no idea where to go. I don't take that for granted. If I could find some answers, it would bring me peace." I hesitated. "I have an appointment next week with an investigator. There's nothing more I can find out on my own. And he may not be able to tell me anymore than I already know. But I don't want to regret never having tried to do everything possible to find out where Wyatt was going that day."

"I want you to really think about what you're about to do. Are you ready to live with whatever he finds out? Especially now, before this baby's even born? What if that gift belongs to Wyatt's son, not someone else's? What then? It would break my heart to know you're holding your son or daughter in a few months, wondering about some other child. You don't have to do this now. Or ever."

I loved Mia, but she pushed me in a way that almost made me feel guilty about wanting to find out the truth. In all the times we'd discussed my contacting an investigator, she never seemed open to considering what it meant to me. She wasn't comfortable knowing the truth would cause me pain, and I wasn't comfortable with the pain not knowing the truth would cause me. I promised her I'd think about it.

Before we hung up, she said, "Lily misses you. We all do. As soon as your mom's recovered, we want you to come back to Houston. You can make a life here. And you won't be constantly surrounded by people and places to remind you of Wyatt."

When I started driving, I found myself headed to my grandmother's instead of my parents' house. She opened her door and, without either one of us saying a word, she gathered me in her arms.

"I'm tired, Granny. I'm so tired," I said, just letting the tears fall. I followed her into her bedroom. She pulled down the comforter; I slipped off my shoes and let her tuck me in like she did when I was young. The pillow was cool against my face, her hand warm on my cheek as she bent to kiss my forehead. She left, closing the door behind her, and I fell asleep like someone who'd had too much to drink.

CHAPTER 31

I stayed with my grandmother for the weekend, even though it meant sleeping on her sofa. After orbiting around my mother for a week, made more difficult when Laura had left for the day, I appreciated a conversation that didn't require filtering through "what reaction is this going to generate?"

The morning after my blackout sleep, Granny and I walked to breakfast at Elizabeth's Restaurant, because who wouldn't want to start a day with praline bacon and Bananas Foster Stuffed French Toast? We left her condo early to beat both the sweltering heat and the late risers who crowded the upstairs bar satiating their table wait with Bloody Marys and Cucumber Coolers. Even though I could still see my feet over my baby bump, I had to remind myself to step carefully over cracked sidewalks, buckled and bowed by the gnarly roots of oak trees.

On the way, I talked to her about my prenatal visit and all the angst that surrounded hearing the baby's heartbeat, and my phone call with Mia.

She reached for my hand as we crossed the street. I looked down at her hand wrapped around mine and smiled. "Thanks. Guess those maternal instincts kick in, even when they don't need to, huh?"

"You're about to make me a great-grandmother, even though I'd be great anyway"—she winked—"so I need to practice now." She pushed back a riotous growth of Confederate jasmine that spilled over a leaning fence onto the narrow sidewalk. The rich sweetness of the flowers perfumed the air, the scent so pungent I was grateful to be over my early weeks of nausea.

"This isn't something you have to do alone," she said. "You know, you could have asked me to go with you to that appointment. Especially since your mother can't be there with you right now."

"Let's not pretend her surgery is the reason she didn't go with me," I said and opened the restaurant door for my grandmother.

"Don't you give up on her." She slipped off her sunglasses, her sharp eyes focused on me. "She'll come around. Trust me."

Just when I thought I'd familiarized myself with the coverages my dad provided for businesses, he popped up with questions about which of his business clients' crime-coverage policies needed to be reviewed or renewed.

"Crime insurance? Really? The same as when they're held up at gunpoint like those people at Café Jacques who were eating their Trout Almondine one minute, and the next they were facedown on the scored concrete floor?" I turned to the computer to search for the files thinking about a to-go order of a seafood platter for lunch.

"Unfortunately, no. Some policies do cover kidnappings, but our clients are interested in being protected against embezzlement, forgery, counterfeiting, inside jobs," he said, flipping through the mail I'd handed him.

"Too bad it doesn't cover jilted brides . . . Now that's a crime."

I didn't realize my comment was a few decibels above a whisper until my dad remarked, "Not even wedding-protection with change-of-heart insurance covers what happened to you."

"Figures," I said as I waited for the list he wanted to finish printing.

I gave him the first page and he started to walk back to his office. "Bring me the other pages when they're finished printing."

He was just a few paces away when my brain processed what he'd told me about wedding insurance. "Dad, wait."

He turned, his eyes scanning the list.

"How did you find out about that change-of-heart coverage?"

After his awkward and sudden onset of coughing, he rubbed the back of his neck and looked at the floor. Hoping, I was sure, a wormhole would appear that he could disappear through and land in Maui.

"Don't tell me one of your clients wanted to know, because that 'it belongs to a friend' excuse didn't fly for me in high school. Ever."

"We, your mother and I, um, we looked into it. I mean, we are in the insurance business. We should be aware of everything that's available." He folded the paper he held in half, his thumb and forefinger carefully creasing it. "But, and you probably already figured, we decided it didn't, um, provide what we needed."

"Hedging your bets, were you? Interesting." I handed him the rest of the list that had finished printing. "I'm not angry, because it doesn't surprise me. I get it. That's what you do. It makes sense you'd want to know about it. I wonder, though, if you had the coverage, would you have told me? And if you and Mom were all about 'protection,'" I said, making air quotes with my fingers, "how is it you never talked to Wyatt about something as basic as life insurance?"

He didn't falter on that question. But anguish replaced the embarrassed guilt that reddened his face earlier. "I did talk to him. Wyatt said he had a small policy at work, nothing great, as we found out. We were going to talk when the two of you returned from your honeymoon."

At dinner that night I told my parents about the baby's heartbeat, how it sounded like a herd of horses galloping on sand.

"Scarlett, that's exciting, isn't it?" Dad reached across the table and squeezed her shoulder, almost knocking over his glass of tea.

"Be careful. You could have spilled that all over us," said my mother, moving her own glass closer to her plate. "Yes, it's very nice to hear," she said, with the enthusiasm of "Place your tray table in the upright position."

Remembering my grandmother's words, I slapped my hand over the mouth of my inner teen, and with a voice that could melt frosting, I said, "Thanks." I pushed my chair away from the table, then stopped. "Mom, I thought of you. How listening to this baby's beating heart, I understood what it felt like for you to hear mine. And all those feelings I experienced, I hoped were the ones you did, too."

She turned the cup in her hands, watching her coffee slosh from side to side. The ice maker whirred, filling itself with water, the coffeemaker sputtered the end of its cycle, and my mother sighed and bit her lower lip.

"Blessed. I felt blessed." She looked at me, her eyes clear, and said, "And scared. Because I loved you so much from that moment, I was afraid I might never have the chance to hold you."

I'd emotionally braced myself for one of her caustic or dismissive responses. It took me a few seconds to recover from the shock of her being honest and vulnerable. I wanted to tell her that she had the chance to hold me now. To help me not be afraid.

But I was afraid. Afraid that the judgmental mother lurked under the surface of the one who had just spoken.

"I understand," I said and kissed her on the forehead before I walked away.

CHAPTER 32

Not a happy start to my morning to be told by my grandmother—or as she said, "warned"—that she and her gray-haired posse planned a road trip to Gatlinburg, Pigeon Forge, and the Smoky Mountains, then a stop in Hot Springs, Arkansas, on the way home.

"You're leaving me? When did you decide to do this?"

"I wasn't going to take the trip because of your mother's surgery, but Laura's a go-getter, and all I do is get in the way. So when Beverly had to cancel at the last minute because she broke her ankle at Zumba, I figured I'd slip on in her place. You'll be fine. Maybe you and your mother will be able to make some progress. Hope so, because I'll be gone almost two weeks."

"Two weeks?" Panic tiptoed in and started making itself at home in my stomach. "But I have that appointment. And then I'll be going to Houston just a few weeks after you get back, and—"

"Honey, you know I love you, but you need to find a friend your own age while you're here. And I want to spend some time with friends my age, too. I've never been to Dollywood. It's on my bucket list," she said.

You would deprive this woman of her bucket list?

Sometimes my good conscience showed up at times I'd rather it stayed home.

"What's this on the calendar?" I pointed to the monitor where Dad had entered *Golf w/ EG* at ten o'clock, then blocked himself out for the day. "I have an appointment during lunch. How's that going to work?"

"It's not. You didn't tell me you needed to go somewhere. We have to talk about these things ahead of time. Can you reschedule this appointment? Is it something with the baby? I'll cancel the game if I need to—"

"No, it's not life or death." My grandmother and Mia were the only two people who knew about the PI appointment. I didn't want to tell my parents, but I'd kept it such a secret from them, I'd forgotten to tell Dad I'd need time off. "I'll call this morning and set up another time."

Clothes not only make the man, they tell you where he's going. When my father walked in without his briefcase, wearing his Lake Hills Country Club polo shirt and khakis, I should have known this was not another day at the office for him. *And that's why you need a private investigator, Olivia, because your powers of observation suck.*

"Let me know when it is, and I'll make sure I'm here." He whistled on his way to his first cup of coffee.

"You're leaving early, plus you're not coming back for the rest of the day? How am I supposed to answer all these questions? I don't think you want me to call you when you're teeing off or putting or whatever—"

"Olivia, calm down," he said, grinning as he stood waiting for the coffee to finish and practicing his swing with his invisible golf club. "You'll be fine. Just take messages. If it's something urgent, text me or call, and I'll take care of it." He shaded his eyes, hand on his forehead, and pretended to look down the fairway. "I haven't been on the course in weeks."

"Wouldn't have ever suspected . . ." I mumbled, still annoyed, but mostly with myself for having to reschedule. The first call was challenge enough, but having to make a second call? *It's your own fault.* And when I climbed out of my ego for a minute, I saw his smile and how relaxed he seemed, and I realized this outing was the perfect mental health day for him. When I worked, as in my real job at Visual Strategies, we'd joke about our "too well to work" days instead of taking off for sick days.

"Oh, I almost forgot to tell you"—he paused to sip his coffee—"I'm playing with Evan. Evan Gendusa."

"That's, um, a surprise. I didn't know he was in town." I busied myself lining up the pens, candy, and business cards on the front counter. "Be sure and tell him hello for me," I said, making an effort to sound friendly without suggesting eagerness. *Which would be dumb, right, Olivia? Especially since (a) your almost husband just died, (b) you're pregnant, and (c) he's engaged.*

"You can tell him yourself. He's coming here to pick me up," he said and started walking to his office.

"Whoa, Dad," I called. "Stop right there. Ya think you could've mentioned that this morning when I was debating what to wear and if I should bother wearing makeup?"

"You women," he said and shook his head. The head shake that meant "You're so silly to worry about that."

"No . . . it's more like 'you men.' It's not as if you haven't been around when Mom and I have these meltdowns. Would you want to show up for an appointment with spinach between your teeth?" I sat behind my desk and opened the bottom drawer to pull my anorexic makeup bag out of my purse.

"Come on, Livvy, you've known Evan since high school. I'm sure there were times when you might have shown up without looking like you were headed to a beauty pageant," he said. "Let me know when he gets here, probably in a half hour or so. In the meantime, I'm going to see what I can accomplish before I leave."

"Sure. I'll just be sitting here looking like, what is it that Ruthie says? 'As ugly as homemade sin.' No problem."

I was rummaging through my purse, not looking at the front door, but then the bell announced someone had arrived. "I'll be with you in a minute . . ."

"That might be fifty seconds too long."

I remembered the scent before I recognized his voice or saw his face. When Evan and I dated, I'd told Mia his cologne made me swoony. "It smells like expensive silk sheets and butter-soft leather with moments of musky oranges." She'd told me she wasn't surprised I felt dizzy if all that was going on in his cologne.

I looked up, and there he stood.

Not at all like I remembered him.

Better.

His brownish hair, once cut short, had grown to a respectable length. He was still thin, but now—at least from the waist up, which was all I could see—he had muscle definition. And the fact that I noticed all of this about him made me feel like a bipolar thirteen-year-old with crush issues and an almost thirty-year-old with cheating issues.

"'Of all the gin joints, in all the towns, in all the world' . . . Great to see you, Livvy," he said. "Your dad mentioned you might be here."

"You, too. Well, not the 'mentioned that you might be here.' The 'great to see you.' That part." *Bravo, Olivia. The epitome of articulate.*

Now what? If I stood, I was too far along for him to think I had a sudden onset of bloating. *He must already know I'm pregnant.* Our parents were friends . . . and then this town . . . By now there might be a Sherpa or two in Nepal who hadn't heard.

If only he didn't look like an improved version of himself.

He's engaged. My nude face and my baby bump didn't matter now, so I stood.

"By the way, congrats on your wedding . . . Your brother mentioned it to me before I moved to Houston. When are you going back to Baton Rouge?"

To his credit, he maintained eye contact instead of resorting to an airport-security body-scan to check out my pregnancy. He opened his mouth to answer, but my father's voice came out.

"Hey, buddy. I thought I heard a familiar voice." My dad welcomed Evan like a prodigal son. Rewarding him with a face-cracking smile, well-pumping handshake followed by the traditional, nonthreatening arms around shoulders, chests bumping, backslapping bro-man hug. "Good to see you. Real good."

"You too, George," Evan said without a trace of awkwardness. Wyatt called my father Mr. Kavanaugh until . . . until he couldn't anymore.

"Evan here thinks he can beat me at my own game."

I might have found the warmth nestled in his voice touching when he talked to Evan, except that I'd never heard it in his conversations with the man I almost married.

"It's been a long time since he's seen me on the golf course," Evan said. "I think your father's underestimating me."

Maybe I had, too.

That longer-haired, well-built man still housed traces of the Evan from years ago. Shades of ego, assuming he's not bound by social conventions and can dispense with "Mr." when he speaks to my father. Even the way he filled a space. A magnet drawing everything to himself.

On the way out, Evan turned around and said, "Olivia, let's catch up another time, okay?"

"Sure," I said, waiting for him to close the door before I finished what I really wanted to say. *You, your fiancée, pregnant me . . . we'll 'catch up' because why? You want the details of my riveting life?*

One thing I knew for certain. I didn't want the details of their charmed about-to-be-married-and-live-happily-ever-after lives.

After they left, I called and rescheduled my appointment with the private investigator. Maybe I'd eventually find out what had destroyed *my* charmed about-to-be-married, happily-ever-after life.

CHAPTER 33

I closed the office early after doodling possible baby names for an hour, went home, and found Laura and my mother on the backyard deck.

"Livvy, hey." Laura waved as I walked out the back door. "Look at your mom. She's breaking out of her training wheels."

Her walker had been pushed to the side, and she managed small steps using her cane and holding Laura's elbow. Two lengths of duct tape, about two feet apart, were her starting and ending points. She stared at that tape as if looking at it harder might bring it closer. A step or so away from the finish line, her mouth twisted in pain, but she didn't stop.

Laura and I applauded when she reached the end, then Laura steered her to a chair. "I'm going inside to grab some iced tea. Too hot, and too early for wine." She winked and disappeared through the door.

I bent over and kissed Mom on the cheek. "Great job," I said. "I'm proud of how hard you're working."

My sincerity seemed to surprise her, because she looked at me and something close to a smile was happening on her lips.

"Thanks. Laura's been a godsend. We were so lucky to find her. Your dad was right; it's easier for someone who isn't family to push you. And she won't let me whine."

Laura walked out with three glasses of iced tea on a tray. "Did I hear you say 'wine'? It's not five o'clock yet, remember?"

"Oh, I remember." My mother nodded, took a glass, and handed one to me. "The first day you were here, I wanted it for breakfast. By the afternoon, I wanted to break the bottle over your head."

"Charming, isn't she?" Laura said and joined me on the glider. "I'm glad the boss let you off early. What's the occasion?"

"The occasion is a golf game, and I begged to close the office early before I fell asleep on the desk and drooled all over the calendar pad."

I asked my mother if she'd known Dad was playing with Evan this morning. "Isn't his law practice in Baton Rouge? And I thought he was getting married soon."

"He mentioned the golf game to me yesterday," she said and wiped her forehead with the napkin that had been around her tea glass. "Evan's mother dropped by a few days ago."

"Lacey? She was the one who looked like she shopped in her daughter's closet?" Laura looked at me and rolled her eyes.

I coughed my giggle into my napkin, surprised my mother didn't jump to her friend's defense.

Mom sipped her tea, sighed, and said, "I guess I have to admit wearing leggings with stilettos and a halter tunic wouldn't be appropriate for women my age." She shook her head. "I know I shouldn't laugh, but . . ." And then she proceeded to do exactly that.

"Sorry I missed that fashion nightmare, but did she tell you anything about the wedding?"

"No wedding in Evan's future." Laura made an X with her forefingers. "Oops, sorry, Mrs. K, guess you should've answered since I only know because I was eavesdropping."

"Lacey blathered her family's business in front of both of us," said my mother. "Anyway"—she paused and adjusted herself in the chair—"Evan's not living in Baton Rouge. He's moved back."

"He's opening a law practice here?"

"No. Lacey said Evan wasn't happy practicing law. His fiancée broke off the engagement. She didn't go into details about that, but I got the impression his fiancée thought Evan might not be able to support her lifestyle. She's from one of those old-moneyed families. Debutante, queen of one of the New Orleans' carnival balls."

"I must have zoned out or been in the bathroom when she told you why he moved back," said Laura, turning to me. "Lacey is one of those people who would go through New York to get to California. Her stories should come with intermissions."

I'd met Evan's mother, usually at my parents' house or club events, but we rarely had much to say to each other. Our conversations usually took place in different time zones.

"Evan's always loved golf. When he was in college, he used to come back for the summers to teach clinics for kids. His father told him the club needed a golf pro because our pro was moving to Florida. Evan decided to apply, they gave him the job, and Lacey said he's doing that until."

"Until what?" I almost couldn't process so much un-Evan-like information. No Baton Rouge living. No wedding. No lawyering.

My mother shrugged her shoulders. "Until . . . I don't know. She didn't say. I think she's hoping this golf thing is temporary."

"Go figure. Funny how things turn out. You and Dad thought Wyatt working as a chef was borderline acceptable, but you were concerned that he didn't have ambition. Now Evan, the man you thought would be the perfect match, seems to be not so perfect after all."

In retrospect, I should have allowed those musings to simmer in my brain before I tossed them out, all raw and unseasoned. My mother's calm and open demeanor since I'd arrived had lulled me into thinking I could speak without editing first.

Wrong.

"Actually, your father and I admire Evan for having the courage to pursue what he loves. And it's refreshing that he isn't concerned about people's perceptions. He's willing to take a risk. Like your father did all those years ago when he left a comfortable position at another agency to start his own business." She set her glass on the deck, grabbed her cane, and started to pull herself up.

"Wait," Laura demanded. "Let me get your walker." She looked at me, mouthed, "What happened?" and retrieved the walker for my mother.

"Mom, what are you doing?" I knew exactly, but I didn't want to argue in front of Laura, more for her sake than either my mother's or mine.

"Olivia, it's steamy outside, I'm tired, and I know Laura has to leave soon. She's going to help me back to bed so I can rest before your father comes home."

"Okay, then," I said in a way that meant it wasn't okay. At all. *Rather than tell me she's upset with me or something I said, she'll leave.*

Difficult to argue with a shadow.

I stayed outside, letting my frustration wear itself out in the tranquilizing back-and-forth motion of the glider. Like when Lily was still new to the universe and had colic, and we'd rock and rock and rock until we rocked it all out. She'd be on my shoulder, and I'd crane my neck to look at her without waking her just to see that perfect O her lips formed when she surrendered to sleep.

I might have fallen asleep myself because I didn't remember Laura opening the door and coming to sit on the glider again.

"She's settled in her bedroom. I stacked a few magazines by her, left her cell phone on the nightstand, and made sure she took her meds. Maybe that's why she was a little bit on edge," said Laura.

"Nice of you to say that, but I'm afraid I'm the edge she's on." I tapped my stomach. "Or maybe it's the baby or both of us. Who knows?"

"Explain that to me again. I'm catching the tail end of a big elephant here."

I gave Laura a condensed version of the past few months, without the details of the gifts and the private investigator. Her expressions morphed from sadness to confusion to anger and back again. "I'm sorry that you're in the middle of this, but then again, I'm not. My mother's a different person with you. Nicer. I'm hoping at least some of it stays after you're not here," I said.

Laura settled her long legs on the chair where my mother had sat.

"Your mother told me about Wyatt dying in a car accident. But she didn't provide details, which, honestly, I wouldn't have expected her to. When I found out from your father that you were pregnant, I thought the baby would be all she'd want to talk about. I mean, you're her only child, and you're having her grandchild. That's something to be excited about. The few times I did bring up the baby or you being pregnant, she'd give me short answers and then move on to something else. At least now I understand why. I'm so sorry, Olivia."

"My father and my grandmother stay involved, but it would be nice, now that I'm going to be a mother myself, to have my mother to talk to. Maybe I should start going to yoga because I certainly can't take up smoking or live on junk food, and I don't want this baby to be born needing stress-management classes in the newborn nursery."

I didn't understand why, after I finished talking, she looked surprised. I began to wonder if she had even been listening to me.

"I have something for you," she said with the excitement of a pre-schooler coming home with an elbow macaroni necklace for her mother.

She pulled a loop of beads out of her purse, placed them in my hand, and closed my fingers over them. "These are worry beads, *komboloi*. My grandfather gave them to me. His father came here from Greece, where they're used for calming and de-stressing. After *yiayia*, my grandmother, died, my *pappou* always carried his with him. Just fidgeting with them helped calm and distract him."

I rubbed the beads with my fingertips, slipping them back and forth on the silk rope on which they'd been strung. The loop was about as wide as my two hands, with one larger bead set off and an attached black silken tassel. "I can't take these. They're from your grandfather . . ."

"Trust me." She reached over, her hands on my shoulders, movement slight, but it drew my head up to look at her. "You can. Greeks don't skimp on worry beads. Some of them cost hundreds of dollars. These don't; they're white onyx. I have beads made of olive wood, coral, and other stones at home."

I rolled the smooth stones between my palms, surprised by the soothing sensation. A tactile sigh. It reminded me of my grandmother brushing my hair when I was young. The soft, slow strokes so relaxing they lulled me into sleep.

Laura showed me how to hold the beads and ways to make them quiet or loud, depending on my mood or stress level. "I love knowing that you have these. And so would my grandfather." She handed them back to me. "I have to leave in a few minutes, but I want you to know I appreciate your sharing with me and how difficult that must be for you. Don't suffer alone. Wyatt would never want that for you . . . Well, I mean, not that I'd know, but from what you told me about him, I don't think he would . . ."

She paused, stared at her cell phone, then back at me.

"I guess what I'm trying to say is, please call me if you want someone to go with you to the doctor or shop or whatever. Provided your mother isn't holding me hostage."

We both laughed. "No, she'd probably say I kidnapped you." I hugged her. "Thank you. Thank you. For everything."

She left but was back before I'd reached the door myself.

"I wasn't supposed to have those beads today. I meant to grab a different set I thought would be perfect for your mother. But earlier today, I saw I'd brought those instead." Laura pointed to the beads I clutched. "I came back to tell you I remembered my pappou saying white onyx takes away sorrow and attracts love and happiness." She grinned. "Is that awesome or what?" she asked and then walked through the back door again.

CHAPTER 34

My mother's nap seemed to have refreshed her as much as the time my father spent with Evan at the 19th Hole, also known as the club's bar, after their round of golf.

My parents entertained each other over dinner, which was some sort of chicken casserole from the refrigerator in a container labeled like a CIA classified document: *THIS BAKING DISH IS THE PROPERTY OF EDITH WEST*, followed by her address and telephone number. I wondered if her husband and children were tattooed.

Since my mother hadn't been playing and wouldn't be able to return to golf for months, she was riveted, listening to my dad's hole-by-hole analysis of his game. I commented that it took as much time to talk about the game he played as it did for him to play it, but I was the only one amused.

He talked about how much he missed being on the course with Mom, and I heard brownie points ringing up like a jackpot on a slot machine. I was semiattentive, more concerned with spearing something with my fork that looked like prunes in the chicken dish, when I heard my name in the same sentence with the word *golf*.

"Olivia, what do you think?" My father was suspiciously beaming.

"About . . ." I clutched my napkin in case I needed it to hide my reaction.

"About golf lessons. You could use your mom's clubs until we had a chance to fit you for your own, and eventually the three of us could play. I think there's even a father-daughter tournament. No, maybe it's father-son, but that's discrimination, right? They'd have to let you play—"

"Whoa, Dad. Your train's leaving the station, and I'm still buying the ticket." I shook my head. "I appreciate the thought, but I don't think this is the right time for me to learn a game that's going to require swinging past my belly in a few months."

"Why don't you take a lesson, then decide if it's something you want to do?" My mother had the gift of asking questions that always sounded like accusations.

"Because I don't need lessons in skydiving to know I have no desire to leave a perfectly stable airplane?" I picked up the plates and carried them to the sink. "Golf doesn't appeal to me." It didn't appeal to Wyatt, either. A commonality that excluded both of us from my parents' idea of an enjoyable six hours whacking balls around.

"Think about it, Livvy, okay? It might be a fun thing for us to do together."

"Okay, I'll think about it." About as much as I thought about shaving my head, but I hated when my dad's appeals were on the tipping point of begging.

"By the way, did you reschedule that appointment from this morning?" Dad asked.

I was grateful my head was in the refrigerator looking for dessert. I mouthed my mother's question at the same time she asked it. "What appointment?"

This moment brought to you by children without a sibling who could have their backs while they're thinking of a reasonable answer.

"I found half a strawberry cheesecake and leftover peach cobbler for dessert," I said, holding one in each hand and closing the refrigerator door with my elbow. Ignoring the question wouldn't make it go away, but I counted on the distraction to buy me time.

"I really shouldn't, but I exercised today, right?" My father glanced down at his stomach and patted it with both hands. "A little of each one for me."

My mother passed, as I figured she would, but it meant she had a chance to ask the question again. "Did you reschedule a doctor's appointment?"

Lying was not only not in my nature, I was a failure at it. I learned early on when I attempted to lie that what came out of my mouth and what showed on my face always contradicted each other. Subterfuge, I was a bit better at pulling off, but under pressure was always a risk. "No, not a doctor's appointment." I busied myself with cutting and serving. Handed my father his plate.

The ripples of my mother's wave of impatience were sloshing on the shore of my hesitation. If she had to ask a third time, I was doomed. The gig would be up, and the ripples would give way to a tidal wave.

"I decided to go see someone . . ." I sat with my mountain of cobbler, rearranging it into a hill as I spoke. "I've had so much happening and trying to sort it all out and then being pregnant. I thought it would help, you know, to be able to talk to someone . . ." Since *someone* became almost the universal code word for anyone in the mental health field, I figured she'd buy in, and I'd told the truth. Or maybe a truth.

"How did you find this person? Who referred you?" Mom leaned over and took a spoonful of Dad's cobbler.

Was she not going to quit?

"Cara, my boss at Virtual Strategies. She'd gone through a messy divorce—"

My father held up his hand. "Could you answer my question? I asked first," he said without glancing at my mother. Wise.

"Friday. My appointment's at eleven o'clock. I should be back by twelve thirty at the latest. I'll put it on the calendar when I get to the office tomorrow morning."

That night before I climbed in bed, I reached for the worry beads from Laura. I wished I'd had them during dinner, but I'd left them on my bedroom dresser because the skirt I was wearing when she gave them to me didn't have pockets.

When I woke up the next morning, they were around my wrist. I remembered holding the beads as I scrunched my pillow under my head and pulled up the sheets. But I didn't remember falling asleep.

Maybe I was just tired or it was the beads or both.

I made sure, though, when I dressed for the day, I found something to wear that had pockets.

CHAPTER 35

I'm going to deliver these contracts. I should be back in an hour. You're good?" My father already had his hand on the door, so he'd expected to hear that I was.

"Yes. I have my to-do list, so take your time." He was halfway out before I finished my sentence.

The first task on my list, not Dad's, was straightening his office. To the clients, it appeared picture-perfect. But open a desk drawer or a cabinet or a closet, and you found a compost stack of paper or risked an avalanche of it, depending. The day I counted six staplers in various nooks around his office, I suspected a problem.

I'd lived with his line of reasoning long enough to understand what happened: "In the time it would take me to find the stapler, I could pull one out of the supply closet and be finished." And it was easier for my mother to continue buying replacements than to look for the lost one. No wonder they worked well together.

I'd almost finished emptying the closet, except for what I couldn't reach without the step stool, when the front bell rang. "Be right there," I called out, dusting all sorts of schmutz from the front of my linen shift.

I primed my welcome-to-the-agency smile and started talking before I rounded the corner. "Sorry, I was in the back. Evan. You're here." My smile soured. "Again."

"Your powers of perception are astounding. As sharp as ever," he said with a lopsided grin that crinkled the corners of his eyes.

"And you are as maddening as ever." *Especially so. Because you look better in jeans than I ever will. And I see you and think things no woman pregnant with another man's baby, even if that man is deceased, should be thinking, much less doing.* "My father left about thirty minutes ago. I'll tell him you stopped by. I'm assuming not for another golf game?"

"You assumed correctly. And I don't need to see him." He handed me a plastic tote imprinted with the country club's logo of a single magnolia. "He left his golf shoes in my car."

I set the bag on my desk. "Thanks, but he could've just picked them up from the club since you work there," I said, making it sound like he worked in a sweat factory that employed four-year-old kids.

I thought he'd be offended by my caustic tone. And, the shameful truth was, I wanted to see him squirm. The once-and-future king of a charmed life who now settled for a job riding around a golf course.

Instead, he launched into a kick-heeled, perky-eyed description of how waking up in the morning to go to work wasn't painful anymore, how he loved being outside and not confined by office walls, and how he enjoyed interacting with people in a way that didn't require taking depositions or hammering them with questions.

"It's been a while since you and I have had a chance to reconnect. How about lunch one day? We could meet at the club or wherever you want. How about Friday?"

Reconnect? Wouldn't that first require connecting? "I already have plans for Friday."

"Already have another date, huh?"

If I hadn't insulted him first, I might've been more offended by his comment. I chalked it up to something I deserved. "As if I'm 'dating material.' I'm sure that eHarmony has me on its 'No Profile Allowed' list."

Evan actually looked confused, which confused me.

"It doesn't have to be lunch. We could have dinner. Maybe go to one of the casinos and eat our weights in boiled shrimp. Like we used to do."

He didn't get that there was no "used to" part of me left, but he still waited patiently for my answer. I dug through the candies in the dish until I found something chocolate. I unwrapped the gold foil off the Hershey's Kiss like there was a Fabergé egg inside. I needed some distraction so I wouldn't have to make eye contact. Especially since one of my early experiences with Evan had been the way he could look at me as if I were the most beautiful woman in the universe. When he started looking at his law books and his LSAT practice tests that way, that's when the music started to die.

"First, my disclaimer that I'm not being fresh when I say this. I don't understand why someone like you wouldn't have a long waiting list of eligible women—"

"Who says I don't?" he said. "And stop unwrapping that candy and look at me."

His voice was gentle and kind, which made it all the more difficult to face him. I popped the candy into my mouth and looked up.

"Why are you making this so difficult? You know me well enough to understand that if I don't want to or if I'm uncomfortable doing something, I won't do it. Having dinner with you is not a charitable deduction on my income tax. I would enjoy a night out with someone who knows me already, even if she does bust my chops now and then."

"This is me waving my white flag of surrender. Saturday night. But not seafood. I retain too much salt. One of the perks of pregnancy. You pick a place, and I'll meet you there."

"Meet me? What kind of date would I be if I wanted you to meet me?"

"This is not a date. Single pregnant women don't date. At least this one doesn't. If you must pick me up, can you make it around seven o'clock? I get hungry early and often."

He smiled and actually high-fived me. "It's a date!"

"It's not a date," I repeated loudly and insistently as he dashed out of the office.

Evan wasn't out the door ten seconds when I reached for my worry beads.

I patted both pockets. Flat. Where were they? I was defeating the purpose worrying about my worry beads.

Dad's office. That's where I left them. In my hurry to get to the front, I'd left them on his desk where I'd been sitting going through some of his folders. I resumed my organizing efforts. It took me about twenty minutes to make order out of chaos, but when I finished, he had a closet that didn't look like an office supply store had thrown up in it.

Dad spotted his shoes on my desk when he returned after his calls. "Evan called earlier to tell me that I'd forgotten these in his car. Told him it wouldn't be a problem for me to stop by the club and pick them up. He insisted he wouldn't mind dropping them off here. Nice of him, especially since our office isn't on the way to the club."

CHAPTER 36

I called Mia on my way home. Not surprisingly, she was skeptical about Evan's newfound career and thought there might be more to the story than being disillusioned with the legal profession.

If Evan's the new golf pro, maybe you should have the investigator check him out, too. Maybe he's been fired. Or disbarred and doesn't want people to know."

I didn't tell her about agreeing to have dinner with Evan. Since one dinner would probably be the beginning and the end of us sharing meals, mentioning it hardly seemed worth the verbal exchange in the first place.

Our conversation was coming to a quick end because both Mia and Lily were having meltdowns. Lily was lining up her raisins on the floor, pretending they were ants going to a party. Mia told her ants didn't have parties, Lily argued they did, and it went downhill from there.

"The nanny is starting this weekend. I'll let you know how it goes. Talk to Laura and see if you can get an idea of how much longer you have to be there. I don't need much time to get a room in the house ready for you," Mia said. "I'm off to teach my daughter the no-playing-on-the-floor-with-food rule."

Remembering Bryce's conversation with me before I left Houston, I wasn't sure Mia had discussed with him her grand plan of my moving into their house. Odds were, she hadn't.

As much as I wanted to return to Houston, I couldn't do it unless I had a place of my own. And even if I needed to be in New Orleans another four or more weeks, it would take that much time for me to lease or buy a place. Not something I could do alone.

Before supper, I called Amanda, my real estate agent, and left her a message asking for recommendations of agents or agencies in Houston.

Brushing my teeth before bed, I felt a ripple in my stomach. "Sick," I said to myself in the mirror, "is not what you need to be right now." It happened a few more times as I settled under the sheets. I was about to check to see what medicine I could take for an upset stomach when I remembered at my last visit, the physician's assistant had told me that before my next visit, I should start feeling flutters. That I would probably think at first they were gas bubbles, but after a few I would come to recognize them as the beginning of the baby moving.

I placed my hands on my stomach. "It's you, isn't it? Well, hello," I said to my little bump. "I'm thrilled you're here." No one could have ever prepared me for that moment: for knowing that I wasn't just witnessing a miracle but that it was happening inside of me. A little life stirred, and my entire life changed.

My perception of private detectives started with film noir, those black-and-white movies narrated by an emphysemic man commenting on some babe with legs to die for. She'd open a frosted glass door and walk into a smoky, messy office, where half-opened, partially derailed venetian blinds covered grimy windows. Maybe a bottle of cheap whiskey on the desk.

Then Richard Castle came along, with his modern Scandinavia-ish desk and supple leather chairs, surrounded by three walls of bookshelves as overstuffed as deli sandwiches.

So when my GPS led me to a nondescript, vanilla-brick ranch-style house on the corner of an equally nondescript neighborhood, I double-checked the address. Maybe flying under the radar extended to his choice of office space? I was already forming assumptions about the man before I opened my door. And they were mostly on the side of glass half-empty.

On the paneled entry door was a simple brass nameplate: The Office of J.M. Tarkington. I realized I'd forgotten to check my teeth in the mirror for lipstick smudges or food that might have hitched a ride between them. I hurriedly swiped my forefinger over my front teeth and pressed the doorbell. The video-camera doorbell. The doorbell I was too busy cleaning my teeth like a cavewoman to notice.

My life had become the lyrics "If it wasn't for bad luck, I wouldn't have no luck at all," from a record by Albert King. Wyatt loved blues and blues rock and sometimes listened to the song "Born Under a Bad Sign." We'd sing that line to each other and laugh. Was God trying to tell me something even then? Was there some sort of genetic predisposition to tragedy, and our child was doomed to live under a rain cloud?

The door opened up and my preconceptions shut down. If I'd worn heels, I might have been taller than the man who opened the door and asked if I was Olivia Kavanaugh. He introduced himself as Jim and invited me in. His hair was shaved so closely it could have been blond or brown or gray. Following him, I wouldn't have known by his slim build and clothes—a navy polo shirt and jeans that fit his body without too much attention to his butt—whether he was in his thirties or fifties.

His office was off the foyer, where a living or dining room might be in someone's home. Mia would have whipped out fabric samples and paint-color chips before Jim had time to sit in his standard-issue desk chair behind his standard-issue desk.

Whatever he lacked in design skills, he made up for in his confident, calm, and caring manner. He asked about Cara—I'd mentioned her name when I scheduled the appointment—but not in one of those efficient ways people who know you've been referred were apt to do. Anyone else, hearing his warmth, might have thought Cara was his sister, not a client.

After asking if I was comfortable, he took a fresh legal pad out of his desk drawer and said, "Okay, let's get started. Do you have the information I asked you to bring?"

I nodded and handed him a manila folder with pictures of Wyatt, a copy of the accident report, and other details he'd asked me to provide. Later, I told Mia the experience was like going to a new doctor because you have some mysterious ailment. And the doctor prods and probes, asking each time, "Does this hurt?" and "How about here?" and he'd sink his fingertips into you over and over, the same questions each time. Sometimes when he pushed, places you least suspected would be tender and sore. And still, after all that, the diagnosis was "We'll have to run more tests."

He promised he would check in with me weekly and told me to call if I remembered anything else or if I had questions. Before I left, he asked me if I was ready.

"Ready? For . . . ? Is there something else we need to do?"

"No, from here on it's all me. Like I said earlier, there's always the possibility that we may not find anything. But if I do, though I think it's going to be more likely *when* I do, you have to decide beforehand if you're ready for the answers. No judgment either way. You do what's best for you, no matter what anyone else says. I can stop at any time."

Driving back to the office, I reached for my worry beads that I'd left in the car. I felt like a patient who'd just been told she had a tumor.

The question of whether it was benign or malignant had already been answered. The other question was, did I want to know and live with it or did I want to risk removing it?

CHAPTER 37

Thirty minutes before Evan was scheduled to pick me up, I lowered the volume on the evening news to inform my parents that he and I were going to dinner.

"That's great, Livvy," said my father, his expression much like the one he wore when he first saw me in my cap and gown before college graduation.

My mother was needlepointing the Christmas pillow she'd started when I left for college. The one she resurrected before my wedding, after Wyatt died, and now. The guest-room closet held a library of pattern books, stacks of canvases, and miles of thread. Dad never cared about her inventory or its cost. "Cheaper than a psychiatrist," I'd overhear him say when she'd come home with a bulging bag from Nona's NeedleWorks. Still focusing on her needle whipping through the canvas, she asked, "What are you wearing?"

"Clothes, since we opted out of the invitation from the nudist colony."

My dad wisely hid his face behind his newspaper, but not before I saw his lips pressed together to stifle a laugh.

"I hoped you might not put on something too . . . revealing," she said. She looked at me. "Maybe one of those tunic tops would be flattering."

Her words were window dressing for her real message.

"He knows I'm pregnant. And this isn't a date, even if I wasn't."

She reached for her cane. I wished I had paid more attention in physics so I could calculate the distance between where I stood and its reach. Instead, she poked my dad's newspaper with it. "Stop pretending you're reading that and help me to our bedroom."

"You're going to bed now?" Dad looked at his watch. "Or are we going to bed now?" He grinned.

I groaned.

"Neither one. Don't be ridiculous. I want to put on my makeup to be presentable when Evan gets here."

"Scarlett, you look beautiful—"

Uh-oh. He hadn't moved from his chair yet to help my mother.

"George, cut it. Are you going to help me or not?"

When Evan rang the doorbell almost exactly a half hour later, my father looked like a man grateful to have been relieved by a new distraction.

I sat on the sofa and watched Evan shake my father's hand and kiss my mother on her cheek, and I listened to him slip into comfortable conversation about his parents and siblings, the club. For a minute, it felt as if I were the only one in the present, and I was witnessing a flashback playing itself out in front of me.

So much was the same. Yet, so much was different.

"This is your car?" I buckled myself in, surprised to be sitting in a small SUV with Evan behind the wheel. "I figured you for something flashy, a convertible or something Range Rover-ish."

"Did you now?" His voice was teasing. "Are you saying this car isn't going to up my game with you?"

"No, because we don't have a game," I said, making air quotes around the word *game*.

"Right. Not date, just dinner. I remember," he said. "And where are we going for dinner? You nixed boiled seafood, and I didn't make reservations anywhere, so we're at the mercy of your palate."

"In that case, let's skip dinner and go straight to dessert."

"How about Dairy Queen for Blizzards? We could order a dozen minis in different flavors," he said.

I would never have expected to experience a twinge of fondness for Evan based on a Blizzard.

The wistful affection I heard in his voice filled a part of me that had been vacant for a long time. It was one of those moments when the issue wasn't the issue. It wasn't so much that he remembered how obsessed I was with Dairy Queen. It was my remembering what it felt like to be with someone who knew my history. Someone familiar.

"Yes," I said, a small sigh of nostalgia escaping. "One of those things I never grew out of."

As the car turned onto Main Street, I noticed a line of white stretch limousines parked outside the church, the one I was supposed to have walked out of as Mrs. Wyatt Hammond. Instead, I had followed Wyatt's coffin down the steps to the cemetery. My pristine white wedding gown and veil, laced with promise, replaced by an inky-black suit, my face covered by a future I'd never see.

"You know, what?" I said to Evan. "Let's find some of those boiled shrimp you enticed me with."

Both too hungry to endure the long drive and wait for the buffet at a casino, we stopped at Dempsey's, a seafood restaurant and bar far enough away from town that we could avoid the locals, but close enough to satisfy our stomachs. Wyatt hadn't been fond of seafood, so we had only eaten there together once or twice. That made being there easier for me.

Most of the staff had worked at that restaurant so long, they probably had served our parents when they came to eat with their parents. I watched Evan as he bantered with the waitress, who was giving him a hard time for not ordering a locally brewed beer. He winked at me once during their conversation, which told me he never intended to order the beer he asked her for. I think she knew it, too, but it was great entertainment for both of them.

I was amused and annoyed. Hunger made me grumpy, but sitting across from Evan made me squirmy. In high school, Evan, *hot*, and *cute* were inexorably linked. I'd replace *cute* with *attractive, charming, self-assured,* and *tempting.* The man you'd want to ask how he likes his eggs for breakfast, minutes into your first date. Then again, he could lapse into *arrogant, demanding, condescending,* and *egotistical.* The last four characterized the Evan I knew in college and law school. I was still uncertain about this new version.

We split a seafood platter for two, Evan making sure he gave me most of the shrimp, and I gave him all the oysters. One of those idiosyncrasies we already knew about each other.

"I'm at an unfair disadvantage here." I pointed my fork at him. "I spotted that ready-to-pounce focus in your eyes. Don't start lawyering me with semantics and telling me things like 'unfair disadvantage is redundant,' okay?"

"Why would I do that? Isn't telling you what you already know redundant?" He maintained his wide-eyed innocence as he speared another hush puppy and chewed thoughtfully.

I knew Evan well enough to avoid the trap of being distracted by his verbal sparring. A pastime he pursued if he suspected discomfort awaited him at the other end of the question.

"That diversion isn't going to derail me. As I said, I'm at a disadvantage because you and the entire town know why my wedding didn't happen. Your brother told me you were engaged. And now you're not. Explain."

He ate a few bites of coleslaw, finished his beer, and said, "You want the unedited version?"

I didn't detect anger or sadness in his voice. He sounded like the waitress asking if I wanted fries or a baked potato. "The CliffsNotes version will do." I'd had enough emotional drama. I didn't want more.

"Quinn and I met my last year in law school. She wasn't the least bit intimidated by my oppositional, rude, and contentious self. In a crazy way, she liked it. Even prodded me into it sometimes. I found out later. I reminded her of her father. Not only was she intelligent and crazy beautiful, she was rich." He was stealing the French fries off my plate as he talked. "What's not to love?" A hint of a smile edged his lips.

"I don't know. That's what I'm waiting to hear."

"Point, Kavanaugh," Evan said and wrote a number one in the air as if on a scoreboard. "I didn't know about the money that followed her until I met her parents. Old money. The kind that people don't talk about, but their daughters are Mardi Gras queens, and their sons become captains of industry. Their house was on the Tchefuncte River at the end of a mile-long driveway through the woods. Anyone on the road would never know what was back there. I guess that was the point. They modeled the house after Twelve Oaks Plantation from *Gone with the Wind.*"

"Get out," I said with savage disbelief. "And this is the edited version? Can we hurry this up? Dairy Queen is calling."

"Bottom line? Quinn wanted to play law, not practice. She's a trust fund baby, with enough for her own babies. But before I slipped that engagement ring on her finger, we talked about building our own lives without relying on family, about children, what we valued . . . It turned out to be blahblahblah. When her parents presented us with a monthlong honeymoon in Europe as part of our wedding gift, I should've suspected that I'd never be able to support the lifestyle she'd known since she was old enough to teethe on a silver rattle."

"Then it was about the money? Or the lack of it?" I picked through the platter hoping to find a fried shrimp buried under the fish, stuffed crabs, and fried crawfish.

"Probably the beginning of the end." He handed me two shrimp on a napkin. "After a year in a law office, I was miserable. How could I have known that I'd love learning about law, love the challenge of it, the logic, and even creativity it required, but hate being an attorney? The stress of billable hours, working late and waking up early, depositions . . ."

He stopped, raised his empty beer bottle to catch the attention of our waitress, and, for the first time since we'd both been back, I glimpsed a shade of disappointment.

"Quinn didn't want to be the wife of a small-town golf pro. Her father offered to set me and Quinn up in our own practice, shift me into a general counsel position at his consulting business, enough money to take six months off so we could travel while I decided what I wanted to do in the legal profession . . . You probably can connect the dots without my detailing the rest of the drama."

"I'm sorry you had to experience all that to discover what really mattered to you." I pushed my plate away to leave room for dessert. "If you had walked through one of those doors Quinn's father wanted you to open, the end result would have been the same. It sounds like you and Quinn had enough in common to attract you to one another. But it's those life-changing decisions that expose the truth about what we value."

Evan nodded. "Sometimes being an adult is highly overrated, isn't it?" He smiled. "And on that note, I'll pay the bill, and off we go to Blizzard Land."

The two of us sat in his car outside Dairy Queen, scooping bites of each other's ice cream and reminiscing. We laughed. Genuine, bellyaching laughter. I'd forgotten that tear-wiping, side-splitting experience of being left nearly breathless.

He insisted on walking me to the front door when we reached my parents' house. "I don't care if it's a gated community. That doesn't excuse me from being a polite man who wouldn't drop his date off at the curb like—"

"This isn't a date," I said, digging in the bowels of my purse for my keys. Hoping to find them soon because the close proximity to Evan made me uncomfortable. In a jelly-kneed, body-humming way. He was waking feelings in me that I'd buried with Wyatt, and when they tried to break ground, I'd stomp on them until they surrendered.

"Okay, if that makes you feel better," he said. "Then can we have another one of these non-date dates again?"

"Found them." I jiggled my keys as evidence. I forced myself to look at Evan and not try to hide my face when I said, "I'm pregnant. Maybe there are reality-television shows where single pregnant women are dating. I'm not auditioning for one of those."

"Then you're saying if you weren't pregnant, we could call this a date?"

This time, I turned to open the door. "No. Can't we just be two friends catching up, entertaining one another, and leave it at that?"

"Sure." He tousled my hair, his hand lingering on the back of my neck. "I had a great time. Good night, Livvy."

I watched him walk to his car, then I closed the front door behind me. As I expected, my parents had gone to bed. *Further proof this was not a date.* I wanted to remember to tell Evan that the next time I saw him.

I changed, finished the face-washing, teeth-brushing, hair-combing routine, and slipped between clean sheets, the lavender scent still fresh. I turned off the lamp, rolled on my side, and tucked my hands under the pillow. I missed those nights falling asleep in Wyatt's arms, his breathing soft and measured, the warmth of his body stretched out next to me.

It had been months since Wyatt died, months before the baby would be born, and then how many months before I felt a man's lips pressed against mine? Or a man's embrace, so close that I could press my hand to his chest and feel his heart beat?

I reached for my worry beads on the nightstand, letting the hot tears roll down my face and onto the pillow. Remembering what I'd told Evan about life-changing decisions exposing the truth about what we value. Wyatt's decision robbed him of life. What did that reveal?

For now, it would reveal nothing. I'd boxed it away. Shoved it into a dark corner of my heart. Along with those two baby gifts.

CHAPTER 38

I was already running late for work when Ruthie called from the Bellagio and told me she'd hit the jackpot on a slot machine. "When those quarters started dumping out, they sounded all kinds of happy. I won over two hundred dollars. Might break even before the day's over." She laughed. "Don't tell your mother, because she'll text me the story about Jesus turning over the tables of the money changers in the temple. I told her last time we took this trip that I tithe on the gross of what I win, not the net."

A sudden rush of loud voices in the background made it hard for me to hear her. "Are you still there?"

She must have walked away because all was quiet when she answered. "I'm here. A couple left the hotel having hissy fits about spending too much money and leaving early. They should've decided their limit before they got here . . . But I didn't call to talk about them." She sighed and then said, "Your mother called me about your date with Evan."

"It. Wasn't. A. Date." The words marched out of me. "It was dinner. That's it. Two friends having a meal. Not something to justify calling you about. Unless she wanted you to tell me something she can't. Or won't."

"You know your mother. Some people look for opportunities. Some people look for problems. Your mother has a PhD in the second one. You might as well sit before I start if you're not already. She's worried and mortified that people will think you're having Evan's baby; she doesn't think dating or dinner with a man is appropriate while you're pregnant. And if people know it's Wyatt's baby, and they see you with Evan, that's a disgrace."

I slammed the bedroom door. "The real disgrace is she's not telling me this herself," I said, irritation and frustration twisting in my chest. "How long is she going to punish me for being pregnant? How long?" I put the phone on speaker so I could tug on my jeans. "It's not enough for her that God's punished me? Now she's His backup? Is she worried her church friends will think I'll be stripping on Bourbon Street next?" I picked up the phone.

"I'd tell you to calm down, but I'd be fit to be tied, too. But here it is. She didn't ask me to call you, but she knows good and well that I'm always honest with you. Plus, I don't keep secrets. You can dress her up and down now that I've told you this, or you can let it simmer for a few days. What's left is what's worth talking about."

I promised her I'd calm down before driving, text her when I made it to the office, and call her if I talked to my mother. I finished dressing and checked my makeup in the bathroom mirror before I left my room. My checks were flushed from the fire my mother's words had lit in me. I breathed into the rage that consumed me and released it, repeating until my body relaxed.

Laura was in the family room with my mother, moving her through her morning exercises. I stopped long enough to tell them hello and that I was late, then I closed the front door behind me. Leaving, I hoped, the negativity that was sucking the life out of me.

Processing it all while I drove home that afternoon, I realized that everything my mother said was about her. About what people would say. To her or behind her back. About what people who didn't say anything would think of her. About having to hold her head high in her country club and church when she thought her daughter had ruined her.

That afternoon and night, I did what Granny suggested. I left everything my mother said to simmer. I ate dinner. Smiled and nodded efficiently through my parents' conversation and excused myself as soon as my fork hit the table after my last bite. "I'll help clean up later, but I'm exhausted and headachy, so I'm going to rest for a while."

I was tired, but I couldn't be in the room with my mother, seeing her through the lens my grandmother had provided that morning.

And I doubted Laura intended for me to use my worry beads for harm.

CHAPTER 39

My mother was improving daily. At least physically. She no longer needed her walker, and using the cane didn't seem as painful for her. She and my dad went out to dinner a few times, and having a social life made her far less grumpy. I still hadn't said anything to her about her conversation with my grandmother. The last thing I wanted was to be accused of causing her a setback because she was so emotionally distraught.

My father left the office early so he could be with Mom for her doctor's appointment. He must've noticed my wide-eyed panic when I realized he would be gone during lunch.

"I know. I know. Don't worry, I've already arranged a lunch delivery for you." Dad patted me on top of my head like he used to do when I was in second or third grade. He'd walk in after work, I'd be bouncing around the den, stopping only long enough to announce that I'd finished my homework. Then a pat on the head for me. A kiss for Mom. Which I never counted as fair because she didn't even do homework.

With a half hour to go before noon, the noises in my stomach grew louder and the candy dish more tempting. I was about to text my dad to ask him where he'd ordered from when Evan came in carrying bags from P.F. Chang's.

"So thoughtful of you to bring me lunch, but my dad said he set up a delivery to be sure I ate while he was gone."

"I know." He nodded and placed the bags on the counter.

"If you already knew, then why did you go to the trouble?" I realized I should text my father and tell him to forget whatever he'd planned because the aromas lurking in those bags smelled delicious.

He took out the containers and lined them up on my desk. "I was about to explain when you interrupted me. Your dad—"

"You're the one he called. Of course. How else would you already know that he'd set this up?" Synapses in my brain finally loaded and fired, and I wanted to, if not die of embarrassment, at least be severely injured.

"You're almost right. I needed to get in touch with him about a delay on a putter he ordered, so I called him this morning. I asked if he wanted to meet for lunch, and that's when he told me he and your mother had the appointment, but you couldn't leave and—"

"And that's when you arranged yourself," I said.

"Once again, you successfully connected all the dots."

"*Ewwww.* Hot-and-sour soup. Not a fan."

"I didn't get it for you. That one is mine." He separated the containers, and that's when I saw he'd written my name on some of the boxes. "It's been a long time, so if I didn't remember correctly, I apologize in advance. Egg drop soup, brown rice, spring roll not an eggroll, and Orange Peel Shrimp." The only thing he'd forgotten was the stir-fried eggplant, but I wasn't going to be so ungrateful as to mention that.

Evan handed me another bag. "Almost forgot this. I put a freezer pack in there, so I hope it didn't melt."

I hesitated. "Is something going to jump out at me?"

"If it does, then I'm going back to the store for a refund," he said. "It's not the Hope Diamond, so don't get too excited."

The last time I saw that expression on someone's face was when Lily handed her parents the Play-Doh pies she'd made for them.

I opened the bag and inside I found a pint of vanilla ice cream and a small jar of dill pickles.

"Silly, right?" A suggestion of a grin and his drumming fingers on the countertop seemed to be waiting for my answer.

I smiled and felt like my heart smiled along with me. "No, and even if it was, it's a silliness that makes me happy."

"Great to know your sense of humor's still intact," he said and smiled. He started placing his containers back in the bag.

"Where are you going?"

"Sorry I can't stay with you. I rescheduled an appointment with someone who couldn't make his later this afternoon. How about lunch on Sunday? If you don't already have plans."

I opened the calendar on my phone. "Nothing. Nothing. And nothing. Lucky you. I'm available."

"Terrific. I'll pick you up for our 'it's not a date' about eleven o'clock. Oh, one more thing . . . I forgot your stir-fried eggplant. I owe you one." He picked up his bag, threw in a few candies from the jar, and left.

I had a voicemail from the private investigator. He wanted me to know he'd been checking telephone records and found out Wyatt had made calls to the hospital in Oakville the day before and the morning of the wedding. He said he'd be back in touch with me soon.

He was obviously planning to visit someone. Who could he have even known there? Already I wasn't sure how much more I wanted to know.

Dad sent me a text that he and Mom were stopping to eat after the appointment. Even at my age, I felt the giddy relief of a teenager whose parents just left for a weeklong cruise. Except the wildest thing I wanted to do didn't involve a party with ten of my closest friends, who invited ten of their closest friends, who couldn't remember the next day where they were or how they got there. All I wanted to do was wallow in the silence, skip the Chinese leftovers for dinner, and eat a huge slab of apple pie covered with whipped cream.

After my dessert for dinner, I soaked under a foamy blanket of bubbles in my parents' garden tub. I was getting accustomed to my rounded tummy, envisioning my little nugget of a baby growing stronger every day. I still hadn't decided if I wanted to know whether I was having a boy or girl. Struggling to accept that my son or daughter might already have a stepbrother was enough.

I slipped on my nightgown, then went to the kitchen to make a cup of hot tea. My mother had left the mail in its usual spot, in a basket on the counter. Every piece of mail except for the junk went into that basket. I rarely gave it any attention because I had already forwarded my mail to Houston, and since I paid everything online, most of what I found in my post office box went straight into the recycle bin.

My parents were still strong believers in paper trails because, as my mother had informed me when I questioned the system, "What if the entire Internet crashes? It could be targeted by terrorists." I told her if that happened, paying bills would probably not be our first concern.

I passed the basket, surprised to see a lone long white envelope propped up against it. "There is no way you jumped out of that," I said. I picked it up. It wasn't with the rest of the mail because it was addressed to me.

No return address. A New Orleans postmark. My name and address had been computer-generated on a label. It was either one of those goofy chain letters that might've fallen into the corner of the mailroom and was just discovered, or it was a generic invitation to attend an exclusive introduction to new beach property for sale.

I almost threw it away, but I could see lined yellow paper inside. Legal pad kind of paper.

Evan.

"Dude, what are you up to?" I shook the envelope to make sure a pound of glitter wouldn't decorate the floor when I opened it. It was too thin for him to have put anything else in there.

I couldn't stop myself from smiling, thinking about what goofy idea had inspired him to mail this. I carried the tea to my room, sat cross-legged on my bed, leaned against the headboard, and opened the envelope. My cell phone was on the pillow next to me, so I could immediately respond to whatever he had plotted.

I unfolded the paper.

I couldn't breathe.

The room began to look like an Impressionist painting. Objects and colors melted into one another like Popsicles left in the sun.

My hand trembled, shaking the page so violently that, if I closed my eyes, it sounded like wind whipping through trees.

I clenched my jaw to stop my chattering teeth. If only I could have clenched my shivering body.

I didn't have to see the signature. I recognized the tightly formed letters, the hodgepodge of cursive and print.

It was Wyatt's handwriting.

CHAPTER 40

Dear Olivia,

I'm not always the best romantic or good at expressing it, but I want you to know that I love you more than I ever thought it was possible to love anyone.

That night I first saw you sitting next to Mia, who was very pregnant with Lily, I asked a friend to serve the two of you. I wanted her to look for a wedding band or engagement ring on your left hand. I know, it probably sounds like something a kid would do. But I didn't want to get my hopes up if you were already with someone else. Even then, I had no idea if I had a chance to get to know you. The one thing I held on *to was that you were friends with Mia and Bryce, and I was friends with his brother. Not many degrees of separation!*

I still can't believe how lucky I am to be with you.

You are a gift to me. I'll treasure you for the rest of our lives together.

I read the letter over and over and over again. As if Wyatt's soul were embedded in each word and somehow I could give life to them all, and he would materialize.

My thoughts were like marbles spilled on tile, scattered in every direction, some of them rolling as if chased, others clanging into one another and going nowhere.

If Wyatt didn't write this letter, then who did? How demented would that person have to be to forge his handwriting? Who would know how we met and then be able to find me at my parents' house?

I recognized the quirks in Wyatt's writing—how he changed the letters *f* and *s*, the letter *a* that sometimes looked like an *o*, his maddening tendency to ignore margins.

But when? Why was it mailed months after he died? Had he given this to someone meaning to get it back?

Or had he given it to someone he trusted for safekeeping? Someone like Jacob's mother?

I thought Wyatt dying on our wedding day was punishment enough. But I was wrong. There was much more: not knowing where he was going that day, the baby gifts, finding out I was pregnant, and now this.

I guess God didn't believe in time off for good behavior. Or He was sending me a strong message that perhaps my good behavior wasn't so good.

Who was I going to talk to about this? Certainly not my parents. I heard them come in from dinner, but I left my bedroom door closed. If they saw me tonight, it would be impossible for me to pretend there wasn't something wrong. And in no way did I want to tell them what that something was.

I didn't have the energy to explain this to anyone. And maybe it was weird because obviously somebody else knew it existed. That Wyatt meant that letter for me.

I also had to face the reality of my not wanting to know who had this letter first. Knowing that could be more painful than the letter itself.

That night before I went to bed, I thought of a wedding I'd attended years ago. The bride announced that single women should sleep with a piece of the wedding cake under their pillows. She told us that the man we would dream about would be our future husband.

I didn't take a slice home because I figured I'd wake up with icing and cake crumbs pasted to my hair. Maybe I should have given it a chance, because sleeping with Wyatt's letter under my pillow, I woke up disoriented. My dreams of him and our lives together were so real, I expected to find him in the bed beside me.

The next day I called Laura from the office to ask if any mail had arrived for me. I asked her to please not ask my mother but just to check the basket. I told her if anything did come for me, I'd appreciate it if she could just place it on my nightstand. I promised her I'd explain, but she said that wasn't necessary.

"Some things I don't need to understand. You're not asking me to do anything illegal or immoral, and you never asked me to do anything crazy. If you want me to do this, I'm certain you have a good reason," she said.

I'd put the letter in my purse, but I regretted having it with me. I couldn't bring myself to open it again. And I couldn't stop thinking about it or opening my purse every hour on the chance that I'd read it again. Not that I needed to. I'd read it so many times the night before, I'd memorized it.

"I'll treasure you for the rest of our lives together." That didn't work out well for either one of us, did it, Wyatt? And if I was such a treasure, why didn't you tell me the truth about that morning? I guess the real irony is that even after dying, you left me a treasure. Our baby.

After a few days of Laura texting me that I didn't have mail, I told her she didn't need to continue looking. But she said she'd check every once in a while anyway.

Not that I wanted more. I'd started to believe that perhaps God was repealing my sentence. Good things were happening: spending time with Evan, hearing the baby's heartbeat, and feeling it move. Maybe God had let me out to play in the prison yard, and now time was up?

I remembered what Jim said about contacting him with new information, which this letter definitely was. He'd be able to figure this out faster than I ever could. The solution was the problem, because if and when he did, I had to be ready to hear the truth. I wasn't.

It was Friday, and we were sitting on the deck snacking on cheese, crackers, and spinach dip left over from yet another drop-off from the ladies' church group.

"Look, if there's a national disaster, I'm hunkering down with that church because they make sure people eat," Laura said.

"The week Mom was in the hospital, we had so many meals delivered my father thought he'd have to buy an extra freezer. It's slowed since then, but there must still be a weekly sign-up sheet because someone will bring over a meal one day, then a dessert another day. If being able to cook is a membership requirement, I'm never getting past the doors." I scooped spinach dip onto my plate. "Besides, that was Wyatt's thing. I thought it doesn't get much better than marrying a man who's as good in the kitchen as he is in the bedroom."

"I'm afraid if Gary does open a restaurant, that might be the end of his cooking at home. Of course, he'd never be home. And if I'm working for him, neither will I. The problem will be we're around too much food. When we'd work catering jobs, we'd sometimes come home with boxes of leftovers. But you can't always live off of stuffed mushrooms and rumaki."

"I didn't know you two worked for caterers. Colin Chapman, the brother-in-law of my friend Mia, owns a company in New Orleans. Wyatt worked for him sometimes. Did you and Gary ever work for him?"

Without taking much time to think, Laura answered, "Um, you know, it's been a few years since we did that kind of work, so I don't remember exactly." She picked up our empty iced tea glasses. "I'm going to dash inside and refill these."

For a woman who could rattle off the names and dosages of all my mother's meds, Laura not remembering a caterer's name was surprising.

When she came back outside, she set the glasses down, and said, "Tell me what's going on with Evan."

I recounted the conversation my grandmother and I'd had, and I ended with, "I haven't said anything to her yet. In fact, Evan's picking me up Sunday morning for breakfast, and I haven't mentioned it to either one of my parents. My dad might hope being with Evan pays off in a few free golf lessons."

"Not that your mother lets all the skeletons out of the closet for air," Laura said, "but she mentions things here and there. Like she did those times she told me about Wyatt's death and your being pregnant. She hasn't talked to me about Evan at all, which is odd. Maybe she thinks

I'd be on your side anyway, which I am, or she thinks your grandmother would agree with her."

"My grandmother hasn't really voiced her opinion. And I didn't ask because I don't think she agrees with my mother, and it doesn't matter. Evan and I are friends, and there's nothing illicit about dinner with a friend. Anyway, it's not like I could get pregnant."

CHAPTER 41

Wear something comfortable. See you at eleven."

Not being pregnant himself, of course, Evan had no way of understanding that nothing in my closet qualified as both appropriate and comfortable for public appearances. Even my go-to leggings left seam indentions on my stomach when I took them off. My tunics barely passed because I found myself growing boobs. An unexpected perk, though a frustrating one. Just when I finally had my dream of legitimate cleavage, it would have been beyond bad taste to display it.

I stood in my closet, eyeing my clothes like they were food in the refrigerator, and I couldn't decide what, if anything, appealed to me.

Olivia, the Nordstrom personal shopper is neither telepathic nor can she teleport. You should have made that appointment with her by now.

The only thing I hated more than shopping for and trying on clothes was paying for clothes I'd shopped for and tried on. I had the money; I'd barely made a dent in what I deposited after selling the house. But it was time to get over my notoriety for being Scroogette of the fashion world, because the bump would soon be a basketball.

Only one alternative, and it required groveling and finesse.

I strolled into the den like a sitcom walk-on with a few one-liners, wearing my pleasant face with its carefully applied smile. My plan was to sashay to the fridge, pretend I was looking for something to nosh on, then with a casual, upbeat tone ask my mother, "Do you still have those shorts that were too big for you last summer? Would you mind if I borrowed them since mine aren't quite buttoning anymore? No problem if you don't."

I didn't remember shorts that didn't fit her, but telling her otherwise suggested she had the body of a pregnant woman. Any hint of desperation in my voice, she'd start asking questions. I couldn't be sure if telling her I needed them for lunch with Evan would work for or against me.

The den was empty. So was the deck. Their car was in the driveway. Presurgery, they'd power walk around the block, but not with the cane. Maybe they went to the neighbor's; she could make that distance. But Evan was picking me up in twenty minutes, and I couldn't wait indefinitely. I'd do a quick recon through her clothes and ask for forgiveness since I couldn't ask for permission.

Their bedroom door was closed. My hand was on the knob, ready to open it when I heard them.

Talking? No. That didn't sound like a conversation. But maybe . . .

I considered knocking, then my brain processed the sounds from inside their room.

Well, good Lawd A'mighty.

One of my grandmother's go-to expressions when shocked beyond belief. But I never expected to think of it or use it because I happened upon overhearing my parents making love.

I tiptoed backward, my hand pressed over my mouth to smother my gasp. All those years I heard stories from my friends, I never believed they were true. And if they were, certainly not something I'd considered an issue with my parents.

I threw on a halter-top maxi sundress generous enough to cover my top and bottom, shoved my feet into my wedge sandals, and left a note on the kitchen table, *Lunch with Evan*, and dashed outside before he could ring the doorbell.

This time Evan appeared in a metallic-white convertible that glistened in the sun. An opal on wheels. A car Wyatt had dreamed of owning.

"You're prompt this morning," he said as he opened the passenger door for me. Watching me gather the dress at my ankles so he could close the door, he tilted his head and asked, "I did mention to wear something casual, didn't I?"

I waited until he'd settled himself behind the wheel. "Yes, but you didn't mention my hair would be slapping my face, and my head would be sunburned."

"And that's why," he said, smiling as he reached into the backseat and handed me a pink twill baseball cap with a little crawfish logo, "I brought this."

He placed the cap on me, curving the bill, and tucking stray locks of hair behind my ears, his fingertips traveling from my temples to my cheeks. So many months since a man touched me with tenderness, I would have taken the hat off just to have him put it on me again.

Get a grip, Olivia. This is Evan. Your friend. You are not allowed to melt because his hands brush your face, and his white V-neck hugs his muscles, and his presence softens your heart.

On our way to wherever he was taking me, I related the story about why I wasn't wearing the shorts I thought I would be.

"Not something I wanted to hear. Especially early on a Sunday morning." This wind-in-my-face business wasn't what commercials promised. It was better. Much better.

"Are you telling me that this is the first time you've experienced that in your entire life with your parents?"

I didn't have to look at him to know he was shaking his head in disbelief. I heard it.

"My bedroom is upstairs on the other side of the house, remember? Maybe I did when I was younger, and I had no idea what was going on. I mean, it's strange to overhear anyone, but when it's your parents, it borders on disturbing," I said.

"Really? Don't get me wrong, I'm not saying we should stand outside the door and applaud or give them a high-five later. But I think it's great your parents have passion. The woman I marry won't look the same in forty years, but I hope her feelings are the same."

"You know, maybe this is one of those situations where the issue isn't the issue." I turned to look at Evan. "The issue isn't what they're doing. We're two grown people living with our parents again."

He nodded and laughed. "Good point. Guess maybe it's time we moved on. Again."

I knew what my options were, but Evan hadn't talked about his plans. I didn't ask him. I wasn't sure I was ready to know the answer.

Riding in a convertible was sensory overload. Especially the sounds, which were almost all noises. Tires swatting over the asphalt, eighteen-wheelers' brakes squealing like an off-key choir, Kanye West booming from someone's radio, horns beeping, grass-cutting tractors on the side of the road. The smells coming from the barbecue restaurant were as inviting as the ones coming from the paper factories were acrid.

The wind devoured our words as soon as we spoke them, making conversation challenging. I didn't mind the quiet. I was enjoying being immersed in the experience. Until, that is, Evan passed at least five restaurants that were lunch possibilities.

"Hey"—I tapped his shoulder—"where are we going? You didn't tell me I needed to bring a snack."

"You're getting to be high-maintenance, Kavanaugh," he semi-shouted. "I already ordered lunch to go from Camellia Bend Café."

"To go where?"

"We're going to Crescent City Park. We can watch the barges and the steamboats and see the city. You need some outside time. And after lunch, I want you to see my weekend job."

"Don't you already work weekends?"

"Yes, but this job is actually every other Sunday."

Next time, assuming there would be a next time, I needed to remember to ask more specific questions about his plans. He might think roller-skating would be fun when I'm eight months pregnant.

Evan pulled into the parking lot of the café, and I pulled into my delusions. *Olivia, what are you thinking? As if Evan won't be dating someone or several someones soon or maybe already is? And, even if he isn't, you're PREGNANT.*

I pulled off the cap and ran my fingers through my damp hair, then pulled down the visor to put it back on again. I watched Evan as he left the restaurant, a brown bag in each hand, and I allowed myself to feel happy.

I told my guilt I'd give it equal time. Later.

CHAPTER 42

From the promenade of Crescent City Park, the city of New Orleans looked like a silver-and-glass Legoland spreading along the Mississippi River. The view wasn't far past the dog run where two honey-colored Labrador retrievers and their owner played fetch, though for the brief time we watched, the human fetched more than the dogs.

We detoured along an asphalt walking path that cut through meandering gardens until we found a picnic area and a table close to a tree that offered some shade. Even in September, the sun didn't give up easily. It wasn't the relentless suffocation of August, but the word *breeze* wasn't in the weather forecast yet.

"Oh, for the record, in case it comes up in conversation with my mother, don't tell her I was sweaty. She'll be mortified. I glistened."

"I doubt your mother and I have a reason to talk about you sweating, I mean glistening. But if I'm desperate for something to say, I'll do my best to remember."

While we ate our wedges of muffulettas and shared a pasta salad, Evan played Name the Building, a game at which I volunteered to lose, and we watched barges pushing ships on the river. Even a cruise liner passed, dwarfing everything around it.

On the way back to the car, Evan said, "We're running ahead of schedule, and I'm feeling guilty not being more specific about today's plans. Let's stop at the mall, a boutique, or wherever you shop, and you can find something more comfortable to wear."

"This is a first. I don't think I've ever had a date who offered to take me shopping."

He looked at me with such smug satisfaction, if we had been anywhere else, I would've turned to see if someone was behind me. "What's that look?"

"So this is a date. When did you change your mind?"

"Don't make me want to knock you into tomorrow. I didn't change my mind. I meant 'a date' generically. As in all the dates I have ever been on. And since dates have never taken me shopping, and you're taking me shopping, it would follow that this is not a date."

"I think the wrong person in this car went to law school."

Except that I would've rather been wrong. Who knew Evan would morph into this person who sat across from me? When we dated in college, we were like schools of fish traveling from one bar or restaurant to another, always surrounded by people. Or when I worked, he'd sit at the bar with his books. Maybe groups brought out his alpha maleness. This Evan probably wouldn't enjoy hanging out with that Evan.

We went to Nordstrom, and I made him promise not to look at any of the sizes I pulled off the hangers. He reminded me we were on a time deadline. With five minutes to spare, I found a pair of navy shorts I could button and a simple white peplum top. I asked the sales clerk to cut off all the tags because I was wearing them out of the dressing room.

"Hey, that looks great and much more comfortable than what you were wearing." He looked at his watch. "We need to get moving. Remember?" He walked toward the escalator.

"Evan, I have to pay for these. If I'm arrested for shoplifting, it'll take much longer to get there."

"I already paid for them," he said.

"Well, you're going to unpay for them." I headed to the cash register holding my credit card out like a sword.

He dashed to catch up with me, closed his hand over mine, and said, "Olivia, I can't be late. You'll understand when we get there. I'm not going to argue with you about the money, especially here. You can pay me back, okay? But we really do need to leave now."

His urgency was much more serious than my "Hurry, it's the last day of the season. We have to get to the snowball stand before it closes" desperate pleas ever were.

"Deal. But only because you look frantic," I said. *And you held my hand in the process.*

The surprise, for me, wasn't so much what he was doing, but the fact that it was Evan doing it.

We had arrived on time at a small park in the city. Really, it was just a one-block stretch of grass with a few twigs masquerading as trees. Evan steered me to a sliver of shade under two large beach umbrellas close to the driving range, but far enough away to avoid a trip to the ER.

Five children, who looked like they were in elementary school, sat cross-legged on the grass. When they spotted Evan, they started chanting, "Ev-an, Ev-an, Ev-an," their golf clubs in two-fisted holds above their heads.

He introduced me to the boys: the twins Quentin and Quincy, Darrell, Andre, and, standing a head taller than everyone else, Cedric.

Quentin, a kid with a faux Mohawk, asked me if I played golf.

"Gracious, no," I said, exaggerating only my voice, not the truth. "I'd have to wear a helmet."

"Maybe if Evan teaches you, he'll have to wear a helmet."

The boys, Evan included, laughed. A lot.

After a moment of getting over myself, I joined them. I had to own that he was right.

For the next hour, I forgot the heat already reddening my arms and legs, even with the shade, and watched Evan interact with these kids. His patience in showing each one the proper swing. Praising them and, when necessary, reminding them they were there to learn golf, not sky gaze.

As time went on, their enthusiasm waned, which I understood since I was glistening like a sky full of stars. But when parents showed up with ice chests, even Evan—whose shirt was more wet than white by now—was distracted.

The boys dropped their clubs where they stood and headed to the promise of a cold paradise.

"Stop. That's not how we end." Evan spoke with authority. And without whining or pouting faces, they picked up their clubs and placed them in the golf bag Evan had brought with him.

They stood next to one another, Cedric in the center, and they repeated, with genuine gusto, everything Evan said.

> I promise to love God.
> I promise to respect my parents.
> I promise to do my best in school every day.
> I promise to be a leader, not a follower.
> I promise to say no to drugs.
> I promise to say yes to golf.

After we all rehydrated and sampled one of each kind of ice cream bar, the kids, their parents, and Evan and I walked back to our cars.

There had to be something Evan wasn't telling me. I'd never witnessed such a compelling change in one person in such a few years.

CHAPTER 43

When we reached his car, Evan grabbed a clean T-shirt from his trunk.

"I don't want to sit in the car wearing this sweaty shirt, and I doubt you'd want me to either."

He pulled off his shirt while I pawed through my makeup bag, searching for lip gloss, finding it, then continuing to search and keep my head lowered so I could sneak peeks at Evan.

The show of abs didn't last long, but I still would've given it a standing ovation. I pulled the visor down to apply my lip gloss as he buckled his seat belt.

"I spotted the keys on your seat. I didn't think you'd mind if I started the car."

"Not at all," he said and patted my hand. "Remember in college after Hurricane Katrina when we didn't have electricity? We all took turns sitting in one another's cars just to be able to turn on the air-conditioners. It was usually the best time to sleep."

"I don't know how it's possible, but I actually had forgotten about that," I said. "It's strange to think that those kids you taught today weren't even born then." I took my cap off and ran my fingers through my hair plastered to my head, the cool air helping to revive me.

Evan pressed a button, and the roof of the car dutifully slid into place over us. We sat in the quiet. The cool quiet. A comfortable silence, where no one reached to turn on the radio to fill the void of no conversation. The only sounds were a soft hiss as the air blew through the vents, the swish of cars moving past us, and the occasional *ga-lump* of the tires over a pothole.

When Wyatt and I rode in the car, we'd let the silence sit with us like a familiar friend, and one of us would reach for the hand of the other. A gentle squeeze conveyed our contentment. I didn't reach for Evan's hand, though I wanted to because I felt the same swell of satisfaction.

I watched out my window as the city flicked by like a film on an old projector. Tattered and torn shotgun houses, some still branded with the Katrina crosses used by search-and-rescue teams, were eerily reminiscent of Passover. Blocks of empty lots where lonely concrete foundations waited for families who would never return. Then, like debutantes at their coming-out parties, renovated shotgun houses and Creole cottages appeared, anchored by stately antebellum homes with massive white columns and wrought iron balconies.

New Orleans restaurants had fascinated Wyatt. Their histories, their menus, even the eclectic ones and the bistros and food trucks seduced him with possibilities. He had wanted to live in the city. I'd been raised in gated communities with country clubs and walking trails. Moving to an area where a murder or a party could be around any corner frightened me. I wanted security, the predictableness of a neighborhood, an ordinary life.

Wyatt conceded and we bought a home in the suburbs over an hour away from work. I told him when we moved that he'd have the best of both, traveling to the city to work, then back home to what he called our Stepford-family life.

That didn't work out well for either one of us.

I shifted in my seat to face Evan. "What led to these every-other-Sunday golf lessons?"

He suddenly looked like someone who'd been keeping a secret so long he was ready to explode. His voice was as animated as his face. "After I started working at the club, golfers would come into the pro shop and buy new putters, drivers, and irons or want to get fitted for an entire new set of clubs. Sometimes they would just give me their old clubs, and others used to joke about how many they stashed in their closets or garages. It just seemed such a waste, especially considering how much they cost."

"Expensive?"

"A new set could cost at least a thousand dollars," he said.

"Yep. That's a bundle to pay for iron sticks to whack those little white balls across grass."

"Funny."

I smiled so he'd know I'd meant it to be.

"Anyway, I searched online for places where I could donate them, and I tripped across programs that were bringing the game to inner-city kids. What really caught my attention wasn't so much that the kids were learning golf. These programs taught them not just etiquette, behavior, and manners about the game, but promoted academics, respect, and good conduct in their daily lives. I mentioned this to some of our members, and one gave me the name of his minister. I called him, explained what I wanted to do, and by the next Sunday, I had a group."

"As much as it pains me to compliment you and risk ego inflation, you're great with those kids. You joked with them, but they knew when to tighten up. You were patient, but I noticed when Darrell started practicing his dance moves, you called him out in a way that was assertive without being angry or annoyed. They respect you."

Evan didn't say anything at first, just nodded. He glanced at me, then said, "Thanks. I appreciate that. I want so much for those kids to succeed. I'd teach them every week if I could. But getting away on a

Sunday at the club is challenging. Until they hire a full-time assistant, I'll only be able to go every other weekend."

When we reached my parents' house, I asked him if he wanted to come inside. "Should be safe with my them by now," I joked.

"Maybe another time? I desperately need a shower, and I wanted to check in with Roy at the club to make sure everything is going well."

I handed him the hat he had lent me, but all he did was put it back on my head again. "That's yours. I don't do pink hats. Pink shirt, yes. Hat, no."

"Thanks for the lunch, the hat, saving me from my fashion disaster, and introducing me to the boys."

"You're the first person I've ever taken to one of their lessons. So if you don't come back, they might think you didn't like being there with them," he said, but with a touch of amusement in his voice.

"Well, maybe you could convince them that it's you I didn't want to be there with."

I meant to sound witty, but the expression on Evan's face told me I hadn't succeeded. It was as if I had slapped him in the face. His eyes widened, his mouth fell open, and he shook his head.

"Evan, I was kidding. Really, I was. I feel so bad. Like I want to tell myself to go away because I don't want to be with me." I reached for his hands, holding on to them, wishing he felt my apology seeping through my skin. "I'm so sorry."

I let go of his hands. His eyes scanned my face, probing, perhaps, for the truth.

"You've been kind to me, and I always have a good time when we're together. I would never purposely hurt you."

"I know, Livvy. I know." He tugged the beak of my hat and offered me a smile, one so slight that it was as if he had to ration them. "I'll be in touch."

I waved as he backed out of the driveway and didn't turn to walk into the house until his car disappeared around the corner.

CHAPTER 44

T hat was some long lunch."
My dad's voice reached me as I closed the door. He grinned, so I knew I wasn't going to hear, "We almost called the police, the hospital . . ."

The back door was open, and my mother walked inside. "Are those new?" She pointed to my blouse and shorts with her cane.

"Hi, Mom. Good to see you, too." I'd already put my hat in the bag with my other clothes, so she couldn't comment on that. "Yes. We were outside almost the entire time, and the maxi dress I wore wasn't made for a picnic. Evan and I went to Nordstrom so I could find something cooler to wear that actually fit me."

Her Richter scale of surprise shot to an eight. "Wow. He didn't mind taking you shopping?" She walked to the kitchen where my father handed her a glass of wine.

"It was his idea," I said. *And you forgot to pay him, so now you have a reason to call and apologize once again for your verbal slam.*

My parents looked at each other, exchanging those glances again.

"Do you think it's appropriate to be spending this much time with Evan?" My mother stared at me over the rim of her glass.

"Why? Do you think it's inappropriate?"

That wasn't the answer she expected, I supposed, because she looked at my father.

She set her glass on the island. "Your father and I are concerned about your being especially vulnerable right now, so soon after Wyatt's death. We don't want you to misinterpret Evan's attention. And, honey, you're pregnant and being seen with a single man who's not even the child's father."

"If Evan and I were having wild sex, which we definitely are not, you could find some comfort in the fact that at least I couldn't get pregnant again. Evan and I are friends. F-R-I-E-N-D-S. He's recovering from a relationship, and I'm . . . I'm . . . I don't even know anymore with everything and nothing going on in my life. Evan and I dated what seems like a lifetime ago. And neither one of us cares what assumptions people are making or what opinions other people have."

My mother refilled her wineglass, replacing the cork with excruciating slowness, diffusing the immediacy of my response. "It's your life. We don't want to see you get hurt."

"It's too late for that, isn't it?" I said.

"Scarlett, Livvy isn't acting reckless," my father said, placing his hand over my mother's. "She's not shopping for a husband with Evan because he's already taken himself off the shelf. He's already told me he's not looking for a relationship. He might not even stay at the club if he decides that's not the future he wants. We need to leave the two of them alone."

"Where's he going?" He never mentioned leaving to me. Tired of shifting from one leg to the other as I stood during this inquisition, I slid myself into the recliner.

"He didn't say specifically, and I don't think he knows himself right now." My father held my mother's elbow, steered her to her chair, then sat on the sofa. "Evan and I talked during our game, and he said he's staying open to however he feels led." He shrugged. "I didn't expect him to be a golf pro forever. The club needed someone fast, and he needed somewhere to go. It worked out. For now."

"And aren't you planning to go back to Houston? If you and Evan are just friends, why would it bother you that he could be moving?" my mother said.

I heard the undercurrent of cynicism, the one she used to suck me under and cause me to drown in my own confusion.

"I don't remember saying it bothered me." I didn't have to verbalize it, though. My expression spoke for me. And she wanted me to know that she knew it, too.

"If I've learned anything these past few months, it's that my plans aren't irrevocable. Who knows? Things could change . . . I could change," I said with what I hoped was an airy and casual tone. "I'm going to rest. Being out in the sun burned off my energy."

"We're going to eat seafood later. Why don't you join us?" My dad, ever the optimistic peacemaker.

"Sounds great, but it's been a long day. I'm always open to leftovers, though," I said. Before going to my room, I kissed them each on the forehead. Displays of affection rankled my mother when she considered being right more important than doing right. Small of me, but I learned the passive-aggressive game well. She proved to be an excellent teacher.

I woke up with the bitter leftovers of my comment to Evan, and I resolved to make it right. But he didn't answer his phone when I called him on my way to work, and I ended up leaving one of those voicemails that sounded as if I'd only learned to connect words the day before. Maybe that would amuse him or provide ammunition for him. As long as he called, I didn't care which one it was.

Laura called me a few hours later and told me she saw an envelope addressed to me, and she would leave it on my dresser. "Unless there's something else you want me to do with it. I have to leave early today, so I won't be here when you get home."

"Is it a plain white envelope with no return address?" I'd be either disappointed or distraught, but I wasn't sure which one I'd rather feel.

I remembered Mia telling me that when she didn't know what to pray for, she trusted God would know her heart. I always thought that was a sly way of making God the fall guy if the choice ended up being one you regretted.

When Laura answered yes, I thought about leaving the office then, because focusing on anything else would be almost impossible. But my father still had two more appointments and someone coming in to pick up a new policy.

Two more hours. One hundred twenty lifetimes.

I couldn't make myself sit at the computer. Every nerve ending in my body was on high alert. When Dad walked out of his office minutes later, he found me with a spray can of cleaner in one hand and a wad of folded paper towels in the other. I must have looked like I was practicing for a clean-off. I'd already finished lemonizing everything in the reception area. My desk was next.

"I usually try never to interrupt a woman, especially when she's cleaning, but I have a favor to ask. Your mother just told me that Laura has to leave early today. She said she'd be fine by herself, but I'd feel much better if someone was there with her, and your grandmother's not back from her trip yet. Could you leave here in about fifteen minutes and go spell Laura?"

"Of course, no problem. Glad to help," I said with an overdose of enthusiasm.

Maybe too much, because my dad tilted his head and squinted as if he were trying to focus to assure himself that he had been talking to his real daughter. "Okay, then," he said cautiously, probably still trying to understand my willingness to spend time with my mother. "I'll let your mom know you'll be there."

I'd been hesitant to approach my father about what I wanted, then he gave it to me anyway. It was a coincidence that felt like a gift.

My grandmother didn't believe in coincidences. She called them God-incidences. "Now, I don't want you to go expecting that God swoops in like Superman and makes all these things happen. Sometimes he just brings people and things together in ways that work out to make these things happen. Sort of like an orchestra provides these beautiful sounds because they have someone bringing them all together and making the timing work."

Maybe God had decided I'd been punished enough. Maybe this was the beginning of all those blessings my grandmother reminded me I was missing by ignoring God in my life. Maybe there was something to this God thing.

CHAPTER 45

Laura had already left, and there was a note from my mother informing me she was taking a nap and to make sure she woke up in an hour.

I didn't have to open the envelope on my dresser to know it was another letter from Wyatt.

What motivated someone who used to joke about his atrocious spelling to write letters?

Usually people who suspected they were going to die wrote letters to their families, like so many hostages did, or someone diagnosed with a fatal illness. Wyatt wasn't either one of those, but what was left terrified me. Almost always, people who intended to commit suicide left notes behind.

What a ridiculous thought. Who would buy someone a gift never knowing if it would arrive?

Without answers, anything seemed possible. But not suicide. Not that.

And if this is one of those God-incidences, then who's conducting this orchestra? How was I supposed to play without the music in front of me?

How is it that right now I wanted to pummel Wyatt until my hands were numb and wrap myself around him at the same time?

I closed my bedroom door, propped a pillow against my headboard, and opened the envelope.

Dear Olivia,

The more time we spend together, the more grateful I am that you are in my life.

I admire you for working so hard during college to earn your degrees, for pursuing what you want and having goals and dreams, and now some of them include me.

Because of your belief and faith in me, I'm finding the courage to go after what I want. To be the kind of husband you deserve, and the father that, one day, our children will look up to.

I want to be a better person because of you.

I don't ever want to lose you. I would be devastated.

I crumpled the paper and threw it on the floor. I buried my face in my pillow, not to sob, but to scream. Until my lungs begged me to stop, my throat seared from the flames that all my words ignited. Except that I couldn't. Not here. Not now.

What is the point of this, Wyatt? Why did you write these? And why did you give them to someone else?

I couldn't do this alone. I called Mia.

"Livvy, this is so crazy," she said, not even bothering with hello. "There's been an accident on the loop, and I've been stuck in this traffic for thirty minutes already. I was just about to call you. We haven't talked in ages, and I want to hear all about what's going on, and I'll fill you in on how the nanny and Lily are doing—"

"Mia, stop. I have a lot to tell you. I'm going to need you to listen all the way through before you start asking questions."

"You sound awful. What's happened? Is something wrong with your mom? Are you okay? The baby okay? Do you need me to be there with you? I can get a flight tonight if you need me to—"

"You've already asked me five questions, and I haven't even started." I shook my head, smiled in reaction to Mia's impulsive inability to listen. "And I don't have much time to talk."

I started with Evan. Leaving the law practice, the broken engagement, and our non-dates. I told her about the awkwardness the last time we were together, and the guilt trip I hadn't had a vacation from since that day. "So proud of you. I know how difficult it is for you not to speak. I only have one more story."

I smoothed out the letter I'd scrunched up earlier, and I read both of the letters to her, explaining how and when I'd received them.

"Thank God, this traffic is finally moving, and there are no drive-through daiquiri shops in Houston. After hearing all that, I'd need a gallon to go. My brain is on overdrive trying to process everything you've told me."

"I hired that private investigator. Do you think I need to take these letters to him?"

"Excuse my teenaged response, but, duh . . . of course you do. Why didn't you take the first one? Never mind, don't answer that. This letter business is creepy, Livvy, creepy. I don't think God has angel mail carriers delivering letters from dead people. Maybe there were things about Wyatt none of us knew. All I know is you have to turn those letters over to that man, and as soon as your mother can move around on her own, you need to move back here. Away from voodoo-hoodoo land."

"Unfortunately, her recovery is more involved than I expected. I'm not sure how much longer it will be until she can return to the office to actually be of help. And the more time I spend here, the more time I spend with Evan, and I'm not sure that's a good idea. He's hardly the same person he was in college. And I wouldn't have thought it possible, but he's become this magnetically attractive man. He's generous, funny, and . . ." I wasn't sure about adding *sexy.*

"And he's maybe not staying there? If he does, where do you see this going? I don't want to hurt your feelings, because I know he's calling these outings 'dates,' but will he still want to keep 'dating' when you're nine months pregnant? Would he even envision himself being a father to this baby, or is he just going to be Uncle Evan?"

"I don't know. I haven't played this whole thing out, but I'm very much aware that being around Evan makes my pregnancy hormones think they're at Disney World, and they're not patient waiting for the gate to open."

She laughed. "That hormonal surge was one of Bryce's top three things he loved about my being pregnant. The other two were feeling Lily kick him when we spooned in bed and coming home to a clean house when my nesting kicked in."

"My mother is expecting me to wake her up in three minutes. She's probably already awake, and setting her stopwatch to see if I'll be on time. Please tell Lily I will talk to her soon. Thank you, Mia. I don't want to know what I would do without you."

"I love you, too, Olivia. Now go love yourself enough to take control of all these things happening in your life."

CHAPTER 46

Tell me we're auditioning for a new reality show, 'How to Embarrass Your Daughter,' because if we aren't, we should be." My father was clearly losing his mind.

"Come on, honey. What else are you doing? You've had a few outings with Evan, but it'd be good for you to learn a sport. Get some exercise, enjoy being outside," he said, mostly talking to the wall he was measuring. "Besides, your mom can't play, and I'd love the company."

I was helping him hang pictures, the ones that had led to my mother using a step stool she'd tripped over, which had led to her surgery. My father told her that was the most expensive artwork they'd ever purchased.

While she pointed her cane to places she wanted the paintings, I followed my father around with the jar of picture hangers and the hammer and measuring tape. "Wise move waiting until you were holding the hammer to announce you'd signed me up for golf lessons."

"He wouldn't listen when I suggested he talk to you first," said my mother, who never held back from a head-shaking I-told-you-so opportunity. "He said you wouldn't mind because Evan would be teaching you."

"Evan?" My mouth dropped and stayed open so long it could have been a haven for generations of flies. "Hand me the hammer now. I'll put both of us out of my misery."

"Stand back and tell me if this is centered," he said, adjusting a painting of St. Louis Cathedral.

"No, move it a smidgen to the left," I said. "Dad, in a few months I won't be able to see my feet, much less a golf ball. If you want someone on the course with you, I'll drive the cart."

He wasn't having it. For every objection I raised, he responded with, "But you haven't even tried it yet. Give it a chance."

By the time we finished hanging all four paintings, each one depicting a French Quarter scene, I learned I would be meeting Evan at the golf course first thing in the morning. Dad would load my mother's golf clubs into my Jeep, and Evan would unload them at the driving range.

I wanted to argue that, if I couldn't pick up a golf bag holding a set of golf clubs, I shouldn't be playing. But the longer my father talked about my lessons, the more excited he grew. I didn't have the heart to deflate him. The man would never experience any of the father-son bonding over football: beer drinking, belching, or whatever they did. Later, it occurred to me that, like a single parent sometimes had to play both roles for a child, a single child had to play both roles for parents.

"My appointment for the ultrasound is the day after tomorrow," I reminded my parents on my way to bed. "If you want to come with me, let me know. If you're there, you'll find out if you're having a grand-daughter or a grandson. If not"—I paused for the sweetest of smiles—"it might be months before you find out."

"Is that some form of emotional blackmail?" The question from my father sounded lighthearted. His face conveyed otherwise.

"Absolutely not," I chirped. "It's the truth."

I hadn't heard from or seen Evan since I insulted him in our driveway after our Sunday outing. I hoped meeting him at eight o'clock in the morning on a driving range counted as justified retribution.

I looked like a rerun from the last day we were together. Same blouse, same shorts, same hat. If nothing else, golf lessons would require me to expand my wardrobe. I had no idea if a line of golf clothes existed for pregnant women, but my father's credit card needed to be ready since these lessons were his idea.

Evan was already there when I arrived. He was talking to two men in a golf cart, gesturing like he was giving them directions. Then he patted the roof of the cart and off they went. Watching him in those moments when he hadn't seen me yet, I was reminded of my conversation with Mia. No doubt, even in the early morning, wearing his collared golf shirt and his khaki shorts, his hat folded and shoved in his back pocket, he was swoon-worthy.

I still wasn't sure why he insisted on calling our time together "dates"; maybe he used the word to annoy me. We barely held hands the few times we'd been together, which was strange in itself considering our college relationship history. Maybe I was one of his volunteer projects. Someone lost, who needed attention. Someone he could help.

What did it say about me that I could fathom a relationship with another man when I was pregnant with Wyatt's baby? Evan didn't ask a lot of questions about the baby, and I didn't volunteer much, either. Shouldn't that be a red flag or at least a yellow caution light?

If he hadn't looked up at that moment, I would've driven right back home, called him, and said I didn't feel well. Because I didn't. I'd managed to make myself feel sheepish and embarrassed by the time he told the golfers good-bye.

All of my hand-wringing about lingering awkwardness between us dissipated as soon as he opened my car door. "I'm so glad you're here after your dad told me his surprise for you. I wanted to call to warn you. But if you hadn't reacted with honest shock, like I'm sure you did, he would've known I'd told you. I wish you could've seen his face. He was almost as excited as the day he told me he was going to be a grandfather."

I doubt Evan realized why, but my father had managed to shock me again. He'd actually shared with someone that he was looking forward to this baby. Hearing that made this morning a small sacrifice, in light of the overwhelming joy of knowing that at least my father wasn't embarrassed by my pregnancy.

Evan toted the golf bag, and we walked toward the driving range.

"Did you know I was going to need this after Sunday when you gave it to me?" I tugged on the pink cap and tucked my hair behind my ears.

He set the bag on the ground between us and shook his head. "Nope. This actually didn't come together until yesterday." He opened a nearby ice chest and handed me a bottle of water. "Drink some of this before we get started. It's warmer out here than it seems at first, especially when you're standing in one place. Definitely don't want you to get dehydrated.

"I probably shouldn't be admitting this, but I've never taught golf to a pregnant woman. An obviously pregnant woman," he said.

"Then I hope my father's getting a special rate," I teased as I pulled my hair into a ponytail.

"Are you kidding, Kavanaugh? I told him I charged extra for you because you'd probably question every instruction I gave you."

I pretended to pout. "But that's one of my most endearing qualities."

"Sure it is." He rolled his eyes. "Let's get started before the it's too hot to breathe."

Evan pulled a club out and said we'd start with the grip. He didn't warn me it was the hokeypokey for my hands. Palm there, curl your right pinkie here, roll your thumb there, index finger here . . . If I'd been made out of Play-Doh, it would have been far easier for him to manipulate all eight fingers and two thumbs.

"Okay." I think he was speaking as much to himself as he was to me. "I'm going to show you how to address the ball." He took a wooden tee out of his pocket and jammed it into the grass in front of me.

"Address the ball? This game is quite stuffy, isn't it?"

"Olivia," he said, choking down a laugh. "You can release the club now before your hand cramps."

"Hey, I'm trying to be a good student. You didn't tell me to let go." I dropped it on the ground and did finger aerobics until the blood circulated again.

Words dropped out of his mouth and fell into a wormhole between the two of us. I held up my hand. "Stop. I lost you at where to put my left foot . . . though by the end of this lesson, I might have a place."

He started over again, his voice shifting as if he were teaching a Remedial Golf 101 lesson.

"I'm not sure I'm going to be successful at a game that requires me to remember where every appendage of my body is at any given time, before I can even hit the ball," I said, my frustration making my gut hurt even more.

"Relax. It's all about muscle memory. And practice," said Evan. "You've only been at this for, let's see"—he looked at his watch—"fourteen minutes."

"It would be easier to whack you over the head with this club than to hit that little ball."

"Yes, but then you'd be arrested for assault, and orange is not your color."

A golf cart pulled up near us, and one of the two women in it stepped out and asked Evan if she could speak to him for a few minutes. He reminded me to drink water, then excused himself, saying he wouldn't be long.

Swinging a golf club, especially when I missed the ball more times than I made contact, digging up wads of dirt in the process, was more strenuous than I'd anticipated. But then the most exercise I'd participated in the past few months was running after Lily or walking to and from the car. So when my stomach felt tight, I was surprised the rest of me wasn't sore.

I bent to pick up the ball at my feet when a searing pain shot through my abdomen. I supported myself with the golf club until it passed and decided the lesson was over for the day. Subjecting myself to torture should only be required if I intended to become a Navy SEAL, not a golfer.

Evan was a few steps away when I doubled over with the next pain. "Olivia." He stood next to me, one arm wrapped around my waist and the other holding my shoulder. "Are you having muscle cramps? Sometimes dehydration causes that. Did you finish that bottle of water?"

I nodded, took a few deep breaths. *You're fine, Olivia. Relax. Stay calm.*

"I'm getting you another one."

But the next cramp hit, and seconds later I knew why. I waved the water away. "No, that's not what I need."

Evan started unscrewing the top.

"Didn't you hear what I just said? It's not dehydration, Evan. I'm . . . I'm bleeding. I'm bleeding . . ." I sank to my knees, holding my stomach as if somehow I could prop the baby up. Keep it from leaving me. *I don't even know who you are, little nugget. Don't go yet. Please. Please. Stay with me. I've already lost your daddy. I can't lose you, too.*

I reached in my pocket for my cell phone and handed it to Evan. "Call my father. Tell him to come get me now."

Evan took the phone. "We're not waiting for anyone to come get you. I'm here, and I'm taking you to the emergency room. We'll call your doctor and your parents on the way."

"Okay," I whispered.

"I need you to listen to me. I'm taking this golf cart to the parking lot just around this bend to get my car. Don't move."

It seemed like he had just told me he was leaving when I heard him call my name.

"Livvy, I'm here."

I started to stand.

"What do you think you're doing?"

"I can do it. I can walk." By now the insides of my thighs were wet and sticky.

"Are you always this stubborn in an emergency? I know you can walk, but you're not going to." And with that, he scooped me into his arms and carried me to his car.

"Evan, your seats. I'm . . . I'm a mess."

He released my legs, opened the door, and guided me into the seat. "I don't care about the seats. The entire car could be a mess, and it wouldn't matter to me. You matter to me," he said as he leaned over, buckled my seat belt, and reclined the seat. As soon as he was in the car, he started it and pulled out my cell phone. "What's your doctor's name?"

"Baby. She's listed under 'baby.'"

"Well, that's a relief," he said as he held the phone to his ear. "For a second there, I thought that was her name—hello, I'm calling for Olivia Kavanaugh. She's a patient of . . ."

"Dr. Schneider," I answered before he could ask.

"She's, um, bleeding and cramping. We're on our way to the emergency room at Lakeside Hospital. I'm handing the phone to her now."

Before he backed out, he kissed me on my forehead. "Hang in there, Livvy," he said, his voice soft and low. "I got this, okay? You're not going to be alone."

But I am. I am. I'm losing this baby. I'll never know this child I've carried with me for months. All I have of Wyatt. Almost gone.

CHAPTER 47

Dad and Ruthie were in the emergency room waiting area when the EMTs wheeled me through the doors.

I looked at them, and Dad saw the question in my eyes. "Your mother didn't come because she said she'd slow us down. Really, honey, it was more important to her for us to get here as soon as possible."

"She asked us to call as soon as we saw you, so she could talk to you," my grandmother said.

"First, I'm going to take her to admit to get all the paperwork started so she hopefully won't have to wait too long. The doctor said she would meet us here as soon as possible," Evan said.

"My dad or grandmother can help me, Evan. I appreciate everything you've done, but you don't have to stay."

Evan crouched in front of the wheelchair, his eyes reminding me of Laura's when my mother was discharged. "How long have we known each other? Isn't this what friends do . . . help?"

"But you've already helped, and I'm sure you have a lot to do at the club. It's not like . . . It's not like—"

"What? It's not like it's my baby? Is that what you're trying to tell me?" The pain I saw in his eyes that Sunday in our driveway resurfaced.

"I know I can leave. I choose to stay. Because you're my concern . . . pregnant or not." He stood. His expression somber. "If you really want me to go, I will. Only because I respect what's important to you. You tell me."

Another cramp curled through my abdomen, circled around itself over and over and over, each time tighter than the last. I heard a sound like an injured animal, a high-pitched growl, and realized, as I lost more blood, that it was coming from me.

When the cramp unrolled itself, I reached for Evan's hand. "Stay."

"Why is God still punishing me? What have I done now to deserve this? Was it something I hadn't done? I don't understand." I'd moved past tears, past sobbing, to a convulsing, ragged-breath squall.

I'd been moved to one of those curtained-off partitions where human suffering became a shared affair of faceless voices.

The nurse gave me a hospital gown and pads that hooked to some contraption that looked like a garter belt for Wonder Woman. She asked me if I wanted her to contact the doctor about something for pain.

"The cramps are doubling me over sometimes. Are they going to get worse?"

"Depends. It's not the same for everyone, and if she's not going to be here for a while, you might want to consider something to take the edge off. It's best to stay ahead of the pain, if you can. I'll call her, and I'll let you know what she says."

"Okay, but tell her I'd rather drink a bottle of wine or two martinis than deal with some of those pain medicines."

She nodded and smiled. "Will do."

I'd asked my grandmother to come with me, and she rubbed my back and shoulders while I lay on my side, being sucked in and spewed out by one whirlpool of cramps after another.

She didn't say much, but she didn't need to. Her gentle touch, reaching every so often to smooth my hair back, was all the conversation I needed.

Evan and my father rotated in and out for a few minutes at a time, looking so helpless and worried that I was beginning to feel sorry for them. My dad seemed relieved when my grandmother suggested that he and Evan go to lunch and bring something back for her.

Evan came back to ask what I wanted. My grandmother told him the nurse had suggested I not eat in case I needed anesthesia later.

"Do you, uh, want something to read? I have a few golf magazines in my car, or we can stop while we're out and pick something up for you," he said.

"That's very sweet of you to offer, but I'm hoping the doctor shows up soon, and I can"—*What? Get this over with?* I waved my hand—"can something."

"I got it," he said and patted my shoulder.

"If you're not up for doing this favor I'm about to ask, it's fine. I know it's probably been a while since you've talked to or seen Mia and Bryce. But would you mind very much calling Mia for me?" I stopped to clear my throat. "I . . . I can't right now. And if she calls and doesn't know . . ." I couldn't finish the sentence.

"Of course. Of course. Your dad has your phone. I'll get the number and call. Do you want to talk to her? I'll bring your phone back here if you do."

I shook my head. "Not yet. Tell her I'll call after I'm home. She'll understand."

Evan rolled his eyes. "The Mia I remember might understand; that doesn't mean she'll listen. Your dad and I will run interference for you." He squeezed my hand. "I'll keep you updated. We shouldn't be long."

"Take your time. It's going to be a while yet. For a man who owns an insurance business, he's one of the worst drivers ever, even when he's not in a hurry," Ruthie said.

"My grandmother thinks anyone who doesn't exceed the speed limit by at least seven miles shouldn't be on the road," I said.

"My kind of woman," he said and flashed one of his epic grins.

When he walked out, Ruthie smiled and said, "You know, I don't remember that man being quite that charming."

"He wasn't. He's just proof we can change. I'll fill you in"—I groaned, more from the dread of feeling the cramp start. I pulled my knees into my stomach, clenched my teeth, and vaguely remembered my yoga teacher telling us to "breathe into the pain." I should have made an effort to attend more classes, because the pain was winning.

The nurse came back and said Dr. Schneider had approved some over-the-counter meds and a prescribed medicine. "If you don't want anything now, just hit the Call button when you do."

She left, and I asked Ruthie to raise the bed so I could sit up. An ultrasound technician came in and said Dr. Schneider was on her way, and she wanted me to have an ultrasound before she reached the hospital. The tech rolled the cart in, apologized for the cold gel she rubbed on me, and moved the wand over my abdomen.

I turned my face away from the screen. My grandmother watched from where she stood behind me at the head of the bed, and one glance at her face was the only screen I needed.

"I was scheduled for an ultrasound tomorrow to find out if the baby was a boy or a girl. Can you tell me?"

"You'll need to ask your doctor when you see her," she said, turning off the machine and wiping off the gel. "She was just a few blocks away when she called. Shouldn't be much longer."

Ruthie wiped her eyes with the corner of my bedsheet.

"Did you see a heartbeat?" The question tiptoed out as if it could walk past the truth without waking it.

She shook her head.

You're gone. You're really gone.

Your little heart stopped beating, and my grown-up one wished it could have beat enough for both of us.

My love wasn't enough to save you or your daddy.

I'm so sorry. I'm so, so sorry.

CHAPTER 48

Ruthie gave me a wipe for my bubbling nose, settled my bedhead hair, and held my face in her hands. "I'm not going to tell you that it's going to be okay. I know what this is like. I had miscarriages before and after your mom, and I've never forgotten those babies. You're going to have to let yourself grieve for this baby. Eventually you'll tuck it away in your heart, and it's going to be with you always. And when, one day, you hold a baby you've given birth to, you'll see this baby," she said as she patted my stomach, "in your heart, in the eyes of the one in your arms." She leaned over and hugged me.

"But this baby is Wyatt's baby. And I'll never have the chance to have his baby ever again. I guess it wasn't enough for God that I lost Wyatt. And I don't know what I did to deserve all of this. I'm not even going to ask how much more He can punish me, because I don't want to know."

Dr. Schneider whooshed through the curtains.

"This is never the way I want to see my patients early." She pulled down the side bed rail, perched on the bed, and patted my leg. "Olivia, I want you to listen to me. Even though I know you're going to question yourself for too long, you did not, did not, do anything to make this happen. Nothing. You didn't say anything to make it happen; you didn't think anything to make it happen. Nothing."

She stopped and looked at my grandmother, then back at me. "I'm glad your grandmother is here to remind you later what I'm telling you right now. And she will have to remind you because it's going to take you a while to believe it."

She went on to tell me the reasons for miscarriages, and that she'd know in a week or so if there were any chromosomal abnormalities. "This doesn't mean you can't get pregnant again or go full-term or that you're destined to miscarry."

"The baby . . . Was it a boy or a girl?"

"I can't tell from the ultrasound. You're about twenty-two weeks, but it looks like the baby stopped developing maybe two weeks ago or even before then. We'll know when the other tests come back."

"My baby's been dead for weeks? Is that what you're telling me?" It was as if she walked in with a glass full of a vile and putrid liquid, and she dumped it on me completely unaware. "How is it I didn't realize that?" I covered my face with my hands. The guilt felt worse than any of the cramps I'd had since this started.

"You had no way of knowing. Possibly if you'd been pregnant before, you might've noticed that you weren't growing or hadn't felt the baby move, but it's not unusual."

Another cramp. I held my stomach and winced, knowing it would get worse before it got better.

Dr. Schneider stood and waited for the pain to subside. "We need to talk about your options. I can release you to go home, and you can do this naturally. Or there's a drug I can give you to induce a natural delivery. The third option is a D&C, which stands for dilation and curettage. The procedure takes about twenty minutes, requires a general anesthesia, and you'd be released in less than four hours."

I wanted option four. The one where she waved her magic wand and it all went away.

"Can she have some time to think this through?" my grandmother asked.

The doctor nodded, but I said, "I don't need time. I want this to be over. I've had enough of dying. When can you do the procedure?"

"I could do it sooner with a local. You have to wait at least another two hours for the general."

"I'd rather wait and be totally knocked out."

She then explained that someone would be coming in with papers for me to sign, outlining all the risks and giving the hospital permission to do the procedure. She said the anesthesiologist would probably stop by to introduce herself.

"I'm going back to my office to see patients while I'm waiting. I'll let them know when I'm on my way, so the nurse can give you a little happy shot in your IV before we roll you in."

She left, and I closed my eyes. If only I could sleep.

It's not enough, God, that my baby has to die. Do you have to make it so painful and difficult for it to leave my body?

"Livvy, do you want to call your mother, or do you want me to talk to her? Laura could drop her off here, and she'd still have time to see you before everything starts."

I didn't open my eyes. I shook my head. "No. She told me that my being pregnant was a sin. I'm only living with her now because of her surgery. She won't have to worry anymore about what everyone at her church will say. I guess God hears her voice before mine. She's getting what she wanted."

Gran held my hand. "Honey, your mother loves you. I don't think she would ever ask God to send you this kind of pain."

I opened my eyes and stared at the ceiling. Patches of light crisscrossed the white ceiling under the fluorescent lamps. "I don't want Mom here. You and Dad can tell her whatever you want. That the procedure would almost be over by the time she'd get here. That it would be uncomfortable for her in the waiting room. Whatever. But I can't do it."

When did I move to the North Pole?

I shook so violently, I must have been on a full-body vibrator. Someone kept repeating my name, but I couldn't answer because my teeth chattered as if they were trying to keep pace with my shaking. I whispered, "I'mmmmmm c-c-c-c-cold." I would have said it again, but my throat burned.

"Olivia, wake up. Olivia . . . There you are."

I opened my eyes. A stranger's face, mustached and bearded. *Who is this?*

Whoever he was, he could read minds, because he introduced himself as Mason, my nurse. I already liked him because he was layering me with warm blankets and tucking them in around me.

"We need you to come all the way back to us, and then your family can take you home."

I felt crampy. *Baby. Miscarriage. D&C.*

I didn't think I liked Mason anymore. He kept waking me up to face a reality I wanted to ignore.

I went home in fresh clothes, made possible by Evan, who'd driven to my house to pick them up from Laura, then dropped them off at the hospital before he went back to work.

My father drove while Ruthie sat in the backseat with me, holding a container the hospital had given her in case I vomited on the way home. I didn't. She told me later she was more relieved than I was.

Time is funny. When you don't pay attention to it, it speeds by. When you're watching it, it's like sixty seconds takes five minutes. Over the next two days, I didn't even know two days passed. Days and people and conversations and meals were all different color finger paints I dipped in. I swirled them around and up and down, and by the time I was fairly lucid, it was a canvas of confusion.

The flower arrangement Bryce and Mia sent staged a coup and took over my entire dresser. I couldn't see myself in the mirror without moving it or standing on my tiptoes. Laura said there was so much candy stuffed in there, the American Dental Association would have awarded it first place for their Most Likely to Bring in New Patients Award.

"Where'd it go?" I poked through the flowers and came back with pinpricks of blood from the thorns, but no candy.

"We put some in the refrigerator, we gave some to your grandmother, and . . ."

"Y'all ate the rest?" I sounded like Lily.

"We gave some to Evan when he stopped by," she said, like I should applaud them for their generosity.

"When was Evan here?"

"The day after you came home. You don't remember? You kept asking him how the boys were doing, and none of us could figure out who you were talking about. At one point you told him you weren't going out on dates with him anymore. He said that was no problem; he wouldn't ask you to go on dates anymore."

"Did I respond to that? Do I want to know how I responded to that?"

"You did, but I couldn't hear you. Whatever it was, it made him laugh."

"Please tell me now if there is anyone else I should be embarrassed to talk to."

She shook her head. "You had a few phone calls, and I think you talked to Mia for a few minutes. Those pain pills were taking you someplace."

I nodded. "It was an easier place to be."

CHAPTER 49

I overheard Laura and my father talking in the den when I was on my way to the kitchen. I stopped to listen. Eavesdrop. I stopped to eavesdrop.

"Scarlett is doing great. And while I don't think she's ready to go back to work, I do think she's going to be okay here by herself," said Laura.

"I agree. If only there was a way you could help Olivia as much as you've helped her mother. It's been over two weeks, and she still doesn't want to leave the house and spends almost all of her time sleeping."

"I wish I could, too, believe me. But broken hearts have to heal themselves. She's experienced more grief in less than a year than most people do in a lifetime."

"I'm afraid that until she solves the mystery about Wyatt, she's not going to be able to move forward. Evan left this morning, so he won't be around to entertain her or—Olivia, hey, Laura and I . . ."

My father saw over Laura's shoulder that I'd walked into the room. She turned around, a flicker of surprise in her widened eyes, and smiled. Guarded, the kind of smile you flash at people when you're unsure if they like you.

I rubbed my arms with my hands to stem the wave of tiny chill bumps that flowed down them. "Where did Evan go?" My question came off as rude as my interruption of them.

"He said he was going out of town for a few days, but he wasn't very specific about why. Said something about having some business to take care of," my dad informed me.

"Okay. Whatever," I said with a voice as flat as I felt. *Why didn't he tell me he was leaving?*

I shuffled past them to the one thing lately that filled the void, the constant emptiness that defined me. Food. It was only a temporary fix, but I could count on it at least three times a day, more if I stayed up late. No more wedding diet, no more pregnancy restrictions. Being ten pounds thinner didn't save Wyatt, and not drinking martinis didn't save our baby, so what was the point of all that deprivation?

My head was in the refrigerator when Laura told me she was leaving for the day. Still holding the door open, I turned around and said, "See you tomorrow," with the enthusiasm of a woman who had been given a dust mop for Christmas.

Since I couldn't decide between the leftover mushroom pizza and the spinach-and-artichoke casserole, I grabbed them both and kicked the refrigerator door closed.

"Want some?" I asked my dad, who stood at the island, watching me load my plate with two slices of pizza and a generous serving of casserole.

"No," he said, staring at my hefty portions, not even trying to hide the look of surprise on his face. "Um, if you want to save that for some other time, you can join your mother and me for dinner tonight. After your mom wakes up, we're going to that new Italian restaurant that opened a few months ago. Some of our friends have eaten there and really enjoyed it. Why don't you come with us?"

I licked the spoon I'd served myself with, closed the pizza box, pulled out a fork, and stood at the island to eat. "Thanks, but I'm just going to eat this now. I thought about picking Ruthie up later, and we could go to Dairy Queen."

"Olivia, look at me." His voice was a plea as much as a command. "I know two weeks isn't a long time for you to process what happened to you. But you need to start taking some steps to making a life for yourself. Laura isn't going to be here much longer, but I know it's not fair of me to expect you to stay here indefinitely. In fact, I plan to ask Laura if she wants to work at the office. That would free you to go back to Virtual Strategies or, even though I would miss you, find that place in Houston you talked about."

He was right, of course. But I wasn't ready for him to be right. Especially after hearing what he said about Wyatt. The remark about Evan, though, made me wonder if it was my dad who was behind the times Evan and I had spent together. Had he asked Evan to "entertain" me? *Might as well get that question answered now, Olivia, before Evan comes back and you make a fool out of yourself.*

I focused on picking all the mushrooms off my pizza slices so I wouldn't have to make eye contact. "Sure, especially since Evan's not around to 'entertain' me. Was he doing that for me or for you? I'm guessing, since he didn't make an effort to tell me he was going out of town, he needed to let you know he wouldn't be around to keep me busy."

Dad stood on the other side of the island going through his mail that he'd brought home from the office. When he didn't answer right away, I looked up, wondering if he had heard me at all. He grinned as he continued to flip through the stack of envelopes.

He had to have heard me. It's not like I was whispering. Why wasn't he answering me? "Something funny in the mail?"

"I don't know if I should be flattered that you think I had the wherewithal to make a man like Evan do something he doesn't want to do. Or insulted because you think I'm capable of such a thing."

He turned the last envelope over, straightened the pile, then wrapped a rubber band around it before he looked at me with disappointment deep in his eyes. "You might want to check your phone. Evan called every day for a week before leaving. He left voicemails. I'd say that's making an effort, but you never called him back. I told him I thought you were on some self-imposed phone deprivation, but the way it seemed to Evan was that you weren't interested in talking to him. And, for the record, I'm sure Evan had plenty of options when it came to people he might entertain. He chose you."

I scraped my leftovers into the garbage disposal feeling a bit like trash myself after hearing my dad; I figured I should be grateful there wasn't a human garbage disposal he could shove me into.

CHAPTER 50

The real miscarriage was in the way people talked about it.

Whose idea was it to say, "I'm so sorry you lost the baby"? As if I didn't know where it was? Because I put it in such a safe place I couldn't find it again? And it was all my fault, too. Because "you" lost it. Not, "I'm so sorry your gene pool screwed up," or "I'm so sorry that this awful thing happened to you."

The day I came home from the hospital, I remembered putting my phone on Silent. Anyone I needed or wanted to talk to either lived with me or showed up at my house at some point. And because I had the volume turned off, I spent more time looking for it than using it. So, after my father informed me I'd missed people who actually wanted to talk to me, I made an effort to locate it and check my messages and voicemails. And, of course, there were several missed calls and two voicemails from Evan. I couldn't even bring myself to listen to them. What did it matter? He was already gone.

There were two missed calls from Jim, the private investigator. He said he had big news and wanted to talk to me as soon as possible. That was two days ago. The thought of calling him appealed to me as much as eating chocolate-covered ants. I already suspected "big news" wasn't synonymous with "good news," and I was right.

He'd found Wyatt's name on a birth certificate as the father of Jacob Pierce, whose mother was Jenny Pierce. Jacob was now four years old.

I thanked Jim but told him I couldn't hear any more. Not now. Maybe not ever. I told him I wanted to close the case.

Ruthie called and asked me to be her date for a fundraiser at the country club. "Your parents are going, and they invited me and my checkbook. Before you get your knickers in a knot that they didn't invite you, they didn't think you'd be interested. But I decided I'd take the chance to guilt you into getting out of the house. Because you wouldn't turn down a date with your grandmother whose opportunities for dating are getting narrower and narrower."

"When is this lame event?" I was having a Lily afternoon and painting my toenails rainbow colors. When I wiggled my toes, my foot looked like it was waving a gay-rights banner.

"In about an hour. And I've checked your dance card, and it's completely empty. I'm sure you'll be able to fit this in just fine. I'm gonna pick you up in forty-five minutes. The invitations said it's a jeans night, so don't worry about pulling out your little black dress."

"If my parents are going, I can just ride over there with them. It's close, it won't be torturous." Much.

"Yes, but wouldn't you like to have an escape plan to avoid being stuck there all night?"

When Ruthie picked me up later, I told her that my parents, who looked shocked that I was going, said they were leaving early to get a table. "A table for what? What is this fundraiser?"

"I was so glad you didn't ask me that on the phone. And it's too late now because we're already on our way, and you can't jump out of the car. It's called Cards and Cocktails, and it's to raise money for the local libraries because their funding has been almost nonexistent, thanks to the state's emphasis on education. Also nonexistent."

"This is what my life has come to? Sitting in a room and watching people play poker for money or something?" I shook my head. "Could this night be any lamer?"

I shouldn't have asked. She explained we would actually be playing card games. "We can start out playing with your parents, but then everybody's free to sit where they want. And believe it or not, there's a crew of young people your age who come in with their bottles of wine and whatever they want to eat that the club doesn't serve." Ruthie pulled into a parking spot. "And I tell you"—she slapped me on my knee—"those kids get rowdy."

I'd hit the triple play of humiliation. On a date with my grandmother, to a card-playing fundraiser, at which people my own age would be, wondering if I was following my parents around because they picked me up for my first outpatient weekend.

Ruthie trotted to the door. Dressed in her white leggings and black oversize sweater, she looked, from the back, like a woman half her age. While I walked behind her looking like a woman twice my age. She waited at the door for me to catch up with her and prodded me, saying, "Life is too short for you to be moving slower than a Sunday afternoon."

I remembered one of my friends in college talking about the Rapture, a time when people would suddenly start resurrecting to the heavens. I couldn't understand why people would want that to happen.

Until now.

I hadn't been quite sure how playing cards resulted in a successful fundraiser. But counting the cost of the tickets, the cost of the cocktails, and the payoff of the cocktails in loosening wallets as the night went on, it made more sense.

The young crowd was young even by my standards. Most of them were in their midtwenties, so it was a relief that, with the exception of my parents' friends, no one would know me.

My father decided we needed to start with gin rummy because it didn't require a great deal of serious attention. Something else I didn't understand until the room filled with the sounds of backslapping, welcome-hugging, laughter of every variety, and a few cheers. While it made concentrating difficult, the noise meant people were actually talking to one another and having fun without television screens or even their cell phones.

I also appreciated that the cacophony limited the frequency and topics of conversation at our table. We'd about exhausted our supply of mundane, trivial, and nonexplosive topics when Dad mentioned again about Laura working for him. "Olivia, in a few weeks you can decide if you want to go back to Houston, live here, or"—he paused as if he'd just heard the celestial choir singing in his ear—"my gosh, you're free to do whatever you want. Travel to all those places you've always wanted to visit."

"Sure," I said, breaking the deck in two to shuffle the cards. "I could join Ruthie and her buddies as they see the world."

Ruthie shook her empty beer bottle in our waiter's line of vision. He nodded and disappeared. "I don't know about that. I might have to get permission, because I'm not sure all the ladies want a beautiful young woman around their male friends. Could you imagine? Between the two of us, we'd about have the market cornered on those cruises." She took the new bottle from the waiter. "But I do agree with your dad. You need to take this time for yourself."

I started dealing the cards when my mom said, "You're going to be sad for a while, but think about all the possibilities you have. Maybe this happened for a reason."

"Somebody please tell me she didn't just say that," I snapped.

Their silence was deafening.

CHAPTER 51

Before the tables next to us could experience Act One of our family drama, I stood and asked Ruthie if she was ready to leave. "It's close enough that I can walk, if you'd rather stay."

"I'm sure what your mother meant was . . ." My father looked at her as if waiting for her cue to provide an explanation.

"Dad, don't. It doesn't require interpretation."

"Scarlett," my grandmother said softly, patting her daughter's hand, "sometimes the reason is just because we're human, and our bodies aren't perfect. Do we really want Olivia to believe that God caused her miscarriage? And, really, this isn't the time or place for a life or a Scripture lesson." She reached in her purse, gave my father a check, and said, "Here's my donation. I'm going to drive Livvy home. I'm not sure yet if I'll be back."

"Let's talk about this tomorrow, okay?" my dad said, looking between my mother and me.

"I'm sorry if I hurt her feelings, but—"

"Maybe you could try saying that to me. I'm still standing here. But don't bother, because I'm leaving." I'd worn the bracelet from Ruthie, the one with *Be still* engraved inside it. I wrapped my hand around it to settle myself.

Ruthie and I walked to her car, neither one of us saying anything then or on the ride home. I thought of the trip Lily and I took to the Butterfly Museum when she wanted to know if coming out of a cocoon was painful for a moth. Sitting in the quiet, I imagined how peaceful being in a cocoon must feel. Sheltered. Protected. I could hibernate for months, and when I was ready to emerge, I could fly. Wherever I wanted to go.

"Do you want me to come inside with you?"

"Thanks, but I'll probably treat myself to a pint of ice cream, a good book, and an early bedtime. Sorry our date turned out to be such a bust." I leaned over and kissed Ruthie on the cheek. "I love you."

"And I love you." She reached over and hugged me. "Call me tomorrow. Maybe we do need to talk about taking a trip together. While I'm still young enough to look like I could be your sister."

I smiled. "You know, that's the best idea I've heard in a long time. I'll talk to you later."

I changed into scrub pants and a T-shirt, and on the way to the kitchen, a text from Evan popped up on my phone. `I'll be back one day next week. Would like to see you. Will call.`

Was I ready to see him? I didn't know. As long as I was pregnant, the idea of falling back into a relationship with Evan seemed improbable, if not impossible. At least from my perspective. But now? I was barely in a relationship with myself. Would the dynamics of our being together change? I was afraid of a "yes" answer as much as I feared a "no" answer.

Clearly, Olivia, if you can't choose between Cake My Day and Cherry Garcia, you're not ready for any kind of commitment.

But who said I had to choose? Instead of eating right out of the pint carton, I put half of each flavor in a bowl. Score one for Team Olivia.

I hadn't checked the mail for weeks, because I couldn't face another envelope addressed to me. But, of course, there one was. Postmarked two days ago.

Tonight I didn't have to silence my anger and frustration. I shook the letter at the ceiling and, with all the energy I had left, I shouted, "Stop. Whoever you are. Stop sending me these letters. Why are you doing this to me? I hate these letters, and I hate you."

This time, I didn't bother going to my bedroom. I opened it while I sat at the kitchen table.

Dear Olivia,

Remember the day I asked you to marry me?

We were having lunch under our favorite oak tree along the lakefront. I asked you to close your eyes and keep them closed until I told you it was time to open them. And you were full of questions. What's going on? Why are you doing this? How long am I supposed to keep my eyes closed?

I kept saying that you just needed to trust me. I would never set you up to hurt you. And if I asked you to do this, you had to trust that I had a good reason. You wanted to put your hands over your eyes, but I said no because I knew you well enough to know that you would figure out a way to peek through your fingers.

When you opened your eyes, you saw rose petals scattered all around you, and I handed you one red rose that I'd tied your engagement ring to. And when I proposed, Colin walked up and snapped our picture.

I need you to remember that day, how you trusted me, and what I told you about never wanting to hurt you.

Too late now, Wyatt. Too late.
You should have asked for forgiveness.

I was sleeping when my parents came home and still sleeping when they left the next morning for church.

A text from Laura woke me up, asking if I'd gone to church with my parents. She wanted to come over with someone she wanted me to meet.

I messaged back that I wasn't in the mood to meet a new man, so if that wasn't the motive, she was welcome.

She said she would be there in twenty minutes, and she was punctual as always. At least it was enough time for me to throw on what I wore last night and brush my teeth.

Why was she ringing the doorbell when she had a key? That very question was about to pop out of my mouth when I opened the door and found Laura with a woman about our age. A petite blonde, her hair cut almost boyishly short, and she was holding the hand of a child. He looked like he could've been three or four. I immediately recognized his eyes. Those startling ocean-blue eyes.

They were Wyatt's.

Everything in front of me rippled back and forth like waves blown by the wind. I steadied myself against the door and fought to focus. I heard Laura ask if they could come in, but I wasn't looking at her. I was breathing in this little life in front of me. His dark brown hair was wavy and his bangs skimmed his eyebrows. He wore a blue plaid button-down oxford that looked like it had been tucked into his jeans at some point, the shirttail hanging out on one side. His free hand was in his pocket, and he looked from his mom to me and back again.

I invited them in, but even as I led them to the den, I felt split in half. One half of me was hurtling back to a past before Wyatt met me, and the other half looked at the future Wyatt couldn't have imagined.

Laura introduced us to one another, though it seemed obvious whom we were meeting. When she finished, I said, "What I don't understand is how the two of you are here together."

"Before I answer, would you mind if I settled Jake at your kitchen table and gave him something to do?" Jenny's voice was calm; her eyes didn't dart nervously back and forth between Laura and me, and she didn't perch on the end of the sofa as if she could be ready to bolt at any minute. She was articulate, self-assured, and composed. Everything that I wasn't at that moment.

She took an iPad and juice box out of her purse and held Jacob's hand as they walked to the table. I appreciated that she didn't engage in those mommy antics—the ones where moms, their voices dripping with syrup, speak loudly about how smart their children are to the kids themselves because they want the adults in the room to hear. Backhanded bragging.

"This is the most awkward situation I ever want to be in for the rest of my entire life," said Jenny as she sat on the sofa. "I'm sure you have a lot of questions. I would, too. But before I start explaining, I promise you that everything I'm telling you is the truth."

While Jenny was talking, Laura had been in the kitchen pouring three glasses of iced tea and setting out a bottle of wine and three glasses.

"I thought you had a rule about wine," I said, watching her pour herself a glass.

"I do. I'm breaking it," she said, and pulled a kitchen chair into the den and sat.

"I asked Laura to introduce me and Jacob. She mentioned you might be moving to Houston, and I didn't know when or if there would be another chance for us to meet in person. Without Laura and Gary, I might not ever have known what happened to Wyatt," Jenny explained. She glanced at the kitchen table where Jacob sat engrossed in whatever he was doing.

"I'm still confused. When and how did the two of you meet?" I asked Jenny. "And if Laura told you about Wyatt . . ." I turned to Laura. "You knew Wyatt?" It was an accusation, not a question.

"I knew about Wyatt, but I had never met him. He and Gary met a few months before your, um, wedding when they worked together at Sadie's, that new restaurant that was opening on the edge of the French Quarter."

Had it not been for Jacob and my not wanting to upset him, my controlled seething would have released itself in a loud angry voice. "You've been in my house, with my family, you and I have talked. I trusted you, and you're just now telling me this? Who are you that you could betray me and manipulate my family? What kind of person is capable of this level of deception?"

"You have every right to be upset with me. And for whatever it's worth, I promise to explain. I wanted you to hear the whole story from Jenny, not just from me. I'm here with her because I know she can't answer all the questions, either."

"Olivia, I'm not going to pretend I have any idea what you must feel like right now. I hope you can understand I wanted to tell you everything to help you feel better, not worse. Wyatt and I were never married; in fact, we were never a couple, for that matter. Until I talked to him about Jacob's surgery, we hadn't seen or been in touch with each other since that time years before when we were together one night. We met at a party, we ended up at my apartment, and by the time I realized I was pregnant, he had left for New Orleans weeks before."

The woman who never loved Wyatt, who spent one night with him, had his child. His son. I loved him, spent years with him. I had nothing. Whatever memories I did have of him now were tainted. Again, where was this merciful God I kept hearing about?

"When the pediatrician told me that Jacob needed his tonsils and adenoids removed because of his sleep apnea and infections, I started looking for Wyatt."

Jacob wiggled out of the chair and walked over to his mother. He tapped her on her shoulder and, holding his hand alongside his mouth, he whispered in her ear. Jenny nodded.

"Jacob, I didn't introduce you yet. This is Miss Olivia, and this is where her parents live. And I'm sure they do have a bathroom." She smiled at him, and he rewarded her with a dimpled grin.

"Do you want to come with me, and I can show you where it is? That way your mommy and Miss Olivia can keep talking. You okay with that?" Laura asked.

He looked back at Jenny, who nodded, and then turned to Laura. "Yes. I go with you," he said softly.

As they walked away, Jenny said, "His voice used to be so nasal, and he snored constantly. But both of those are much better since the surgery."

"He looks"—I stopped to clear my throat—"so much like his father."

I wondered if Jenny really remembered the shape of Wyatt's face or knew about the tiny scar on his eyebrow or the way his eyes could magnetize you and draw you into his arms.

Would Jacob ever know anything about his father?

CHAPTER 52

Laura, Jacob, and his juice box went to the back deck and sat on the glider. Not being able to see him was almost as disconcerting as it had been watching him. But Jenny had much more to say, and I had much more to learn.

"It wasn't so much that Jacob's surgery was critical, the doctors also had questions about Wyatt's medical information, which I knew nothing about. And, even though I was sure my insurance company would cover everything, I wanted to be honest with Wyatt about the possibility of needing some financial help. I own an event-planning business, but if I don't work I don't make money."

"I can't imagine that Wyatt was too happy to find out that you kept a secret from him for years," I said. "Insensitive, don't you think?"

Jenny's eyes widened.

I waited, thinking she might fire back at me, but she just looked down for a moment, smoothing the imaginary wrinkles on her dress. I wanted to start a fight with her. To break her cool, confident composure as she sat there telling me things that destroyed my life. The conversation was surreal. I felt as if this were one of the events she had planned, and we were going over the details of Wyatt's participation in his own death. But I couldn't allow, for Jacob's sake, the rage and resentment to surface.

I poured myself a glass of wine while she told me that Wyatt was angry at first when he found out about Jacob. "Maybe it wasn't the right thing to do, but it was the best right thing at the time," she said. "It was Wyatt's idea to come up that morning. It was important to him to see Jacob before he went to surgery, and he was confident he'd be back in time for the wedding."

"That didn't work out for any of us, did it?" I didn't look at Jenny when I spoke. My eyes were fixed on Laura and Jacob in the glider. After a few sips of wine, I realized that Cabernet for breakfast wasn't the direction I wanted to go in, and it was making my already queasy stomach worse.

Jenny didn't answer. She didn't need to. "If you have any questions—"

She might as well have asked me if I had a pound of flesh to share. "Are you kidding me?" I felt the heat moving up my neck, my eyes narrowed, and I heard my voice, gritty and loud. "My entire relationship with Wyatt is now a question. Not to mention that he'd probably still be here if it wasn't for you."

I poured my wine down the sink. Checked the time on my cell phone. I didn't want my parents walking into this circus of tragedies. I closed the cover on the iPad that Jacob had been playing with and handed it to Jenny. "I'm entirely overwhelmed. I can't talk anymore. I'm not sure what you want from me. After all, you have more of Wyatt than I'll ever have."

Jenny slid the iPad into her purse, stood, and said, "I didn't come here wanting anything except for you to know the truth. My business is successful. The only time I ever asked Wyatt for money was because of Jacob's surgery, and even then, only if it was more than I could cover. I don't expect or need money now. I thought you should know about Jacob so you could decide if you want to be a part of his life." She pulled a business card out of her purse and handed it to me. "I could tell just by the excitement in Wyatt's voice when he talked about you and your wedding how much you meant to him. If you decide you'd like to spend more time with Jacob, let me know. I think Wyatt would have wanted that."

I watched her walk outside and talk briefly to Laura, who hoisted Jacob to her hips. They came inside, and I realized there was a question I needed her to answer. While Laura took Jacob to the car, I asked Jenny, "Are you the person responsible for sending me those letters from Wyatt?"

Jenny's reaction was the only answer I needed. I could tell by the tilt of her head and the confusion in her eyes that she had no idea what I was talking about.

Laura.

Who else could it be?

Grateful my parents hadn't returned yet, I grabbed my keys and started to head out of the house, when my stomach revolted. I dashed to the bathroom and leaned over the sink, my body shaking, my face drained of color, and I couldn't stop the bitterness that forced its way out of my throat.

When my stomach emptied itself, I sat on the edge of the tub and waited for the nausea to pass. It was like my body didn't know the difference between drinking too much the night before and the power of rage and betrayal. They were both equally toxic.

I made it to my car, and I headed in the direction of the country club to find Evan. I pulled into a parking spot, and then realized not only was he not there, but I shouldn't have been: I was depending on Evan's sympathy to pull me through, to coach me through the problem, like I was used to Mia doing, and hoping I could avoid confronting it all together.

So now what?

Are you seeing this mess, Wyatt? A mess you left me to clean up because you were afraid to tell me the truth. It didn't have to be this way, you know. Because if you would have been honest with me, you might still be here today. Was that deceit worth dying for?

CHAPTER 53

The one question I didn't have answered was whether or not Laura was responsible for sending me those letters. And, if she was, I didn't understand how or why.

That Monday, my father drove my mother for another postsurgery doctor visit, so I was alone at the office. I called Laura and asked her to meet me there. She didn't ask what I needed to talk to her about. I wasn't surprised.

From the moment she walked in, the weight of all she knew and hadn't told me felt like a seismic rift between us.

"Those letters. Did you send them?"

The answer was in her eyes before she spoke.

"Yes. I'm sure you're angry, and I can only imagine what you would really like to tell me. Please, just give me a chance to explain."

I nodded. "But one question first. Did Jenny know anything about the letters?"

"No, and she still doesn't. Not that I meant to keep them a secret from her, but they weren't meant for her. But she would've wanted you to have them, too."

Inside, I was biting my fingernails and pacing, wondering exactly what I was angry about. Was it that Laura mailed those letters to me, or was it that she knew they existed before I did? Had Wyatt, somehow, first shared them with her? If that was the case, then Wyatt was complicit in this as well. But dying took him out of the blame equation.

Before she started talking, she plucked a few tissues from the box on my desk and held them in her hands. I'd always thought of Laura as someone, not so much stoic, but in control of her emotions. Sharing this story wasn't going to be easy for her.

"I have to go backward before I can go forward. When I found out about working for your parents, I didn't connect the dots until after I had taken the job. But, knowing what I knew, I thought it would give me a chance to meet the woman Wyatt had loved so much. I came into this not really knowing what you knew already. After the few things your mom said about him, well, I hesitated to mention anything to her until maybe the two of us had spent more time together. I couldn't figure out how to find out what you knew, and then Evan came into the picture. So I thought I should wait. But then the longer I was with your family, the more I realized you didn't know anything about Jenny or Jacob."

"You knew them when you and I first met?"

"No." She shook her head. "Until we came to your house, I'd never met them in person. And if Gary hadn't found that yellow legal pad in Wyatt's locker at the restaurant after he died, neither one of us would have known much about them at all. He and Wyatt talked a lot, and Wyatt told him about Jenny and Jacob and how afraid he was to tell you. He told Gary that he never thought someone like you would ever love someone like him. And, once he told you about Jacob, he didn't know if you would stay with him."

"Well, he certainly didn't give me a chance . . ." I wanted to break the pencil that I'd been rolling between my hands into pieces. *So, Wyatt, you died thinking I never trusted you. What did I ever do to make you feel that way?*

"I think he wanted to. That's why he was writing, not so much to send you those as letters, but as a way to clear his thoughts in his own mind before he told you. Gary said he was so desperate, wrestling with how to tell you about Jacob so close to the wedding—"

"If you had all that, why send those letters so mysteriously? What right did you have to withhold them from me?"

Laura bit her lower lip, gazed at her hands where the tissues had been twisted like a rope. She sighed and then looked at me. "You can blame me, and I won't say it's undeserved. If there was a mistake, it was only because I wanted you to understand how much he struggled. If I'd given everything he wrote to you all at once, I just figured you'd read the last thing he wrote first, and the others wouldn't matter."

"Laura, I don't even have the vocabulary to express what I'm feeling. She has Wyatt's child. I have nothing. At least when I was pregnant, I had a part of him. Even though, and I've never admitted this to anyone, I struggled knowing I was carrying the baby of a man who drove away from his own wedding. But I told myself that baby hadn't asked to be here. It didn't deserve to be responsible for the stupidity of its parents. It deserved to be loved. And I couldn't even do that enough." I pounded my fist on the desk, my pens jumping up in the air, my coffee leaping out of the mug. This rage was a hand grenade whose pin had been pulled, and there was nowhere for it to go. I had no tears left. Just a raw, aching wound.

Laura reached into her purse and handed me the familiar white envelope. "I wanted to give you this the day I was at your house with Jacob and Jenny. I promise this is the last thing he wrote." She wiped under her eyes with a tissue, stood, and pushed her hands into her jeans pockets. "I never meant to hurt you. I hope someday you can forgive me."

"Forgive *you*?" I said with disdain. "I can't even forgive myself yet."

Dear Olivia,

Gary, a friend of mine you'll meet at our wedding, told me that sometimes it helps to write difficult things you need to say. I started writing a few times, but I couldn't make myself get to what I really wanted to talk to you about. The truth is, I'm scared. Our wedding is just a few weeks away, and I'm afraid that after you read this letter or I find the courage to tell you face-to-face, our relationship will be over. I love you so much, and the idea of losing you forever is as painful to me as what I need to tell you.

Maybe I should have said something to you as soon as I found out, but there was so much going on with the wedding, I couldn't bear to bring it up. And the closer our wedding day came, the harder it was to say anything.

Even writing this, I'm stalling. So, here it is . . .

I have a son named Jacob. He's almost four years old. The morning of our wedding he's scheduled to have surgery at a hospital in Oakville, where his mother lives. I plan to drive there early so I can meet him before the surgery. Of course, it's not so far away that I won't make it back for the wedding. The last thing I'd want would be to destroy the day we've planned for so long.

Jenny, his mother, and I met at a party over four years ago. We spent the night together, and the next morning I drove in to New Orleans. We never spoke to or saw one another after that night. Until she called me a month ago, I didn't know Jacob existed. She said she didn't see a reason to disrupt my life, she had family support and was self-sufficient. Jenny said she knew neither one of us were going for happily ever after.

She wanted some medical information, and I told her that if she needed help with the medical expenses to let me know. Jenny told me if I couldn't come, she understood. If we wanted to meet Jacob later and be a part of his life, she would be open to making that happen.

Of course, I had no idea all those years ago that someone as beautiful and smart and amazing as you would come into my life to stay. You *are the most important person in my life. Even now I still can't believe how blessed I am.*

I hope that when you read this or I'm explaining this to you, that your heart will be open. If I made the wrong decision by waiting to tell you, then I ask you to please forgive me. I would never, purposely, do anything to cause you pain.

I love you to the moon and back.

CHAPTER 54

Always a man of his word, Evan called when he came back home and asked me if I wanted to go to dinner.

"I'm sorry for missing so many of your phone calls before you left. I appreciate the dinner invitation, but there's just too much going on right now. Can I call you when I'm not so scattered?" I held my breath waiting for him to answer.

"Since I have no idea how long or where you plan to be scattered, I'll call you back when I can," he said, with a trace of his familiar sarcasm.

I was relieved that I hadn't pushed Evan off the ledge yet. That he was willing to give me another chance. Reality was, I didn't know if I was ready for another chance or for any chance at all with anyone. I was putting myself back together piece by piece, and I didn't want to mash something together just to fill an empty space.

I had made one decision, and I sent Mia a text to let her know: Please ask Bryce if he can start looking again for a place for me to live. I'd like to be back there within the month. I'll call soon

with more information. Tell Lily I miss her.
Love, O.

Days later, I drove toward Oakville. The last time I'd traveled this road, I was pregnant, and I didn't know anything about Jenny or Jacob or Laura. All these months later, it was challenging to find the spot I was looking for. I pulled over on the side, careful to keep my car off the road. I had to walk only a few yards before I spotted the cross.

This time I brought a little garden shovel with me. I cleared away leaves and branches in front of the cross, dug a hole, placed our rings in it, and covered them up. I also had remembered to bring something to sit on. I spread the blanket and sat, knees to my chest, my arms locked around my legs.

I suppose you already know how much has happened since I was last here. I met Jacob and Jenny. One look at him and there was no denying that you were his father. He has your wavy hair, those killer blue eyes of yours, and he can entertain himself on an iPad.

I understand, like Jenny told me, sometimes we don't always know the right thing to do. We just do the best right thing we can at the time. I read what you'd written before our wedding. Laura made sure of that. But I wish you'd trusted me enough to tell me about Jenny and Jacob before our wedding. Look what happens when couples don't trust one another enough to survive the hard stuff together. I would have preferred to find out about them with you than without you.

I brought the rings back because I wanted something of us here. I'm going to give Jenny some things of yours for Jacob. But now that our baby's gone, these are all I have that belonged to the two of us.

Our baby was a girl. I figured you had the right to know first. I haven't told anyone else, but then no one is really asking that question. It's probably crazy, and you're the only person to know this, but I felt like I had to give her a name. All I knew of her was her heartbeat, but I thought that made her important enough and alive enough to be called something more than a fetus. I named her Stella. It's just the name that came to me one night when I missed her so much. Later I found out the name means "star." That made my heart happy because even though she's no longer with me, when I think about her, I can look at the stars and imagine that she's looking back at me. Always shining. Always bright. Always Stella.

Driving home, I thought about how my plans for happily-ever-after never materialized. I had to find a way to get out from under this black cloud, this major time-out that God had assigned me to for whatever wrongs I'd committed. Evan was supposed to call me, and I was so tempted to let myself fall into a relationship with him. Presumptuous of me, though, to think that might even be an option.

But what was I going to bring to a relationship with Evan or with anyone for that matter? A broken woman, always looking over her shoulder, wondering when or where the next hurricane would sweep her life off course? I didn't know if I was ready to face another happily-ever-after that turned into happily-never-ever.

Mia, Wyatt, and my parents believed love was protection. Protection from the truth, sheltering me from the pain even if it meant being dishonest. How ironic that the only people who ultimately didn't hide the truth from me were Ruthie, Laura, and Jenny. They made me walk through my grief, not around it.

Not ready to confine myself to my bedroom or sleep away another afternoon, I drove into New Orleans to walk down Magazine Street, six miles that curve along the Mississippi River, and to window-shop the antique stores, gift shops, and quirky clothing boutiques. On the way there, I passed by the running shop where Wyatt and I had been fitted for shoes years ago when we decided to train for the Crescent

City Classic. We ultimately didn't participate in the 10K race, but we did start running a few days a week.

Considering my clothes were loving me a bit too much as they insisted on hugging my hips, I decided the time had come to put some distance between us. Almost two hours and a dent to my debit card later, I left with new shoes, new socks, and enough Lululemon attire to make Ruthie proud. If I had to sweat, I wanted to look cute doing it.

At Mignon Faget's, I splurged on a sterling-and-pearl necklace for Lily with a strawberry snowball dangle, fleur-de-lis earrings for Mia, and etched fleur-de-lis tumblers for Bryce. Gifts could never repay them for all they'd done and were going to do for me, but I knew they'd appreciate these special remembrances of home.

I drove past Ruthie's on the way home to surprise her with my haul today, but her car wasn't in the driveway. She had a social life that required a planner and pep to keep up with, and she managed both.

My parents weren't home either, so I schlepped my bags to my bedroom, changed into slouchy clothes, and stalked leftovers in the refrigerator. They'd left me a note that my mother had physical therapy, then they were going to dinner and a movie. I was on my own.

I found a container of seafood jambalaya, zapped it, and was carrying my plate and iced tea to the table when my phone dinged twice. A text from Mia: ?????? Her way of telling me she wanted to know what was going on. And another from Evan asking me to call him.

So much for my appetite.

Evan answered after the first ring and told me that he was leaving town again. "Can we plan something for when I return? If you're not interested, tell me now. I don't want to keep calling you if you want to stop."

I pushed my rice around with my fork, wishing I could find an answer buried under there somewhere. "It's not that I don't want you around." I hesitated. I wasn't sure what to say or if he would even understand. "Evan, it's just—"

"I know. It's a bad time," he said wearily. "I hope you can find some good times in your life, Livvy. I wanted to tell you not to worry about those golf lessons. I know you only took them to make your dad happy. If you're still interested, tell your dad he can arrange something with the assistant in the pro shop; he has some openings."

"I never meant that things wouldn't get better." Whatever the relationship was that had existed between us started to slip through my hands.

"I'm sure they will. In the meantime, I'm ready to enjoy my life. I want to be with someone who wants to spend time with me."

"When will you be back this time?" I felt the desperation of not wanting to let go, yet not having what I needed to hold on.

"I'm not really sure. Four, maybe five days," he said.

"Well . . ." I tried to hold on. To offer some hope.

"Take care of yourself, Olivia."

And he was gone.

CHAPTER 55

After Evan hung up, I scraped my dinner in the sink, flipped on the garbage disposal, and wished I could stuff my sadness in with it. I barely slept, waiting for a decent hour so I could call Ruthie.

Early the next morning, I called and asked her to please not go anywhere until I could get there and talk to her.

She sat in the wingback chair she'd pulled close to the sofa, where I stretched out, her feet propped up next to mine. "Ruthie, my life is a runaway horse, and my boots are stuck in the saddle backward."

"Honey, I'm not used to cowboy analogies. Why don't you just tell me what's going on."

"I'm tired of not taking control of my life, but I don't know how. I'm tired of feeling sorry for myself. But when does it end? I feel like I'm on God's permanent detention list."

"It's not God punishing you. Even if He was, you'd cut Him a break because you're flogging yourself enough for the both of you." She shook her head. "I hate to tell you this, girlie, but this is life. Sometimes it's so wonderful your heart can't stretch enough to hold all the exquisite joy, the spectacular of the ordinary. Other times, it's so difficult that just opening your eyes in the morning is a miracle. Feel like you're spending your life walking up the escalator backward, watching everyone pass you up, going where you want to go, and getting what you want."

I pushed myself to sitting. "So now what? I turn around on the escalator? Where's my 'get out of hell' pass?"

"Being a victim is a decision. Happiness is a decision, too. I don't believe in Santa-Claus God, but He does want us to be happy. Imagine having to hear the prayers of a zillion million miserable people. Of course, He'd rather watch us laugh until we can't breathe. But that doesn't mean that there aren't tragedies in our lives. But He's there with us for that, too. Maybe you're not ready to hear that yet. You need to decide what you want for your life. In the end, you have to choose joy."

The next morning I woke up early, put on my running clothes, and drove to a nearby park. The sun hadn't broken through the clouds yet, which made it a perfect time to start, because the mornings were cool and breezy. I mostly walked, sometimes picking up the pace to run until I couldn't breathe, but the distance wasn't as important to me as the decision to lace on those new shoes and move myself out of the house.

The ducks at the pond waddled toward the paved pathway when the early-morning exercisers passed them, squawking like they were berating us for not dropping off food. It had been years since I'd been there. The city had added a playground, a rock-climbing area with rope bridges and swings, and sheltered picnic areas with barbecue pits nearby.

Jacob would have fun here.

My own thought startled me.

Sometimes Ruthie would say that God whispered in her ear. Mostly she said that when it was something we questioned the sanity of, like God whispered in her ear that she should learn how to hang glide before she died. My mother had told her if God said that, there wouldn't be much time that passed between her hang gliding and her dying.

When Wyatt and I started dating, I had stopped attending church. Wyatt said we could be spiritual without being religious, and that worked for me. Until it didn't. After Wyatt's accident, it seemed that God slammed the door on me. Or at least on my chance to experience any joy in my life. So God and I had been on talking probation for a long time, and I didn't think either one of us had reopened the lines of communication. Maybe it was Wyatt's voice I was hearing?

I remembered my conversation earlier with Ruthie about choosing joy. Wyatt and our baby were gone forever. That tragedy would be with me always. But I could decide to open myself to all that was left of Wyatt on this earth, and that was Jacob.

A phone call later, Jenny agreed that she and Jacob would meet me Saturday at the park for a picnic lunch and for a surprise neither one of them knew about. Wyatt's gifts.

Mia sent a text telling me to check my email for links to properties that Bryce wanted me to look at, along with a video of Lily singing "Itsy-Bitsy Spider." Except her version was, "Itsy-fitsy sfider clumbed up the water sfout." She ended her song telling me how much she missed me, and she wanted her nails painted. Lily's face exploded into view, and she whispered, "My nanny don't do it right."

I laughed. Her nanny probably had her number already and was limiting her color choices.

I promised Mia I'd look. She knew I was notorious for having unanswered personal emails going back for weeks. She continued to send me her ? ? ? ? texts until I reassured her I was waiting for everything to stop hitting the fan and then I'd make a FaceTime reservation with her.

Shopping for groceries after I had been running didn't rank as one of my smartest ideas. But when I invited Jenny and Jacob to the park, I'd used the word *picnic*, which suggested food and snacks and drinks. I was determined to be prepared the day before and not scurry around Saturday morning only to find myself at some fast-food drive-through placing a large to-go order.

No wonder mothers have panic attacks. An entire aisle displayed box after carton after pouch after cups after bowls of kid treats, packaged in loud colors and featuring suspiciously happy cartoon characters or zoo animals or playgroups. Some were unapologetic sugar overloads. Others were fat-free, sugar-free, organic, gluten-free, non-genetically modified, soy-free, vegan, fair-trade certified. Pity the child who showed up with a fruit roll-up at lunch time. The kid might as well have worn a T-shirt that screamed, "My parents don't care about me."

I called Jenny to ask her if there was anything Jacob was allergic to or that would send him into some shame spiral if he ate it.

"Crazy, isn't it? As if there isn't enough for mothers to feel guilty about already," she said and went on to give me some suggestions. "And, Olivia, it means a lot to me that you invited us."

Oddly, Saturday morning my parents said nothing to me as they watched me making peanut butter and jelly sandwiches, which I cut into triangles, packing grapes and carrot sticks and apple slices and animal crackers in little plastic bags, and making wraps with chicken and avocados. It wasn't until I brought an ice chest into the kitchen and filled it with juice pouches and a bottle of wine that my father, as he refilled his coffee cup, remarked, "I assume that's not all for you."

"And you assumed correctly," I said. I slipped my arms through the straps on the backpack where I'd stashed all the food, picked up the ice chest, and headed for the side door that led to the garage. After I had everything loaded in the car, I opened the door, popped my head through, and said, "I'm going on a picnic. With Jacob, Wyatt's son, and his mother, Jenny."

I didn't linger to see their expressions. It was a mean and petty thing to do since I hadn't told them anything about Jenny and Laura's visit. But for once, just once in this entire tragic mess, I knew something about Wyatt before they did.

Jenny arrived just a few minutes after I had parked. I told her we'd meet at the duck pond, hoping that feeding the ducks with Jacob would be an easy icebreaker.

At first he didn't want to let go of his mother's hand when I showed him the bag of stale bread and asked him if he wanted to feed the ducks with me. I stood between the edge of the pond and where Jacob stood and started tossing out bits of bread. After a few tosses, I felt a tug on my shorts and heard "Can I have some?"

I looked down to see Jacob standing next to me, those saucer blue eyes looking up at me and his little hand outstretched. I handed him a few pieces of bread and told him to toss them as far as he could. Jenny followed him and was taking pictures. He giggled and laughed and seemed to have no fear, unlike me, who was certain at any time he was going to lose a few fingers because he didn't let go of the bread fast enough.

Before we ate lunch, he climbed over, around, under, and through every piece of equipment on the playground. He wanted to try the rock climbing next, but Jenny suggested we eat first. I was so grateful she did because I was exhausted just watching him.

I think I fell in love with him when, during lunch, he asked his mom if he could come back and play with Miss "Olibeya."

"I would like that very much," I said and tried very hard to keep the emotions that swelled my heart from leaking out of my eyes.

Jenny and I, for most of the time we spent together, didn't talk about Wyatt. We were just two women getting to know each other. As usual when you first get to know someone, there was still that veneer of awkwardness. At one point, she mentioned something about liking country music. Had I been with Mia, my response would have been,

"Just poke my eardrums out now with a guitar string, would you?" But I kept myself in check and mumbled something about not being familiar with the latest country hits.

When Jacob started to get cranky, we knew it was time to go. By the time Jenny buckled him in his car seat, he was about three long blinks shy of falling asleep. She thanked me again for reaching out. "I don't know if you realize it, but you're the only person right now in Jacob's life who can tell him about his father. That's something I could never give him." She brushed Jacob's bangs out of his eyes and looked back at me. "I've learned that God places people in my life at a time I really need them. I wish the circumstances that brought us together would've been different. I'm sure you do, too. But I'm glad to have met you and to know that you want to be a part of Jacob's life."

"Honestly, God and I have been on a break. Even though my grandmother tells me that I'm the only one on the break. Either way, what I'm beginning to realize is that I may not always understand everything, but my life can't wait around until I do. I have to admit, I wasn't so glad to meet you at first," I said. "But later I thought about your coming to my house, and I begrudgingly admired the courage it took for you to do that."

She smiled as she opened the door of her car. "It was a tough day. For both of us."

"Wait," I said, remembering the gifts I needed to give her. I handed her the package from Babycakes and told her that it had to be reordered after Wyatt originally ordered it, and it didn't arrive until weeks after he died. "This one," I said and handed her the other gift, "was . . ." I had to clear my throat, and this time I really couldn't stop myself from crying. "This was in Wyatt's car when they found him that morning."

She gasped as she took the gift from me, placed it on her driver's seat, and hugged me. "I'm so sorry. I had no idea that you've been burdened with this since Wyatt died."

"I'm glad Jacob fell asleep," I said as we both sniffled and wiped our tears away with our hands. "He might've thought going on picnics was very sad for the two of us."

We said good-bye, and I started to walk to my car when she called my name. "Olivia, don't ever sell yourself short. You have more courage than you realize."

CHAPTER 56

What did I have to offer Evan or any man for that matter if I was still trying to figure out who I was? Maybe the time had come for me to not define myself by the man in my life.

I didn't want Evan to think that he was responsible for my avoiding him. Even if all I walked away with was our friendship, it was important to me that he knew everything that had been going on in my life.

After my run the next morning, I called Evan and left a voicemail asking if we could meet for dinner when he returned. I was on my way to my grandmother's to tell her the story of Jenny and Jacob when Siri read his text message to me: Might be here longer than I expected. Will get back to you.

Well, at least it wasn't a "forget you ever knew this number" message. I had no idea where *here* was nor whether he'd get back to me in a day a week or a month, but I knew Evan was a man of his word.

I found Ruthie kneeling on a foam pad in her front yard, yanking weeds out of her garden. Too late, I realized why she was so excited to see me.

"A brand-new pair of gloves that should fit you perfectly," she said, smiling as she handed them to me. "I'm about to introduce you to the best and cheapest therapy you'll ever have."

"So where is he?" I asked as I pulled on the gloves that unfortunately did fit me. "This therapist of yours?"

She sat back on her heels, hands on her hips, and said, "Well, bless your heart. Do you think if he was here, I'd be in this yard pulling weeds?" Ruthie pointed to where she wanted me to start. "Now, what is all this news you had to tell me?"

With just a few water breaks in between, I finished telling her everything that had been happening, and she had a weed-free garden. "I'll take those gloves. Come inside for some air-conditioning and carrot cake."

After being outside, walking into her kitchen felt as if I were stepping into an igloo. My arms looked like they had been dusted with garden dirt, and even though Ruthie had given me a hat to wear, my face felt like it'd been steam ironed.

"I want a huge glass of water, but I'm passing on the cake. I'm too hot and too gross to think about eating anything."

"That's fine," she said, handing me the water. "But you haven't told me anything your parents said about any of this." Ruthie sat with her water and a slice of carrot cake, and wiped her forehead with a paper towel.

I looked at the table and wished I had something to eat just to avoid making eye contact. "They don't know anything except for one small piece of information." I confessed my pre-picnic bomb dropping.

"Olivia Ruth Kavanaugh, that's meaner than a bucketful of rattlesnakes. I know your mother has given you grief at every turn, but I don't care anymore who started all this. Somebody needs to stop it. Even if that somebody is you. It's time for you to prove to your mother that you're taking control of your life. She doesn't have to like it, but if you're going to play her games, then you haven't made much progress."

⚜

Laura insisted on being with me when I talked to my parents. "I owe them and you that much, especially since they asked me to work at the insurance office. If they're not going to be comfortable with that decision after we tell them everything, then we all need to get that straight now."

I suggested we might want to have our worry beads with us. "Or if you have two more, bring them along. We could lower all of our stress levels at one time."

"Not a bad idea, as long as you don't think they might want to strangle us with them."

I told Ruthie I wanted her to be a part of this, too, so she wouldn't have to hear the story through my mother's filter. A filter that needed to be changed more often than it was. It was Ruthie's idea that we all meet at her house because it was neutral turf.

Since my spiteful remark the day I'd left for the picnic with Jenny and Jacob, my parents and I had resorted to well-orchestrated dodging of one another and the if-you-can't-say-anything-nice rule. Ruthie said she pitied my father. "Poor man. He's parted the Red Sea like Moses, making sure you and your mother aren't engaging in fighting, but he can't figure out how to bring it back together again."

Laura took the lead. She called my parents and asked them to meet us at Ruthie's, saying it would be best for all of us to be someplace different. "So no one has the home-field advantage," she offered by way of explanation.

My parents said little throughout the entire unfolding of the Wyatt saga. Their reactions were mostly a gallery of expressions, from confused to shocked to sad and back again.

I told my parents that when I first heard the story from Laura, and after she had given me Wyatt's last letter, I asked her to leave our house. "I was devastated that someone I trusted and considered a friend could be manipulative and deceitful. I had to get out of my victim mentality to see that Laura's intention was never to hurt me. I may not agree with how she handled everything, but she acted out of genuine care for me and wanting me to know the truth."

"And not that anyone here's asked for my opinion," said Ruthie, who put her arm around Laura's shoulders, "I don't think you and Scarlett should hold any of this against this young woman. We all know that she was the best person we could have had to take care of Scarlett after her surgery."

"I appreciate your vote of confidence," Laura told Ruthie. "But," she said, turning to my parents, "I understand if you want to rethink your offer of my working for you in light of everything Olivia and I told you tonight. I want you to be able to trust me. If you can't, I understand."

"One more thing," I said. "Maybe this would be better said at another time, but since we seem to be working on forgiveness tonight . . ." I moved so that I sat across from my mother. Her hands were folded in her lap, and I placed mine over them. "Ever since that night I told you and Dad I was pregnant, you and I might as well have been thousands of miles apart from one another. Maybe I don't know or understand God the same way you do, but I don't believe God wants us to use Him as a wedge between us. You're my mother, and I never needed you as much as I did those months I was pregnant. I was stubborn, too, but I want to have a relationship with you. I hope we can forgive one another and move past all this. It's up to you now."

"Scarlett, it's time for you to tell your daughter the other reasons why her being pregnant was so difficult for you."

I looked at Ruthie, then at my mother. "More secrets?"

My mother shook her head. "I never meant them to be. I thought at some point, when you and Wyatt were planning a family, we'd talk. Then everything happened, and you were pregnant, and I didn't want to tell you then."

In between pauses for water and tears, my father's arm around her shoulders, she told me about her four miscarriages in six years, all happening between six and seven months. How she'd decided she couldn't endure losing another baby, and three months after her last miscarriage, she was pregnant again.

"I was devastated. I even told God not to make me wait and hope for months only to lose another baby. Just get it over with early. I don't know how your grandmother and your father survived me. I was a miserable person."

They both nodded.

"I was so afraid that pregnancy would end like every other one, I refused to be happy. And I put God on notice that if I didn't come home with a baby in my arms, we were done."

Ruthie laughed. "I'm pretty sure God got a kick out of that one."

"Probably so," my mother said and smiled softly. "Because you were the baby I came home with." She reached for my hands. "When you told us you were pregnant, all I could think about was having lost all those babies and how awful it was for your father and me. And you were dealing with Wyatt's death. You didn't need any more stress hearing about my miscarriages. Not then. And even though I still believe in God's commandments, maybe in a different way than you do, I was wrong to shut myself off from you. Just like when I was pregnant with you, I couldn't get past my fear."

I hugged her, and she wrapped her arms around me, and I understood what my grandmother had told me: "In the end, you have to choose joy."

CHAPTER 57

Do you want to meet me at JB's Steakhouse or do I pick you up? I don't know what your latest sensitivity level is when you hear the word 'date.'" Evan sounded weary or frustrated or both.

"If you pick me up, it's a date, but if I meet you there, what do we call it?"

"Look, Kavanaugh, I'm too tired to play semantics. I've been driving for the past six hours, and I'll get home in enough time to shower and meet you or whatever. Just tell me what you want to do."

"Then why don't I pick you up? That's an option in the twenty-first century."

"You know, you're absolutely right. Our reservations are for eight o'clock, so pick me up around seven thirty."

With the help of even a little time spent running and Spanx, I wiggled into my favorite little black dress. A simple sheath with six narrow straps across each shoulder. I slipped on a pair of black ankle-strapped high heels and the pearls my grandmother had given me on my sixteenth birthday, and I almost didn't recognize myself in the mirror.

My parents were eating dinner when I went to tell them I was leaving. My father actually whistled, and my mother smiled and motioned me to move closer. "You look beautiful, Olivia."

I bent down and kissed her cheek. "Thank you," I whispered.

I called Evan from my car to let him know I was in his driveway.

"You're not coming in to meet my parents? They have about thirty questions for you, and they want to be sure I'm home before curfew."

"Do you want to have dinner or a one-man night at the improv? I'm counting to three . . ."

He was out the door before two, and when I saw him, it was as if my entire body had been dipped in warm honey. His dark suit was tailored to accentuate his broad shoulders and trim body. He was stunning. And when he sat in the car, I forced my eyes to the road because if I looked at him, there would have been no hiding the thoughts my eyes would have revealed.

Our conversation in the car was limited to discussions of our parents, my running, and any other topic of little consequence. I asked him about where he'd been, but he said he'd go into all that later.

When the valet opened my door, and I walked around to Evan, he looked at me so long, I felt as if he were drinking me in. Not totally unpleasant, but enough to make me glance down to be sure I hadn't drooled on myself watching him walk to my car. I brushed the front of my dress.

"Something wrong?"

"Absolutely not," he said and caressed me with a slow, easy smile. He reached for my hand as we walked to the door. "Hungry?"

Oh my, you have no idea, do you?

At the table, he ordered a bottle of wine and, after our glasses were filled, he leaned forward. "You look better than anything on the menu," he said.

I slapped back my sarcasm before it spoiled the moment. Even though it would have deflected my awkwardness much better than my wineglass dinging the edge of my plate when he dropped that line.

"Thanks," I said. "You don't look too shabby yourself." *Olivia, really? That's the best you could do?*

Fortunately, the waiter appeared for our orders and saved me from humiliating myself more and provided a break from my awkwardness.

"One of the reasons I wanted to have dinner with you was I felt like I owed you the truth about why and how I came back from Baton Rouge." Evan refilled our glasses, then said, "I want you to know the real reason I decided to leave the law firm."

"Okay," I said and already felt my heart preparing to go on lockdown. I wanted to ask him to cut to the chase. If this was his good-bye speech, I'd rather leave on an empty stomach. But he'd already sat back in his chair, ready to give his testimony.

"I was the defense attorney for someone I knew was guilty. He was acquitted, then three months later he stabbed his pregnant wife. She and the baby died. I couldn't sleep for months. The guilt almost killed me, and that's not hyperbole. That's when I knew I had to leave to save my own life. My fiancée thought I'd get over it. That practicing corporate law would make a difference. Maybe it would have, but I knew in my gut that I needed to do something different with my life. I ended up at the club. They needed a pro, and I needed something to do. I never intended to stay, and I thought my being there was an absolute fluke until you showed up. I was such a pompous idiot in college, and I'm sorry for that because I realized too late that I had lost any chance with you."

"In all fairness, I was pretty inflexible myself. I thought a relationship should be the romance for the ages. When I met Wyatt, it was comfortable. He was always ready to do whatever made me happy, and I wasn't used to that. Then Wyatt dies on our wedding day with a mess of unanswered questions, and I find I'm pregnant and, well, you know the rest. Not exactly the romance I intended it to be." I shared the Jenny, Jacob, and Laura story, which took us all the way to dessert.

"And here we are, figuring all this out, and before long we're going to be almost four hundred miles apart. Our timing hasn't been good, has it?" I said, trying to decide if my Spanx could tolerate cheesecake.

"But I think your moving to Houston is the right thing for you to do," Evan said, with a bit more enthusiasm than I expected.

I mentally drummed my fingers on the table, impatient now to leave because what I thought might have been a beginning was now looking like the end. "Of course, it doesn't seem like there's any reason for me not to go." I hoped I sounded mature in my bitterness.

He asked me when I planned to go back, and then he ordered coffee and flan.

Might as well order two desserts, Olivia. I told our waiter I wanted espresso and the praline cheesecake. "Bryce has already sent me some places he scouted out. I figure sometime in the next four weeks, I should be able to make a decision about where I'll live."

"Bryce is doing the same thing for me," Evan said.

"So, you're looking for a place in New Orleans?"

"I'm not staying here," he said. He sounded too chipper about his willingness to jet off to wherever this new life of his was.

"Then where?"

"I interviewed for a teaching position at the University of Houston law school. And I'm starting this spring semester."

"You're moving to Houston?" The anxiety let go of my lungs, and I wanted to both strangle him and hug him for leading me through this torture.

"So, what do you think Kavanaugh? I still owe you some golf lessons." He smiled and reached across the table to lock his fingers with mine. "And stir-fried eggplant from P.F. Chang's."

"What do I owe you, then?"

"Another chance," he said.

CHAPTER 58

On my way out of town, I stopped at the mausoleum to leave a bouquet of wildflowers with a letter tucked inside. I set the flowers in the vase attached to the stone front where Wyatt's name had been engraved. I traced each letter of his name with my finger and, when I finished, whispered, "Good-bye. I love you."

Dear Wyatt,

I'm on my way to Houston, but I didn't want to leave without stopping to tell you good-bye. I almost didn't write this letter because, at first, it seemed ridiculous. For one thing, I have no idea what the postage rates are to mail something to eternity. Plus, it's not like I can't talk to you anywhere I am.

I guess this letter is as much for me as it is for you because I'm starting, not a new life, but a different one almost four hundred miles away. And there's this part of me that feels like I'm leaving you behind. Not just geographically, but emotionally. I haven't figured it all out yet, but I suppose that will take time like everything else has.

I finally met Jacob and Jenny. He looks so much like you, and I see so much of you in him. The way he bites his lower lip when he's totally focused on something. How he tilts his head when he's asking a question. He already has your compassion. When we were at the park, he heard a baby crying, and he asked Jenny if he could hug the baby because it was sad. Jenny is self-assured, kind, and so grounded. She's an amazing mother, Wyatt. She is playful and yet firm, she's patient, affectionate, and she's invited me to be a part of their lives. Jenny wants Jacob to know about you. When I gave her those two gifts that you had picked out for him, she hugged me. Those two packages were albatrosses that weighed me down for months. But when I saw the surprise and gratitude in her face, I knew that you had done the right thing.

Being with Lily and Jacob, I've learned that I enjoy the company of children. Who knew?! My parents, understandably, are surprised that I want to shift from public relations to preschool education. Ruthie told them there really wasn't that much difference. That teaching was PR with a different age group. I'm going to miss her, but I did tell her she's the reason I opted for a two-bedroom condo. She has no excuse not to visit. When I get settled, I'm going to look into certification programs.

Evan's moving to Houston in a few weeks. He's going to start teaching in January. We've been spending time with one another, but neither one of us is ready to rush into anything. We're going to see where these new lives take us. He's a different man than he was when we were together before. We've both been changed by unexpected tragedies, but we're learning so much about ourselves and one another through them.

God and I are working things out. Or, as Ruthie reminded me, "God worked things out a long time ago, girlie. He's been waiting for you to catch up." After you died, and I

found out about Jenny and Jacob,
I thought I lost the life I'd dreamed
about because God had decided I was
next in line to be punished. Thing
is, I was doing a great job punishing myself. God didn't need to step
in. But I'm realizing I don't have to
understand; that's the whole point
of faith. Like in Raiders of the Lost
Ark, when Indiana Jones is told he
has to take a leap of faith and step
out over that enormous chasm even
though he doesn't see the bridge. He
does, and it's there. So, I'm learning.
One step at a time.

I love you, Wyatt. I still miss you,
miss who we were together. I miss
Stella. Even though I never had a
chance to hold her in my arms, I held
her in my heart. And that's where you
are. Tucked away with her in a place
where only the three of us can meet.

While I was writing this, I remembered these lines from a poem by e. e.
cummings that will forever remind
me of you and Stella:

"i carry your heart with me(i
carry it in my heart) i am never
without it . . ."

I love you,
Livvy

EPILOGUE

Almost two years later . . .

Granny Ruth says lightning can't strike twice in the same place. We all know that's a myth, but nobody would dare say that to her. It's her way of telling us that everything's going to be okay.

And we don't just want to believe her.

We all need to believe her.

Because, once again, we were all there. Waiting for you. All the plans we'd made, reserving a special suite, the balloons, the confetti.

Six hours later, you finally, blessedly, and miraculously arrived.

All seven pounds and fourteen ounces of you.

Your father whispered, "Thank you for our beautiful son," and placed you in my arms. Arms that had been empty. Arms that waited and longed for you.

Evan Samuel Gendusa, born on New Year's Eve, was about to meet his family.

ACKNOWLEDGMENTS

Once upon a time, I had an idea. It grew up and over and into this novel that I am now thrilled to share with all of you. The characters in *Since You've Been Gone* refused to be silent, tugging on my writer's sleeve like impatient children determined to be heard.

And heard they were. First, by my enthusiastically persistent agent Jessica Kirkland of the Blythe Daniel Agency. She encouraged me at a time when I wondered if the gig was up. Her honesty and fearlessness are admirable. Because of her, Erin Calligan Mooney, acquisitions editor at Waterfall Press, gave these characters life, and Megan Makeover, my developmental editor, gave them a purpose. To everyone at Amazon who had a part in bringing this novel to readers: thank you for your kindnesses. Waterfall Press has blessed me.

Thanks to Phyllis Puglia Welsh who answered some legal questions for me, and her husband, Dennis, who invited us out to eat and cooked for us, sending home leftovers enough times that my husband actually ate cooked food at least once a week.

God bless Jenny B. Jones, who faithfully answered my neurotic and frantic texts, emails, and phone calls. If she can't talk me off the ledge, she pulls me through the window every time. Also, thanks to

Nicole Deese for her patience, and Amy Matayo for her pre-deadline encouragement.

I appreciate my teacher friends, readers, and cheerleaders who haven't forgotten me since I retired. Carole, Carrie, and Shelley never fail to check in with me to make sure I haven't bashed myself on the head with my laptop.

Last, but certainly and never not least, my children and children-in-law, who understand when I've slipped into my writing coma. I even remember their names: Michael, Sandy, Erin, Andrae, Shannon, Sarah, John, and Amanda.

I'd like to thank our dog, Herman, but he was the one member of the family who felt obligated to annoy me. I don't recall how many times I had to delete lines of "rob,rob,rob,rob,rob . . ." from my manuscript because of his incessant barking.

Then there's my husband, Ken. Even though he decided that we should move and continue to manage three vacation rentals while I was on deadline, I am happy to report that he is still very much alive and loved. He's been on the front lines for the agony and ecstasy of my writing life. I so owe him. For everything.

Eternal gratitude to God for reminding me that I'm not Him, for the countless blessings in my life, and for allowing me to write about His grace and mercy.

And to all the readers (and the audio listeners), I am humbled by and grateful for your support. Thank you for changing my life.

ABOUT THE AUTHOR

A true Southern woman who knows any cook worth her gumbo always starts with a roux, Christa Allan is an award-winning author who writes stories filled with hope, humor, and redemption. Her novels include *Test of Faith*; *Threads of Hope*; *Walking on Broken Glass*; and *The Edge of Grace*.

Christa is a mother of five and grandmother of three, and she recently retired after twenty-five years spent teaching high school English. She and her husband live in New Orleans in a home older than their combined ages. They spend their time dodging hurricanes and pacifying their three neurotic cats and Herman, their dog.